The Undergrounders
&
the Malice of the Moth

C T Frankcom

First edition December 2020

Front cover design by Sam Waters.

Graphics from www.pexels.com, www.Brusheezy.com

Inside cover illustration by C.T. Frankcom

Special thanks to T. Frankcom, T & J Shardlow and M & J Frankcom

Other titles in this series:

The Undergrounders & the Flight of the
Falcon

The Undergrounders & the Deception of
the Dead

For Mum & Dad x

Prologue

From: The Moth
To: The Flame
Re: The Jaybird {Encrypted}

I have the Jaybird.
If you want her, you will have to meet with me – face to face.

End.

From: The Flame
To: The Moth
Re: The Jaybird {Encrypted}

I give you credit for your tenacity, but you are the last person I would agree to meet.
If you want to make a trade, I suggest you lower your expectations.

End.

From: The Moth
To: The Flame
Re: The Jaybird {Encrypted}

My expectations are that you will bend.
I know you want her alive.

You have seven days until my offer expires, then I will dispose of her myself.

End.

From: The Flame
To: The Moth
Re: The Jaybird {Encrypted}

As ever, you show yourself to be foolish and naïve, just like those before you. No one gives me an ultimatum, least of all, you.

End.

Chapter 1: Broken

The sound of shattering glass sent needles running through George's nerves, yet he felt no pain as the blood sprang from his knuckles. All he could feel were the claws of the monster that raged inside him, tearing at his gut and making every one of his muscles scream out in anger. It had got the better of him again, building and brewing until it exploded from within him, taking over his limbs and lashing out without his consent.

As the shards of glass bounced off the carpet and settled at his feet, George stood and stared at his fractured reflection, unable to recognise the face that glared back at him.

"George, what have you done?"

The sadness and shock in her voice made him recoil in shame. He couldn't look at her as he ran from the house and didn't dare to look back as she called after him. He knew it would kill her to watch him go, but he needed to get away before he did anything worse.

George sat alone in the alleyway. He felt safer there – safer for him and for anyone who knew him. It had gone too far, and this time he didn't know how he was going to make amends.

God, George!

He stared down at his battered knuckles, watching the blood slowly congeal into the folds of his skin. After seeing so much blood in recent weeks, he thought he'd be used to the sight of it. He knew the smell and even the bitter taste of it, but that didn't stop his stomach from turning.

His fingers felt raw, and the cold wind that whistled up the alleyway was slithering its way between every breach in his clothes. He could feel it seeping beneath his woollen hat, crawling up around his ankles and slipping down the back of his coat, but he still refused to move. Maybe if he stayed there, hidden in the shadows, everything would just disappear – his anger, his fear, his frustration – maybe he would emerge from the darkness and everything would be erased – no Victor, no Jin-é and no missing mother.

Sitting with his back against the brick wall, he listened to the distant sound of traffic. The roofs above jutted over the alleyway, shielding him from the driving rain, but he had given up on keeping dry. He wrapped his arms around himself and buried his face.

What have I done?

His mind staggered backwards and he felt nauseous with guilt. He hated making Gran angry. She did so much for him, no more so than in the past few weeks.

It had been three weeks since George had returned from Paris, but his pain and frustration hadn't numbed with time. If anything, he felt more rage and hopelessness as every day passed. Every dawn brought another day without knowing where his mother was or if she was safe, and the thing that made him maddest of all was that everyone else seemed to be getting on with their lives as if nothing had happened.

Even the sound of the traffic made his skin prickle. How could people be out shopping, going for coffee, dashing to pick up their kids from school when his mum was somewhere out there: trapped, imprisoned – or worse?

Clamping his hands over his ears, he tried to drown out the sound of tyres splashing through kerb-side puddles. He wanted to drown it all out, but one sound punctured through the rest: footsteps, and they were headed his way.

George raised his head to see a shadowy silhouette marching towards him – hood up and ankle-length mac flapping about madly in the wind.

Great!

Forgetting about his shredded knuckles, he scrambled to his feet and stumbled towards the bend in the alley. He didn't need some do-gooder asking him if he was ok.

"Wait!" the stranger shouted, his voice lost in the whistle of the wind, but George just put his head down and sped up, trying to escape the heavy footsteps that thundered against the cobbles behind him.

"Leave me alone!" he shouted over his shoulder, as he broke into a sprint and lunged for the end of the alleyway.

"George!" the person yelled.

Huh?

George tried to stop himself as he stumbled out onto the busy high street, but it was too late. He collided full-on with a pram, nearly sending the mother and baby careering into the road, but before George could apologise, someone had him by the arm.

"Got you!"

George looked up. Half-buried beneath the hood of his mac, was George's dad, Sam.

"Dad?"

"What do you think you're playing at?" Sam asked, with a look halfway between confusion and disappointment.

"Um … I…" George stammered.

"You need to apologise to this young lady."

But the woman wasn't hanging around. She scuttled off with a look of horror on her face.

"Look at you," Sam said. "You're a mess!"

George glanced at his reflection in a nearby shop window. With his hat pulled down low and blood on his hands, he looked like a criminal.

"I'm sorry, OK," he scowled, yanking his arm out of his dad's grip.

"For what exactly?" Sam asked, raising an eyebrow.

"Bunking school, losing my temper – I don't know – what else do you want me to own up to?"

Sam squinted, trying to shield his eyes from the onslaught of rain. "There's no need to be like that."

"Like what?"

"Sarcastic," Sam frowned.

"So, what do you want me to say?"

The wind blasted a bucketful of rain into George's face, and Sam grabbed him again and pulled him into the doorway of a vacant shop. "I don't want to fight with you, George."

"Oh, really?" George said, wiping the water from his eyes.

"Yes, really, but it seems that all we do right now is exactly that."

"Well, maybe if you hadn't gone behind my back and–"

"I don't think we need to go over this again."

"No, you've obviously made up your mind," George said, pulling his hood up over his beanie, "but that doesn't mean I have to agree. It's my life."

Several other pedestrians staggered past them, battling against the elements.

"George, you're obviously not coping and you need–"

"I don't need counselling!" George said, raising his voice and making the passers-by look in their direction. "And I definitely don't need Miss O'Donnell dragging me off at breaktime in front of all my classmates. Do you have any idea how embarrassing that was?"

"I believe she can help you."

"With what?"

"Your anger," Sam replied, calmly.

"I don't need help with my anger!"

Sam glared at George. "I think that Gran would disagree with you, especially after this morning's episode."

George's nostrils flared, and he could feel the heat in his cheeks.

She told him.

"That was … an accident," he said, his jaws tightening.

"You lost control."

"What, like you never do?"

"This isn't about me," Sam growled.

"It never is," George bit back.

"I'm trying to get you help!"

"I don't need help!" George snapped. "What I need is for you to find Mum!"

Suddenly, he could feel it again. The same thing he'd felt that morning: the creeping burn of rage that seemed to crawl through his veins and erupt at the surface without warning; as if it wasn't him but some monster inside him, taking control of every muscle. He gritted his teeth and dragged air in through his nostrils. He didn't want to lose it in front of his dad – that would only prove that he was right and George was wrong – but before George had a chance to recompose himself, he could feel his dad's grip on his shoulders.

"Listen to me, George," Sam said. "It's not shameful to need a little help. You've been through hell."

George looked up at him. "But…"

"I understand," Sam said.

"Do you?" George asked, trying to unclench his jaw.

Sam stood back. "Listen, when your mother died … I mean, when we thought…"

"Yes?"

"Well, I didn't exactly deal with it too well myself. I refused help and … well, it didn't leave me in a good place."

George looked up at Sam.

"I don't want the same to happen to you," Sam continued. "That's all."

George felt his muscles ease and the monster slowly lose its grip.

"I get it," he sighed. "but it's my choice, Dad."

"Yes, I know, and I should have asked you first. I'm just not sure how many more mirrors we can spare," Sam said.

They stared at each other from beneath their dripping hoods.

"I'm sorry," George mumbled.

"I'm sorry too, but will you just think about it for me?" Sam asked.

George shrugged. "I guess."

Sam dragged his hand down his face and squeezed the rainwater from his beard. "Now, will you please come home and apologise to your grandmother?"

George hung his head. "There's nothing I can do to make it up to her."

"That's nonsense, and anyway, she sent me to find you, so you can come quietly or I can drag you."

George opened his mouth to protest, but another gust of wind slapped him in the face, so he decided to do as he was told.

George trailed behind his dad as they battled their way along the sodden high street, skipping puddles and dodging past the other pedestrians who were rushing to get out of the weather. By the time they reached Sam's old van, they were both soaked through.

George slid into the passenger seat and slammed the door. It felt good to be out of the rain, but his wet clothes clung to his skin, making him shiver.

Sam started the engine and cranked up the heater. "You need to sort out your hands."

"I'm fine," George said, wedging his battered knuckles beneath his shivering legs.

The rain had stopped by the time they glided into Chiddingham. Sam slowed the van and pulled up to the kerb a few doors down from their cottage. He glanced down at his phone. "I need to get back to the office."

"A lead?" George asked, hopefully.

"Maybe," Sam replied, sliding his phone back into his pocket.

George looked down at his hands. "Dad … you said you wouldn't shut me out … and I feel like…" He looked up at Sam. "I need to know, Dad. I need to know that we're making progress. It's driving me mad."

Sam sighed. "Let me get back to the office … I'll find out what updates Cate has … we'll talk when I get home."

"You promise?"

Sam nodded. "Now, get outta' here."

"Here?" George asked, staring down the lane towards their cottage.

"You can walk the rest of the way," Sam said. "I reckon you need a minute to decide what you're going to say to your grandmother."

George stood and watched his dad's van disappear down the lane. He looked up at the leaden clouds as they raced across the sky.

How can I make this right?

Flexing his sore hands, he glanced towards home.

Just say sorry.

Straightening up, he strode towards the gate with his keys in his hands, but as he reached the front door, he saw it. Leaning up against the wall, under the lounge window, was a pile of shattered glass and the remnants of an ornate, wooden frame. His heart sank, and he thought about turning and disappearing back up the path.

"Georgie!" It was Gran.

She stood at the open door, sadness and relief etched through the wrinkles that bordered her warm eyes.

They stood for a moment, looking at each other, and George crumpled inside. He loved her more than anything and hated himself for ever making her sad. She was everything to him: a mother when he needed care, a father when he needed advice and a friend when he needed cheering up.

"I'm sorry," he croaked, searching her eyes for forgiveness.

"I know," she said, opening her arms. "I never doubted that."

George fell into her arms and squeezed her. "I'll fix it. I promise."

"It doesn't need fixing," Gran said, releasing him and looking down at the shattered mirror.

"But your dad made it. It was the only thing you had left of his. You said it meant so much—"

"It's not important, Georgie," she said, wrapping her soft hands around his cheeks. "You're all that's important to me – you and your father."

"But you said it reminded you of him – of your dad."

"People don't live on in *things*, Georgie. They live on in you: in your heart, in your memories. That's what keeps them alive."

"But—"

"I won't hear any more about it," she said. "Let me see those hands."

"I'm fine," George said, looking down at the fists that had caused all the damage.

"There's no glass in those cuts?"

"No … I promise."

"Well then, you better come in and see what your birthday surprise is."

"What?"

"I won't let an old mirror ruin my only grandson's birthday."

"But…"

"Just come in."

George shuffled into the hallway and shook off his wet coat. "I need to get these trousers off," he said, unbuttoning his jeans.

"Er … I wouldn't do that right now," Gran said. "We have company."

"Surprise!"

George looked up to see the kitchen door flying open and his friends piling out into the hallway.

"Happy birthday!"

From: K07
To: J21
Re: Stolen Goods {Encrypted}

Update 1.0

The Louvre have finally confirmed that four of the Rothkos have been identified as counterfeit.

All four belong to the Russian billionaire, Ivan Pozhar. He had lent them to the gallery for the exhibition.

End.

From: J21
To: K07
Re: Stolen Goods {Encrypted}

Response to Update 1.0

Are we to assume that the Bird targeted these four paintings for a reason?
Let's look into any past history between the two men.

I'm heading out early. Let me know what you find.

End.

From: K07
To: J21
Re: Stolen Goods {Encrypted}

Response to Update 1.0

You'll be the first to know. In the meantime, try to take some time with your son. I'm sure he needs it.

Send him my best wishes.

End.

Chapter 2: Distant Memories

George wasn't sure that he cared much for birthdays. His had never been a big affair. He'd never had a party or even a gathering of people to watch him blow out his candles. Gran always made him a cake and his dad would give him a gift that Gran had undoubtedly bought, but that was the sum of it.

As his friends surged down the corridor and engulfed him in a hug, he immediately felt guilty.

What must they think of me?

He'd bunked off school for the past two days and had ignored all of their calls. He knew he'd spent the last three weeks becoming more and more withdrawn and bad-tempered, and he'd watched them start to tiptoe around him – anxious and wary. And yet here they were, showing him how much they still cared.

"Guys, I… wow… um…"

"Look, we got you this," Felix said, nudging Will.

"Yeah, we clubbed together," Will said, pulling a parcel from inside his bag.

"I hope you like it," Lauren said, reaching to take George's hand.

"Ahh, I'm filthy," George said, pulling away. "I mean…"

"Why don't we all go into the kitchen," Gran called from behind them. "There's cake."

George ducked into the bathroom and cleaned up his hands. By the time he came back out, Gran had made drinks, the candles were lit and the kitchen was filled with chatter.

"Missed you at school," Felix said, as he wedged himself in beside George, who was now leaning against the radiator, desperately trying to warm up his damp legs. "You been OK?"

"Yeah, I'm fine," George replied.

"You sure?"

"Aren't you allergic to cats?" George asked, quickly changing the subject.

"I took a pill," Felix said, grinning. "Should mean I'm good for an hour or so."

"Appreciate it," George said, smiling back and scanning the kitchen for any sign of Gran's scruffy cat. "Marshall's probably hiding from you lot anyway. He's totally anti-social."

"Right, let's have you, boy!" Gran said, beckoning George over to blow out his candles.

They sang him Happy Birthday, and Gran took the cake for slicing.

"Here," Felix said, bundling the roughly wrapped parcel into George's arms.

"Will wrapped it," Francesca said, apologetically.

Will looked offended. "What's that supposed to mean?"

"It sucks!" Josh laughed. "That's what she's trying to say."

"I didn't say that," Francesca squeaked.

Jess was rolling her eyes. "Just open it."

"Yeah, we want to eat your cake," Josh smiled.

George flipped the gift over. "You really didn't have to…"

He tore back the paper and blushed. It was a brand-new backpack with 'Champion' emblazoned across the front.

"Champion … get it?" Josh asked.

"I think he gets it," Francesca replied.

George had lost his last bag in the chaos of the Paris attack.

"You like it?" Lauren asked.

"I love it, guys. Thank you."

"Great! Now, cake!" Josh roared.

George wasn't sure exactly when Gran had snuck out of the room, but he spent the next hour surrounded by his friends. They talked and laughed, and for a fleeting moment, he forgot all about the mirror, the blood and the anger, until someone mentioned the unmentionable.

"Any news of your mum?" Josh asked, picking the cake crumbs off his plate with a licked finger.

"Josh!" Francesca scowled.

"What?"

"No, it's OK," George said. "I think we might have a lead, but I'm waiting to hear more from my dad when he gets home."

Before Paris, only Felix had known about Sam's real job with MI5, but it had been impossible to keep the truth from them all after everything that had happened in Paris. They'd been in the hangar when Cate had arrived and had heard the argument that she'd had with Sam about catching George's mother, Jay. George had been careful to tell them only what his dad had agreed to, but it felt nice to have friends who at least partially understood.

"Your dad will come through," Felix said.

"Yeah, they'll track down Jin-è," Will added. "She can't hide forever."

"I guess," George said, his chin sinking to his chest.

"She'll be home soon," Lauren said, reaching out for his hand again.

This time he didn't pull away, but he could feel the sting of his cuts as she squeezed his hand in hers. Trying his hardest to hide the pain, he squeezed back. "I hope so."

With that, George could hear keys jangling in the front door.

"Your father's home," Gran called from the front room.

George could hear his dad's voice as he came through the front door and his stomach tightened.

Does he have news?

"Maybe we should go," Francesca said, looking towards the kitchen door.

"No," George said, instinctively. "I mean, unless you need to."

His friends looked at each other. "It's your birthday," Will said, slapping George on the back. "You call the shots."

"We'll stay as long as you want us to," Jess grinned.

George could feel his cheeks burn, so was pleased when his friends' attention was drawn away to Sam pushing open the kitchen door.

"Hi, Mr Jenkins," Felix chirped.

Sam's faded blue cap had been replaced with a new one that looked rigid and awkward on his head. His beard had been trimmed, making him appear younger and fresher, but the lines across his forehead and bags under his eyes gave away his exhaustion. He stood in the doorway and stared at the bodies that filled his kitchen.

"Er, hi," Sam said, pulling his cap down and squeezing past them.

George caught his eye and opened his mouth to speak, but Sam just smiled and pushed open the back door. "I'll leave you to it."

During the following hour, George spent half the time wrapped up in the warmth and frivolity of his friends' banter and half the time with his mind drifting out towards his dad's shed, wondering whether he had any news.

By the time Sam re-entered the kitchen, George's friends were on their way out.

"Thank you for having us," Francesca said, as they started filing down the hallway. "Hope you have a lovely evening."

Sam stood in the kitchen and watched them all leave. Lauren was the last. She leant in to hug George, but noticing that Sam was watching, she thought better of it and just whispered in George's ear. "See you back at school … I hope."

"Yeah, tomorrow," George said, smiling.

Once they had all disappeared up the path, George closed the front door and turned back to look at his dad, who was still loitering in the kitchen doorway.

"Let's talk," Sam said, standing aside and ushering George back into the kitchen.

He waited until George had settled himself onto one of the bar stools and then leant up against the cupboards on the opposite side of the breakfast bar.

"What do you want to know?"

"Everything," George replied, bluntly.

Sam took off his cap and bunched it up in his hands.

"Well, there's not a lot we know for sure, but our current assumptions are that–"

"I thought you said that good detectives never assume," George said, a little too prickly.

Sam frowned. "Do you want an update or not?"

George sank into his seat and let Sam continue. "We think that Angelika is still in possession of the stolen Rothkos and still in France."

"So, no progress there," George said.

Sam shook his head. "Will you let me finish!"

George folded his arms.

"We've identified the owner of the Rothkos," Sam continued, "and we're looking into any connections between him and Victor."

George fidgeted. He knew his dad had been given the task of tracking down the artwork and the weapon that had been stolen by Victor, but George only cared about one thing.

"What about Mum?"

"I'm getting there," Sam said, wringing his cap into a knot. "Victor still isn't talking, but we think we may know Jin-é's true identity, and we think she might be associated with a gang that smuggle stolen and counterfeit goods across the channel."

"That's progress," George said, sitting up. "Do we know where they might be?"

Sam shook his head. "We've got a few groups under surveillance. We're hoping that she'll show her face."

"Hoping," George said. "Can't we interrogate them?"

"We don't need to alert Jin-é to our presence. We can't afford to force her deeper underground. The more relaxed she is the better."

"Do we have any clue if she's even left France?"

Sam looked up at George from beneath his furrowed eyebrows. "No."

George shook his head. "But, how hard can it be to track her down? I mean, someone must know where she is. Haven't you got spies or agents or someone who can push harder?"

"You know, Cate and I are on the case full-time. Dupont and Elías, and even Eddie, are all doing their best."

George dumped his head into his hands. "It's not enough."

"George, I also have a fugitive, some highly valuable art and a weapon to find."

"But Mum could be ... hurt ... or worse!"

"We don't know that," Sam said, "and let's be clear; for all I know, she chose to go with Jin-é."

George glared at his dad. "What?"

"She chose to run, George. Don't forget that. She could have trusted us."

"That's not fair, and you know it!"

Sam came around the breakfast bar and spun George's stool around to face him. "Look, we're doing everything we can. We can't work any faster than the leads come in."

"But–"

"George, listen to me. You need to trust me. As soon as we have any idea where Jin-é and your mother are and what they're planning, we'll make our move."

George stared at his feet. The wrapping paper from earlier sat screwed up at the foot of his stool. He nudged it with his toe.

He still doesn't believe she's innocent.

"Just trust me ... please," Sam repeated.

George nodded. "Fine."

"Anyway," Sam said, straightening up, "I don't want to argue with you again, especially on your birthday."

"Huh, I thought you'd forgotten," George said, kicking out at the balled-up paper.

"Wait here. I've got you a gift."

George stayed in the kitchen while Sam disappeared upstairs. He felt deflated. He didn't want to fight with his dad again, but he couldn't shake the feeling that he was still keeping things from him. He felt like an outsider: helpless, aimless and with no control, and the leads just weren't coming fast enough.

We need to be out there hunting down clues.

Surely, there was more that his dad could be doing.

Does he even want her to come home?

"Your gift," Sam said, reappearing at the kitchen door with a small cardboard box in his arms.

"What's that?" George asked, sceptically.

"It's something I should have given you years ago."

Sam placed it down on the counter-top and stepped back. George pulled it closer. The sagging cardboard was covered in dust, and the parcel tape that bound it had lifted in places.

George peeled back the tape and peered inside. "What's this?"

"I'm sorry I kept it from you," Sam said, wiping some stray dust from the counter. "However I felt about her … I should have let you know her better."

George folded back the cardboard flaps and carefully picked through the contents: photos, old birthday cards, hand-scribbled pictures in brightly coloured crayons. His breath caught in his throat. There she was: young, fresh, cheeks flushed; wrapped in a hospital gown and holding him in her arms; pushing him on a swing; chasing him across the lawn. Notes she'd written to him and pictures he'd drawn for her. Words between them that had vanished from his memories as permanently as she had. He knew it was all him, but it felt so unreal. A world that he could barely recall – a world that he'd been part of with her, his mother.

By the time he raised his head, Gran and his dad were both standing in front of him.

"Thank you," he croaked.

"I'm sorry it's not some new gaming thing," Sam said with a crooked smile.

"This is far better," George beamed.

"You can put them up … if you want – you know, around the house."

George looked back down at the box. He felt a warmth inside him that he hadn't felt for a long time, but he also felt a twinge of pain.

"Maybe," he said, lifting the box in his arms. "I'll take them upstairs though … if that's OK?"

"Of course."

His birthday evening wasn't so bad after all. They ate homemade pizza and watched a movie, which went someway to distracting George's mind, but well before the end, Gran and Sam fell asleep on the couch, so George flicked off the TV and crept upstairs. By the time Gran came into his room to wish him goodnight, he'd looked through the box his dad had given him several times.

"You OK, Georgie?"

"Yeah, Gran. Thanks … for getting all my friends over."

"My gift to you," she smiled.

"It was just what I needed."

"I know," she said, turning to leave. "You sleep well, my boy."

"Gran," George said, stopping her in the doorway, "I really am sorry about the mirror."

"I told you, Georgie, people don't live on in things."

But as she left, George looked over at the collection of memories in the box on his desk and had to disagree.

From: The Moth
To: The Flame
Re: The Jaybird {Encrypted}

Six days and counting.
Maybe you should bury your ego and reconsider.

End.

From: The Flame
To: The Moth
Re: The Jaybird {Encrypted}

You shouldn't goad me. It will only end badly for you.

End.

Chapter 3: Strange Salutations

Wednesday wasn't George's favourite day of the week, mainly because he had to survive double maths, but at least the half-term break was only a few days away and that meant a whole week off.

One day at a time, George.

He managed to convince Gran to let him have some left-over birthday cake for breakfast.

"Don't let your father see," she said.

"He's gone to work already," George said, gobbling down his cake.

"Are you going to open your birthday cards?" Gran asked, as he pulled on his coat. "There's a pile of them by the front door."

"Really?" George asked, surprised.

"Yes, three or four. They came in the post."

George grabbed them as he left the house and stuffed them into his new bag.

The journey to school had vastly improved for George. He used to sit on his own and try to avoid making conversation with anyone other than Mr Steckler, the old bus driver, but now Lauren saved him a seat every day. All golden, tousled hair and rosy cheeks, she was beaming at him as he climbed onto the bus.

"How was the rest of your birthday?" she asked as he sat down.

"Er, yeah, pretty good."

They chatted the whole way to school.

The morning flew by and double maths was looming after lunch. All George's friends were busy with lunchtime clubs, except Felix, so the two of them hid out in the locker room and tried to avoid bumping into Liam

Richardson and his gang. Liam still had it in for George but was more careful about when and where he picked on him. George's friendship group had grown considerably since the beginning of year nine and there was some sort of safety in numbers, but George didn't doubt that, given the chance of being alone with George, Liam would make up for lost time.

"What did your dad get you for your birthday?" Felix asked, as he tried to lever himself up onto the top of the lockers to join George.

"Oh, a bunch of stuff … just small things really," George replied.

"Anyone else get you anything?"

"Oh, I've got some cards to open," George said, leaning down and scooping his bag off the peg inside his locker. "You can help me open them."

"OK, but if I find any cash – it's mine," Felix grinned, pushing his glasses up onto his nose.

"There won't be anything as exciting as cash inside," George said, handing Felix two of the cards.

The first card was from a friend of Gran's. She sent him one every year, although George could never remember ever meeting her. It had a picture of a dinosaur on the front. Felix laughed and started on the second.

"There's something in this one," he said, ripping open the envelope. "I can feel something – unless it's a birthday badge to go with your dinosaur."

"Shut up! Give it here," George said, snatching it back.

The card was tightly packed in, and George struggled to pull it out. Losing patience, he ripped apart the rest of the envelope, making the card spring out across the locker-tops and a small brown package tumble to the floor.

"What's that?" Felix asked, leaping down after it.

George jumped down beside him, and Felix handed it over. It was about the size of a coaster and nearly as flat, except for a strange looking bulge in the centre.

"No idea," George said, squeezing it between his fingers.

"Open it then," Felix said.

George found the end of the tape that sealed it and pulled. It came off in one piece and the brown paper folded out, revealing a single brass key.

"Huh," George said, screwing his nose up. "What sort of gift is that?"

"Who's it from?" Felix asked, swiping his hand across the top of the lockers, searching for the card.

The card flew off and just missed George's head. He grabbed it and stared at the front. It was a picture of a dog wearing a beret. Flipping it open, he scanned his eyes across the loopy handwritten note.

"Er … Dupont," George said, looking back at the key.

"Dupont sent you a card?"

"So, it seems," George said, perplexed.

"Weird – and what's with the key?"

George read the words again.

Dear George,
Bon Anniversaire!
Dupont.

*PS: The gift is for you and **only** you!*

"What the hell does that mean?" Felix asked, reading over George's shoulder.

"I guess she doesn't want me to show anyone else," George shrugged.

"Bit late for that. How could she be sure that you wouldn't open it in front of anyone?"

With that, the bell rang and the rest of year nine could be heard steaming down the corridor. George shoved the cards into his locker, scooped up the brown paper, re-wrapped the key and stuffed it in his pocket. "We should get ready for maths."

George couldn't concentrate in maths. Miss O'Donnell's soft Irish voice was enough to lull him into a post-lunch slumber at the best of times, but today his mind wasn't even in the room. All he wanted to do was take another look at the key. Dupont's words circled around in his head. She was trying to get him a message, and he guessed that she was trying to bypass Sam.

*You and **only** you.*

He needed to reach Dupont somehow, and he needed to know what the key was for.

"George ... George!"

Miss O'Donnell was standing beside him. She squatted down and met his gaze. Her youthful eyes and smooth, freckled cheeks seemed to always be smiling.

"Sorry," George said, "I was just getting my head around it."

"Around what? The algebra, I presume?"

"Um ... yes."

"Hmm, if you're struggling with it, maybe you should wait behind and see me after class. We can discuss which particular part you're finding difficult."

"Um ... thanks."

Great!

The rest of the lesson seemed to drag, and George's mood was sinking with the autumn sun. He really didn't want to have to stay behind. Watching the rest of his class leave for end-of-day prayers, he slid down into his seat.

"How are you?" Miss O'Donnell asked, pulling up a spare chair.

George fiddled with the end of his tie. "I'm fine. I was just struggling to concentrate. I'll catch up, I promise."

"Hmm, I'm not worried about your algebra, George. I'm worried about *you*."

Not this again!

"I'm fine," he said, "just tired. It was my birthday yesterday. I … had some friends round and–"

"George, I'm going to be straight with you. Your dad called and told me that you didn't want to do any more of the sessions."

George couldn't help feeling bad. He liked Miss O'Donnell and knew that she was only trying to help.

"It's just … I…"

"You don't have to explain. I totally understand. However, I have been asked to keep an eye on you – not just as school counsellor. I am your form tutor, and it's my duty to look out for the wellbeing of my students."

"I'm fine, really," George said.

She sat back in her chair. "You've shown incredible bravery and maturity in recent weeks, but that doesn't mean that you're not allowed to feel angry or sad. It is perfectly understandable."

"I'm not angry – why would I be angry?" he asked, a little too irritably.

She smiled at him. "Hmm, OK … fine. I'm glad you're not angry. But if you are, I'm here to talk."

George pushed his chair back, eager to leave. "Sure."

Miss O'Donnell smiled her gentle smile. "We'd better go. We'll be late for prayers."

She escorted George down the corridor and told him to sneak in at the back of the hall. Shuffling along the back wall, he managed to squat behind a bench of sixth-formers without turning too many heads.

Mrs Hamilton was reading a poem about the beauty of autumn that he'd heard before. Unable to wait any longer, he reached into his pocket and slid out the piece of crumpled brown paper from Dupont's card. Carefully, he unfolded it, revealing the tiny key, but something else caught his eye. Scribbled in faint pencil, across one corner, was a message. George squinted in the dull light of the hall, barely able to make out the words.

If anything goes wrong, deliver this to my <u>son</u>. It is for his eyes only. He is not to trust anyone. It will help him to think of <u>home</u>.

George's pulse raced, making him catch his breath. *Mum!*

His mum had sent him a message. Had she been in touch with Dupont?

"Amen," the whole room chorussed, making George jump.

"I hope you all have a wonderful evening!" Mrs Hamilton boomed from the stage.

Before George had even registered the movement around him, everyone was on their feet and streaming from the hall. Recomposing himself, he gathered up the paper, checked his pocket for the key and shuffled out with the sixth-formers. Desperate to get home, he made a dash for the year nine lockers, but just as he was stuffing all his belongings into his bag, someone shoved him from behind, and he collapsed head first into his locker.

"Ow!"

"Oh, I'm sorry, didn't see you there, cockroach!"

It was Liam, Connor and the Fox twins. George had managed to avoid them all day, but now he was alone and surrounded.

You idiot, George!

"Let me help you out," Liam said, grabbing George by the pockets of his trousers and yanking him out of his locker backwards.

George tried to stay on his feet, but Liam threw him back with such force that he slammed into the lockers opposite and slid to the floor.

Arghh!

He really didn't need this right now. He just wanted to take his mum's note and get home, so he bunched up his fists and slid up the locker face, but as he straightened up, the tiny key toppled out of his pocket and bounced to the floor.

No!

The tinkle of metal was barely audible, but Hayley had heard it. "What was that?"

George slid his foot over the key and tried to distract them all. "What's your problem?" he snapped.

"Problem?" Liam snarled. "It's not me with the problem."

"Yeah – it's you who has issues?" Connor said. "Heard you needed special time with Miss O'Donnell."

"Yeah, Miss O'Donnell your new mummy?" Liam asked, leaning against George's open locker and poking around inside it.

The twins sniggered. George went to open his mouth but knew that he'd only make things worse if he answered back.

Just keep your cool.

All he cared about right now was not losing his mum's key.

They can make all the fun they want.

"What, no smart answer?" Liam asked, turning to face George.

George was blocked in – the twins to his left and Connor to his right.

Where are the others?

"He's done all his talking with Miss O'Donnell. You all talked out?" Connor teased.

George frowned.

Just ignore them.

"Oh, it's OK, George," Liam whispered. "Your secret is safe with us. We won't tell anyone that you have your special little sessions with the school shrink."

George could feel the familiar stirrings of the monster deep in the pit of his stomach. He chewed at his tongue and tried to put it back to sleep.

"She's my maths teacher," he said through gritted teeth.

"Oh, OK," Liam snorted. "That's what we'll tell everyone – shall we? Wouldn't want you getting *upset,* would we?"

"Yeah, wouldn't want to upset poor, fragile George," Connor added, dragging his hands down his cheeks and pretending to cry.

George could feel his blood pumping through his neck. His monster was wide awake now and pacing back and forth.

The key – just hold on two more minutes – the others will get here.

"What do you reckon it's worth – keeping your secret quiet?" Liam asked.

"Huh?" George said, trying to peer past the line of lockers and out of the door. He could hear voices and the clatter of footsteps.

"You deaf as well as special?" Liam said, shoving George in the chest.

George glanced down at his feet as he staggered backwards.

"Not so brave without all your bodyguards, are you?" Connor added.

George froze. The key was just poking out from beneath his shoe.

Hayley followed his gaze down. "What's that?"

"Nothing!" George replied, trying to slide his foot back over it.

"He's hiding something!" Annie squealed.

"Give it here," Liam said, bending down.

"No!" George shouted, and without stopping to think, he shot his knee upwards to block Liam's path. *Crunch!* His rising kneecap caught Liam square on the nose. Liam staggered backwards, clutching at his face, and collapsed, backside first, into George's open locker.

"Argh!" Liam roared. "You've broken my nose!"

"Get out of my way!" George steamed, snatching up the key and pushing past the twins.

Flailing about like a toddler mid-tantrum, Liam tried desperately to free himself from the confines of the locker. "Stop him!"

But George was already making a dash for the door. Grabbing the handle, he looked back, only to see the twins stumbling over themselves in an effort to chase after him.

Ha!

He squeezed the key in his hand and dragged the door open, hoping to see the rest of year nine coming down the corridor, but instead he ran straight into Miss O'Donnell.

"What's the rush?" she asked, startled.

"I … I'm … late…" he stammered. "I need to get home."

But as Liam appeared with blood trickling from his nose, George knew that he wouldn't be going home any time soon.

From: K07
To: J21
Re: Stolen Goods {Encrypted}

Update 1.1

I've dug up everything we have on the Russian billionaire.

His main business is gas and oil, and although he has his finger in several other pies, I can't see any obvious link between him and the Bird.

End.

From: J21
To: K07
Re: Stolen Goods {Encrypted}

Response to Update 1.1

Something doesn't add up. The Bird must have targeted him for a reason. We need to question him directly. There must be a link.

End.

Chapter 4: The Key to Success

George waited over twenty minutes for Miss O'Donnell to return from the medical room. Liam's nose wasn't broken, but George was in deep water nonetheless. With both his form tutor and his headmistress buried behind the office door, he could only imagine that they were calling his dad right now.

He sat on one of the chairs outside the Headmistress' office and buried his head in his hands. He hadn't done it out of anger. It was a complete accident – just an instinctive reaction – but he knew that no-one would believe him, least of all his dad.

"George," Mrs Hamilton called from behind the heavy door, "come in, my dear."

Her comforting tone did nothing to reassure George. She was just tip-toeing around him like everyone else.

"Sit down, George," Miss O'Donnell said, as she pushed the door closed behind him.

George perched on the edge of the pristine sofa that sat opposite Mrs Hamilton's desk.

"So," Mrs Hamilton sighed, "Miss O'Donnell has told me what happened this afternoon in the locker room."

"It was an accident," George mumbled. "Liam was teasing me and I didn't mean to–"

"Yes, well, I'm inclined to believe your side of the story, but never-the-less, I think you will need to write him an apology."

George's shoulders sank.

Great! I'll never live that down.

"I'm sorry, I really didn't mean it," he said.

"I know, George, and I know how much pressure you've been under recently, so I'm willing to let it go on the understanding that you make peace with Liam and…"

George looked up.

And?

Chewing the end of her pen and glancing at Miss O'Donnell, Mrs Hamilton was obviously thinking carefully about what she was about to say, and George instantly read her mind.

"I'll do it," he sighed. "I'll do the sessions with Miss O'Donnell."

Mrs Hamilton smiled. "I think it will help, George. Just a few – to get things off your chest."

He looked up at Miss O'Donnell and she was smiling too, but for the first time, he saw sadness in her smile, or was it sympathy? He wasn't sure.

"Tomorrow?" she said. "You tell me when is best for you. You can come to my study room; no one will disturb us there."

George nodded. "Tomorrow."

George lurched off the bus and lumbered home. The wind was biting at his face and ankles, and he couldn't wait to get inside. His mother's note had been eating at his thoughts, so he pulled the piece of paper from inside his coat pocket.

Deliver this to my son … for his eyes only … not to trust anyone … think of home.

He stared at the two words that were underlined.

What about home?

He was wandering down the road, heading for home, when his phone buzzed.

"Where the hell did you disappear to?" Felix asked, sounding exasperated. "And what did you do to Liam?"

"It's a long story," George groaned. "Let's just say, I'll have leapt even higher up Liam's hit list."

"Er, I think you were probably already at the top."

"Yeah," George chuckled.

"You wanna' meet up?" Felix asked.

George glanced down at the crumpled paper in his hand. Honestly, he felt like being alone so he could try to work out the meaning of his mother's message. Looking up, he could see home and felt the pull of his room and an overwhelming desire to collapse onto his bed and rummage through the box that his dad had given him.

Oh God! Dad! He's going to go mad!

Suddenly, going home felt like a bad idea.

"When?" George asked.

"Now," Felix said, appearing at George's side.

George nearly dropped his phone. "Jeez, where d'you come from?"

"I was waiting for you," Felix smiled.

"Why?"

Felix's smile seemed to expand across his whole face.

"Well, I may know where your key is from."

The boys were standing in the middle of the pavement, a few doors from George's cottage. One of George's neighbours was out sweeping leaves, so George steered Felix further up the lane.

"How?" George whispered.

Felix lowered his voice. "I was sure I'd seen one just like it, but I couldn't quite remember where. Then it hit me in maths: my dad has one, exactly the same."

"Seriously?" George asked, doubtfully.

"Yep, I'm sure of it."

"And?"

"It's the key to a PO box," Felix said, making his eyebrows jump up and down. "My dad has one for the local charity he runs. It's the numbers on the back. That's what gave it away."

George squeezed the key in his fist. "Numbers?"

"Yeah, look at it. You'll see."

Before sliding the key from his pocket, George checked over his shoulder. The neighbour had his head buried in an overgrown hedge. Happy that no one was looking, George inspected the key. Felix was right. Engraved on the back of the key was a set of tiny numbers. "What do they mean?"

"It's the box location. Put the numbers into the post office website – bang – you've got your box."

George blinked. "You sure?"

"Try it," Felix said, gesturing towards George's phone.

Sure enough, George inputted the numbers and the page spat out a location. "Pendleton," George murmured, his mind spinning.

What has she sent me?

"Huh!" Felix said, looking puzzled. "Why would Dupont have a PO box in Pendleton?"

"Don't know," George said, stopping himself from mentioning his mum's note. "But whatever's inside, I need to get to it." He glanced at the time on his phone and spun around in the direction of the bus stop. "The post office will still be open."

"Hey, slow down there," Felix said, stepping out in front of him. "It's not as easy as that."

"Why not?"

"Well, you don't just need the key: you need ID and proof of address as well."

George slumped down onto the nearest garden wall. "How am I supposed to get that?"

"You can't get hold of Dupont; I'm guessing?" Felix asked.

George shook his head. "Not without going through my dad."

"Then you're gonna' have to think of a way of passing off as her," Felix said, grimacing.

But George knew that it wasn't Dupont's PO box, it was his mother's, and whatever had been sent there, she wanted him to get his hands on it – and without anyone else knowing.

After thanking Felix and leaving him to make his way home, George stumbled back to the cottage, quietly hoping that Sam wasn't back from work. He didn't need a dressing down for his run-in with Liam, but to his great relief, Sam didn't make it home before George and Gran had retired to bed.

By the time George turned out the lights, his eyelids were pleading to give up on what had been another draining day, but his mind had other ideas.

What's in that PO box?

He pulled his duvet tight around his shoulders and tried to nestle into the cradle of his mattress, but even as his muscles began to ease into slumber, thoughts continued to pace up and down behind his eyelids.

I need to get into it.

He turned over and tried to squeeze his eyes into submission.

But I need proof of address.

He flipped onto his other side.

And what address?

He thought of his mother's words again and they weaved their way in between and around his other thoughts.

Home – think of home.

His eyes sprang open.

That's it! It's our address! I need something with our address on!

That one thought stopped all the others dead in their tracks, his head sank into the pillow and he dived into a deep restful sleep.

From: The Moth
To: The Flame
Re: The Jaybird {Encrypted}

I thought I'd let you know that we caught the little rat that tried to sell you my location. I have saved his head as a memento.

And there was me thinking you weren't interested in my offer.

Tut-Tut. Five days and counting.

End.

From: The Flame
To: The Moth
Re: The Jaybird {Encrypted}

Oh, how sad. He was quite amicable (as snitches go).

You can hide away for as long as you want, but you know as well as I do that it is you who is desperate to make the trade, not me.

I can only imagine how broken you are since losing your last deal. Money must be tight. Such a shame.

End.

Chapter 5: Identity Crisis

When the alarm went off on Thursday morning, George woke to find himself lying on his back with his hands clasped around the paper-wrapped key at his chest. He looked like one of those fairytale princesses that lay waiting for their prince to kiss them back to life. His covers fell over him like settled snow, and his back felt as rigid as a board. He'd obviously not moved all night.

"Georgie!" Gran was knocking at his door. "Time to get up."

Not wanting her to come in and find him clutching the key, he leapt up and shoved it under his pillow.

"I'm up!" he called back.

She peeked her head around the door. "I'll do you porridge if you get up in time."

"Er, thanks, Gran."

Ten minutes later, George was dressed and about to head downstairs.

Where can I hide the key?

He didn't want to risk any more close-calls at school, but needed somewhere safe to hide it. He scanned his room, and his eyes rested on the framed photo of him and his mum on the seesaw, making him grin.

No one will touch that.

Pulling open the back of the frame, he whipped out the thin card that held the photo in place and replaced it with the piece of paper and the key.

Perfect!

By the time he made it downstairs, breakfast was ready and Gran was whistling to herself in the bathroom.

George sat at the breakfast bar and tried to stir the heat out of his porridge while Marshall stretched out on the counter-top and cleaned himself.

"Do you really have to do that while I eat?" George grumbled at him, to which Marshall flipped over and flicked his tail in George's direction. As Marshall slid off the counter, with his nose in the air, George spied the pile of unopened post that had been serving as Marshall's mattress.

Dropping his spoon, George shot a look towards the bathroom door. He could hear running water.

Is she having a bath?

Sliding across to the other bar stool, he carefully leafed through the envelopes. He needed something official looking, and something that preferably just had their last name on: Jenkins.

Junk mail, to the occupier, letters to Mrs Cerys Jenkins…

The water stopped running and the door lock clicked.

"Morning, boy!"

George grabbed his spoon and slid his bowl back towards him. "Hmm, porridge is great. Thanks, Gran."

Damn!

"You need to get moving, Georgie. Bus won't wait for you."

Glancing at the pile of post before he left, George wondered where his dad kept his mail.

George made it to the bus stop on time, but Mr Steckler shredded a tyre in his enthusiasm to battle up the hill to school, meaning George missed registration, but he managed to intercept Felix before first lesson.

"I think it's registered to my home address," he said, as they wandered down the corridor towards art.

"Really? Why would Dupont do that?" Felix asked.

"Um … because she wants me to open it," George replied. "I mean, that's what I'm going to try."

"Bit risky."

"What have I got to lose?"

"Hmm," Felix said, unconvinced, "I mean, it's easy enough to get a bill or something with your address on but what about ID? You got anything official looking with your surname on?"

"Like what?"

"A bank card, maybe?" Felix suggested.

"No – but I could … borrow my dad's, I guess."

"That could work – but what if it's not registered in his name? I mean, what name would Dupont put it under?"

The boys paused their conversation as a bunch of year tens pushed past.

"Oh God, I don't know," George said, stuffing his hands in his pockets. "What else can I do? I can't exactly pass off as Mrs Cerys Jenkins!"

Or Mrs Jennifer Jenkins, he thought to himself.

"What if you get to the post office and they rumble you?"

"I don't know," George said, irritated. "Maybe it's a stupid idea."

"You get caught trying to fake it; you could get in big trouble, and you'd probably have to give up the key."

George could feel his confidence draining away.

"Maybe I should just give up."

As they reached the art studio, Josh, Francesca and Lauren were waiting for them.

"Where were you this morning?" Lauren asked, looking concerned.

"Steckler punctured a tyre," George replied.

"Not again," Josh groaned.

"Yeah, you're lucky you had early swim training. We had to walk the rest of the way up the hill."

"Oh, speaking of swimming," Josh said, "Liam turned up looking less than happy. I saw the nice bruiser you gave him."

"Oops," George said.

With that, Will and Jess appeared from the other end of the corridor.

"Liam's on the war path," Jess said.

"He's looking for you," Will added. "Says you owe him an apology."

"Oh God!" George said, glancing over their shoulders. "I was meant to write him a letter. Mrs Hamilton made me promise."

"Here," Lauren said, fishing a pen and some paper out of her bag, "do it quickly, now."

George leant on Felix's back.

"What you gonna' say?" Will asked.

George shrugged. His mood was rock bottom, and he could feel a spike of irritation prickling at his spine. "Er … I don't know … Dear Liam … Sorry your face hit my knee … Best wishes, George."

"Ha!" Josh roared. "Perfect!"

"That won't help the situation," Francesca tutted.

"He's coming," Felix said, straightening up and hiding George from view. George ducked down and tried to lean the paper on his knee.

"Where's Captain Cockroach?" Liam bellowed down the hallway.

"Don't know who you're talking about," Will said, folding his arms and pressing up next to Felix.

"He's gotta' be here," Connor snarled. "He's always hanging around you lot – like some nasty smell."

"Yeah, like a bad fart in a lift," Hayley giggled.

Francesca tutted again. "You're all so immature."

"Oh – really," Annie said, pushing past her twin sister. "You're not so big and grown up yourself. I heard your mum doesn't let you out past ten."

"Yeah, who's the baby?" Hayley teased.

"That's not true!" Francesca said, stamping her foot.

"Whatever," Liam interrupted. "Where's cockroach? He owes me an apology."

"George said to send his apologies – there you go – that's his apology," Will said, grinning.

The others sniggered.

"I swear, Carter," Liam growled, stepping up to Will, "one day I'll mess up that smug face of yours."

"What, make me look like you, you mean?"

George could tell things were about to get messy, and although he didn't want to give Liam the satisfaction of an apology, he didn't want his friends getting into a fight for him, so he quickly finished writing and folded up the paper.

"I'm here!" he called, springing up from behind Felix.

Liam shoved Felix aside. "You hiding back there like a coward?"

"No," George replied.

"Where's my apology?"

George stared at Liam. Both of his already bulging eyes were feathered with spidery-red veins and framed by indigo and amber bruises that made him look like something out of a horror movie.

"Er, it's here," George replied, handing over the roughly folded paper.

"What took you so long?"

"Um … I just wanted to make sure it was …"

"Sincere," Josh said, winking at George.

Liam opened up the note, and George watched the parts of his face that weren't already purple turn a matching shade.

"What!" Liam said, screwing it up in his fist and lunging at George. "You smarmy little…" He grabbed George by the ears, and before George could react, Josh and Will were piling in.

"What's going on?" Mrs Stone, their art teacher, had appeared from inside the art studio. "Put each other down!"

"Liam started it!" Jess blurted out.

"No!" Liam spat. "It's George's fault!"

Mrs Stone frowned. "I'm not interested in who did what. You're all in trouble. You all know that you are supposed to wait in an orderly line outside a classroom until the lesson starts."

Liam fumed. "But, George was supposed to–"

"But nothing, Mr Richardson."

"Ask Miss O'Donnell," Liam demanded.

"What's that?" Miss O'Donnell had come down the corridor to see what all the commotion was.

"Look!" Liam said, shoving the note under her nose. "This is what George gave me as an apology."

George shrunk back behind Felix as Miss O'Donnell scanned her eyes across George's less-than-sincere sentiments.

"You will see me at break, George," Miss O'Donnell said; the usual sparkle missing from her eyes.

George nodded, Liam smirked and Mrs Stone ushered them all into the art studio.

First break came far too quickly for George's liking, and before he had time to regret his actions, he was sitting in front of Miss O'Donnell, trying to find a comfortable position on the lumpy, cushion-filled couch that occupied half of her study room.

"A drink?" she asked, passing him a cup of water.

"Thanks," he grumbled.

There was a large chair behind her desk but she chose to pull a stool up next to George and balance her tea cup on her lap.

"You're not helping yourself, George," she said, dunking her biscuit.

"I'm sorry, it's just–"

"He winds you up – I know."

George looked up from his luke-warm glass of water. "He's just…"

"A bully – I know."

George felt himself relax a little into the sofa.

"I didn't get angry," he said, running his finger around the rim of his glass.

"That's good. I would have," she said, smiling.

George looked at her. She wasn't like the other teachers. He didn't feel her judging him, or grading him like a piece of homework.

"George, my father worked for the … military." She wiped the biscuit crumbs from her skirt and looked up at him. "There were lots of secrets – things that my mother and I couldn't be part of. Do you know what I mean?"

"I … guess," George said.

What's she getting at?

"Well, sometimes I felt that he wasn't there for me – in fact, my parents eventually divorced and he really wasn't there." She swirled the dregs of her tea and downed them in one. "I think I spent most of my teenage years angry." With that, she put down her cup and turned to face him.

"Anger is only worth the energy, George, if it fuels your determination to succeed. Do you agree?"

George nodded slowly.

"Great!" she suddenly said, clapping her hands together and glancing at the clock. "I want you to think about what we've talked about."

"But…"

"When you've thought of how you are going to use your … frustration to fuel something positive, pop-in and see me again." She stood up and offered to take his glass.

"Right, OK, thanks," he said, dragging himself from the swamp of cushions.

He wandered down the corridor with a head full of questions.

What does she mean, fuel something positive?

Felix was waiting in the locker room. "Did you get detention?"

"Er … no," George said, grabbing his books for his next lesson.

He knew he'd got off lightly, but he couldn't help feeling agitated. Agitated at having to constantly fend off Liam, agitated at the lack of progress in finding his mum, and agitated at not being able to think of a way of getting into his mum's PO box. Miss O'Donnell was right: the only way to quell the anger inside him was to take control and make things happen.

"You know what, Felix, I'm going to get inside that PO box. I don't care what it takes. Even if I have to steal my dad's ID or pretend to be my gran or break in or whatever."

"Er … right," Felix said. "Good plan."

"I might need your help though."

"With what? A disguise?"

"No, with holding my nerve at the post office."

As the afternoon progressed, George became more and more fired up. He couldn't sit back any longer and wait for the leads to come in. His mother had sent him a task and he had to succeed, whatever it took.

"Five o'clock," George yelled at Felix, as he leapt onto the bus, "outside the post office!"

Felix stuck both thumbs in the air. "Just text me – let me know that you've got the … paperwork!"

"I'll get the paperwork – you just make sure you're there at five! It shuts at five-thirty!"

"I'll be there!" Felix shouted as he jogged off down the drive.

By the time the bus pulled up outside the newsagent, George had hatched a plan. He was going to spend the next thirty minutes hunting down ID and proof of address for his dad. He had to hope that he could pass off as Mr S Jenkins and that his mother had had the foresight to put the box in their name. All he needed to do was distract Gran while he searched the house, but as he opened the front door, Marshall streaked out, making George jump out of his skin.

Huh?

Marshall never left the house when Gran was in.

"Gran?" he called out, as he threw off his shoes.

Nothing.

Perfect.

Happy that the coast was clear, he dumped his coat and bag and made his way straight upstairs. Unsure of where his dad kept his mail or any form of ID, he headed for his dad's bedroom. He hesitated outside the door. It was firmly closed, and George realised that it was pretty much always that way.

"Secrets," he murmured to himself, before placing his fingers on the door handle.

George very rarely entered his dad's room and wasn't sure what to expect. He imagined a jumble-sale of clothes and bedding flung about in a rush to get out to work, but as he ventured further in, he was shocked to see that there wasn't a crease in the pristine duvet or any sign of discarded washing. Sam was far more organised than George realised.

George scanned the room.

Where would he keep his paperwork?

Even though the house was empty, George tiptoed around the bed towards Sam's chest of drawers. Carefully, he pulled out each drawer in turn and tried to search between the tightly folded clothes and rolled up socks without disturbing anything obvious. As he moved around the room, checking every possible drawer and cupboard, he started to fear that everything useful his dad owned was stashed away in his double-locked shed.

There's got to be something.

As he reached the far side of the bed and checked the bed-side table, his dad's alarm clocked ticked loudly at him: four-nineteen.

Hurry up, George.

Glancing out of the window, he could see Marshall perched on the front gate pillar, waiting for Gran to return.

Tick, tick, tick: four-twenty.

George ploughed on.

Screech!

George turned and peered out of the window again. Marshall had gone and the gate was swinging closed.

Damn it!

Making for the door, he rounded the bed at speed but stubbed his toe on the bed frame.

Ouch!

"That you, Georgie?"

George was bent over, massaging his throbbing toe.

"Hmm!" he tried to call back, but the pain had somehow paralysed his voice box.

"You OK?" Gran asked.

He could hear her putting down her bags and flapping out her coat.

I need to get out of here.

But as he went to stand up, he spotted something peeking out from beneath the bed: a hefty wooden box.

"Georgie!" Gran was on the stairs.

Without hesitation, George grabbed the box, slung it under his arm, dashed from the room, slunk past the top of the stairs and almost tripped in his urgency to get the box under his own bed.

"Where are you?"

"Here," George said, hopping out from behind his bedroom door.

"Oh!" Gran said, looking down at George's floating foot and glancing back towards Sam's room.

Damn!

The door was ajar.

"Your father home?"

"Um, not sure," George said. "I just got in – haven't seen him – unless he's in his shed."

"I didn't see his van," Gran said, still staring at the open door.

"Right, of course – so, no then – guess he's not."

Gran looked back at George and narrowed her eyes at him. "You better not be up to anything, boy."

"No," George chirped, his eyebrows rising up a little too far and his voice even further.

Gran let it go. "You in for tea?"

"Yes, please," he replied. "Any chance it can be a late one though? I said I'd meet Felix quickly in town."

"Of course," she said, before turning back towards the stairs.

George slid back behind his door and watched her go. He waited for the radio in the kitchen to kick into life before he sneaking back over the landing and pulling his dad's door shut.

He checked his watch.

I've got ten minutes.

Falling to his knees, George yanked the box back out from under his bed. It looked like an antique: rich, polished wood; a delicate metal trim and a tiny key hole at the front.

Damn!

Taking a chance, George pulled at the lid – loose but definitely locked.

Where on earth would the key be?

He slumped to the floor and ran his hands through his hair. *Buzz!* It was Felix on text.

'I'm leaving now. U got the ID?'

George squeezed his head between the palm of his hands.

Come on, George, think …

"Paperclip!"

Jumping up, he rummaged through the contents of his desk drawer.

There!

One solitary paperclip.

This better work.

Uncurling it, he jammed it into the hole like he'd seen people do in the movies. Wiggling it around, he pulled at the lid again. Something rattled inside. He tried turning the twisted metal pin from one side to the other, but still the lock didn't budge. Finally, he turned the box on its side and tried to push down on the keyhole from above. Nothing.

How can such a tiny lock be so hard to pick?

He threw the paperclip across his room and collapsed back to the floor.

Rubbish!

But then he saw it, stuck to the base of the box, a simple metal key poking out from a small leather pouch.

"Ha! Not so 'MI5 genius'," he chuckled to himself.

Without wasting another minute, he opened the box and filtered through its contents.

Well I never!

There were several passports, a handful of cash cards from foreign banks, letters from the around the world, and buried at the very bottom, a small handgun. George stared at it all.

Buzz!

It was Felix again. *'We still on?'*

George grabbed his phone. *'Yes – coming now."*

George knew that the passports wouldn't work. He needed something without a date of birth or photo on, so he grabbed a couple of the cash cards and a fistful of letters, re-locked the box and made for the door.

Wait!

He'd nearly forgotten his mum's key. Levering open the back of his mum's photo; he slid the key out and zipped it into his jacket pocket with the cards and letters. Before leaving, he made sure to slide the box back under his dad's bed, desperately hoping that he could return all its contents before his dad got home.

From: K07
To: J21
Re: Stolen Goods {Encrypted}

Update 1.2

The Billionaire was less than keen to speak with us. He claims to have no knowledge of the Bird or know of any reason why he would have targeted his artwork, but my instincts tell me that he's holding something back.

End.

From: J21
To: K07
Re: Stolen Goods {Encrypted}

Response to Update 1.2

Always trust your gut.
Let's put him under surveillance and see what turns up.

End.

Chapter 6: In a Fit of Panic

It was five fifteen by the time George's bike tyres squealed to a halt outside the post office in Pendleton High Street. Felix stood in the doorway, wrapped in a large duffle coat, hat and scarf. George had to check twice that it was him before approaching.

"Felix?"

"Yeah, it's me," Felix replied from behind his scarf.

"You cold?"

"Maybe."

"You sure you want to do this?" George asked.

"You got the ID?"

"Yeah, it's my dad's, so my name is Sam if anyone asks."

"I suggest you wear this," Felix said, pulling a baseball cap from his pocket.

"What?"

"I mean it."

George shoved the cap on his head. "Is this really necessary?"

"Let's just get this over with."

The two boys locked up their bikes and made their way into the post office. There was only one other customer inside and she was being served by the only visible member of staff. George stood in the line behind her with Felix cowering in his shadow.

"Take the scarf off," George whispered over his shoulder. "You look like you're about to rob the place."

"We practically are," Felix's muffled voice replied.

"We're just retrieving what's mine," George said, trying to stand up tall.

"Next," the young woman behind the glass announced.

George watched the elderly customer in front of him wander out of the door before he stepped up to the glass and tried to look the young lady directly in the eye.

"Hi," he squeaked.

"Hi," she said, glancing up at the clock. She was chewing gum and fiddling with a collection of rubber bands around her wrist. "Can I help you?" she said, glancing at the clock again.

George followed her gaze. It was five-twenty.

It's now or never.

"I've come to collect my mail," he said, with only a slight tremor in his voice.

"Local collect?" she asked, hovering her fingers over her keyboard.

"Um…"

"No, a PO box," Felix piped up from behind.

The young lady peered over George's shoulder at Felix.

"A PO box?" she asked looking back at George.

"Yes … please," George replied, smiling as broadly as he could without looking creepy.

She looked at the clock again.

"We usually ask that you don't come just before–"

"I'm sorry," George interrupted, "it's mail from my aunt, she lives abroad … I hardly see her … we meant to get here earlier but…"

"OK, OK," the young lady sighed.

She stood up and George felt his shoulders ease.

So far, so good.

"I'll have to get my manager," she said. "I can't leave the front unmanned."

George tensed up again.

A manager.

She disappeared for a moment, and George and Felix were left standing alone.

"Don't look up," Felix whispered in George's ear.

"Why?" George asked, peering out from beneath his cap and spotting a large TV screen showing a CCTV image of the two of them.

Great!

"Who's the registered owner?" a booming voice said from behind them.

The young lady had returned to her kiosk, but a much larger and older woman had appeared from another door.

"Er … me," George said, trying not to glance up at the CCTV again.

"Follow me, please," she said, beckoning them through a set of double doors and into a side room.

George tried to look like he'd seen it all before but couldn't help being dazzled by the large bank of shiny, red lockers that lined one wall.

"Do you have your key and box number?" she asked.

"Box number," George repeated, looking at Felix, who just shrugged. "Right … I forgot about that."

The lady looked him up and down. "You don't know your box number?"

"No … I … I can't remember. It … it's been a while," George stammered.

"You have the key though, I presume?" the woman asked.

"Yes!" George said, whipping the key out of his pocket so quickly that he nearly threw it at her. "It's here."

She looked at the key, looked George up and down again and then peered over at Felix who was now loitering by the double doors, still wrapped in his scarf.

"OK, I can search by name and address," she said, turning to her computer.

"Jenkins," George said, and then gave her his full address.

As her fingers tapped away at the keys, George watched her eyebrows furrow and her eyeballs flit across the screen. He could hear the whirr of the computer and the sound of his own saliva slipping down his throat as he swallowed hard.

"Box forty-two," she said, turning back to George.

"Ah, yes, that's it," George said, nodding enthusiastically.

"This box really hasn't been accessed in a while," the lady went on.

"Er, yeah, we don't use it much," George said, glancing over at Felix, who was now slipping out of the glass doors.

Where is he going?

"Do you have your ID and proof of address?" she asked.

George dug into his pocket and pulled out the letters and cards. They all came out in a jumbled wad. He tried to leaf through them, looking for something that wouldn't draw too much attention, but his fingers were jittery and he lost grip, sending several pieces of paper and one of the cards tumbling to the floor.

"Let me get that," the lady said, bending down and scooping them up. "You seem to have your hands full."

She looked down at the bank card and letters and over at her screen.

George could feel a finger of sweat trace its way down the back of his neck. He tried to resist the temptation to run, and instead, flared out his shoulders and pushed out his jaw, as if that would make any difference.

The lady looked up at him twice, back at the paperwork then back at her screen.

"There seems to be a problem," she finally said.

The room seemed to fall silent, and George's tongue wrestled with a ball of saliva that had lodged itself at the back of his throat.

"Oh," was all he could say, before the double doors were sliding back open.

"I need your help!" the young girl from the front shouted, and George nearly choked on his spit-ball as he looked up at the CCTV screen to see Felix rolling about on the floor of the post office, clutching at his stomach.

"Wait there, please," the woman said, as she rushed out to see what was happening.

George stood and gawped at the screen. Felix was back on his feet and staggering about like a drunk. *Crash!* He smacked into a rack of envelopes, sending the whole thing flying.

Ping! A clock above George's head struck five-thirty and jogged him back to reality. The tiny key glistened up at him from the creases of his sweaty palm.

"For goodness sake!" he heard the woman cry.

Not wasting another moment, George searched the bank of lockers for any sign of box number forty-two. It wasn't obvious, so he counted from left to right and top to bottom.

This one!

The key slid into the small lock and turned first time. *Clunk.* The door swung open, and staring back at him was a single, white, A4 envelope, lying flat on the base of the locker.

Got you!

Slamming the locker shut, he turned the key, rolled the envelope up and stuffed it inside his jacket before grabbing his dad's letters and cards and making for the double doors.

The scene in the post office would have been hilarious if George hadn't been so on edge. The two women were propping Felix up as he lolled about like a rag doll, his glasses half-hanging off his face and his scarf trailing along the floor.

Composing himself, George marched towards them.

"What's happening?" he asked, in his most concerned voice.

"Is he your friend?" the older woman asked, looking flustered.

"Yes," George replied, trying to take hold of one of Felix's drooping arms.

"What's wrong with him?" the younger woman cried.

"It's probably his … allergies," George said, shifting his shoulder under Felix's armpit and wrestling his wayward scarf out of the way.

"What's he allergic to?"

"Oh …. everything," George said, dragging Felix towards the door. "I'll get him home. Don't worry, he'll be fine!" he called over his shoulder.

"Wait!" the older woman called after them. "Your mail!"

"I'll come back another time!" George yelled, as the door slid closed leaving the two women looking baffled.

"Please tell me you got it?" Felix asked, nudging his glasses back up onto his face.

"Yes," George replied, dragging Felix around the corner. "Please tell me you aren't really having some kind of fit."

"Ha! No!" Felix said, standing up and grinning so broadly his braces flashed in the low sun. "But I was pretty convincing – if I do say so myself."

George could hear the post office door rumbling back open.

"Let's get the hell out of here!" he said, whipping off his bike lock.

"I'm right behind you!" Felix squeaked, as the lady from the post office thundered out after them.

They couldn't have peddled any faster as they fled the high street. Only the steady line of commuting traffic stopped them from breaking the speed limit as they free-wheeled down the hill into Chiddingham.

"That was mental!" George screamed, as they raced along the lanes towards the village centre.

"Ha! You should have seen the woman's face!" Felix yelled back.

By the time they skidded to a halt beside the cricket ground, George's adrenalin had all but burnt out, leaving only a sense of exhausted exhilaration.

"I couldn't believe it when I saw you rolling around on the floor!" George said.

Felix laughed. "I just hoped you'd realised what I was doing."

"What on earth made you do it?"

"I was pretty sure you were getting nowhere, and I'd seen it in this movie."

"Seriously – you're a genius."

"I know," Felix said, proudly.

"I mean it though – I was dead in the water – you pulled it out of the bag."

Felix sat straddled over his bike, gripping his handlebars. "You're welcome. Let's just hope it was worth it. What was inside the locker?"

George stopped grinning and placed his hand on the bulge in his jacket. He had no idea what would be inside the envelope, and his mother's warning swarmed around inside his head.

"Er, I don't know – maybe I shouldn't open it up out here – you know…"

"Right," Felix said, his arms dropping to his sides. "It's not like there's anyone around though."

George looked up and down the lane. "I think that maybe I should … take it home and…"

"You know, George," Felix said, stuffing his hands into his pockets, "you don't have to do this alone."

"I know, it's not that, it's just…"

"Every good detective needs a useful sidekick," Felix added, winking behind his fogged-up glasses.

He saved your skin, George. If it wasn't for him…

"You're right," George said. "Let's go up to the pavilion."

"Perfect," Felix said, grabbing hold of his handlebars again and spinning his bike 180 degrees.

The cricket green was empty, so the boys dumped their bikes and perched on the edge of the pavilion's terrace.

George unrolled the envelope. "Felix, there's something I haven't been totally honest about."

"What?" Felix asked, breathing into his hands to warm them up.

"I think this envelope is from my mum."

"What? How?" Felix asked, puzzled.

"I'm not sure," George replied, "but I think she's the one who asked Dupont to get it to me."

"You think she's heard from her?"

"I don't know."

"So, what are you waiting for?" Felix said, edging closer. "Open it!"

"Yeah, I guess…"

Slowly, George wriggled his finger into the opening of the envelope and ran it along the flap. He thought of his mum and tried to picture her sealing it shut. Even holding it in his hands made him feel closer to her.

"OK," he sighed, slipping his hand inside and sliding out the contents.

"What is it?" Felix asked, peering over George's shoulder.

Three pieces of paper lay on George's lap, and sat on the top, in the dip that sagged between his knees, was a small plastic bag containing a bullet.

The two boys stared at each other.

"Is that blood?" Felix asked, pointing at the flecks of brown that gathered at the bottom of the plastic bag.

George held the bag up and twisted it from back to front. "I guess."

"Why would your mother send you that?"

George's mind vaulted back to his last conversation with her, in the woods in Paris.

I have to clear my name – there are things I've done.

He swallowed hard. "I don't know."

Felix plucked the little bag from George's grasp. "Is it evidence?"

"Maybe."

"What's the paperwork?" Felix asked, placing the bullet carefully on the step between them.

George tore his eyes away from the bullet and picked up the first piece of paper. It was a photo of two men.

"Is that Victor?" Felix asked, squinting at it.

Victor's hard features just peeked out from the shadows of a hooded mac, but George knew that imposing silhouette, that hooked nose, that arrogant smirk.

"Who's he shaking hands with?" Felix asked.

The other man in the photo was taller and broader than Victor, with thick, golden hair, slicked back from his face. A chunky ring graced every finger, and a fat metal watch glinted up from his wrist. The jewellery looked oddly out of place against his bleached-out camo jacket and trousers.

"No idea," George replied, flipping the photo over.

Something was written on the back in bold block capitals.

DARLIK, TURKEY, AUGUST 23RD

"Do you think your mother took the photo?" Felix asked.

"Maybe. She said something about a deal in Turkey. She must have been there, watching Victor."

"And the other guy?"

"No idea," George shrugged.

"What's the other stuff?"

George put the photo to the bottom of the pile. The next piece of paper was a news article, roughly ripped from a newspaper.

George scanned it. Various words were underlined, but it wasn't in English.

"How good's your French?" he asked Felix.

"Not bad." George handed it over. "Um … it says something about a dead body … found in a dockyard in Calais," Felix said, tracing his finger over the words. "Shot … several times."

"Who's body?"

"A seventeen-year-old boy," Felix said, grimacing. "Chinese descent and wait … thought to be from London."

George looked over at the picture. It looked like a criminal mug shot. The boy had thick, black hair; light stubble and what looked like stitches above his eyebrow.

"What's his name?" George asked.

"Um … it says they are waiting to confirm identity – his parents are 'non-traçable' – not traceable."

"Anything else?" George asked. "What's that word there? The one that's double underlined."

"Bande – I think that means gang or group."

George took the article back. Staring at the boy's joyless eyes gave him an uneasy feeling. He shifted his weight and peered out at the darkening green.

"Why has she sent me these things?"

"Maybe it's a clue," Felix said, strumming his fingers against the pavilion step. "What's the last one?"

George picked up the last piece of paper, but the light was fading, so he dug out his phone and flicked on the torch. It was another photograph. Several important looking men and women, all dressed in evening suits and cocktail dresses, were gathered in a garden. Two men's faces were circled in red pen.

"It's that same guy," Felix said, grabbing the first photo from George's lap. "The one shaking Victor's hand. Look."

George flicked the torch between the two pictures. Felix was right. The man in the centre of the shot was the guy in the camo gear from the first photo. He had his hands clasped in front of him, and George could see the rings and a glimpse of the same watch, but this time his sharp black dinner jacket and glowing white shirt made him look more like royalty.

"Whoever he is, my mum obviously thinks he's of some importance."

"And the guy next to him?" Felix asked, wiping the fog from his glasses to get a better look.

The other circled face was that of a much younger man. Tall and willowy, but with a face of stone, his expression severe and his eyes cold. He stood at the other man's shoulder, too close to be a stranger, and George could see that his right ear was completely missing.

"What's the significance of all this?" he asked himself out loud.

"God knows," Felix said, dumping his chin into his open palms and strumming his fingers against his cheeks. "There must be a link, some clue your mum wants you to look for…"

"Or maybe she just wanted me to keep it all safe. It could be evidence."

"Shame she didn't give you a hint. There's nothing else in the envelope, is there? No letter or instructions?"

"Don't think so," George said, upturning the envelope and flapping it about, but to his surprise, something fluttered to the ground – something small and red.

"What's that?" Felix asked.

George recognised it immediately.

Jin-é!

Chapter 7: Exposed

The blood-red card lay harsh against the feathery grass of the green. It stared up at George; the golden moth glinting at him in the torch light. As he reached down to pluck it from the ground, he felt a wave of goosebumps run up from his frozen fingers to the base of his neck, and he could almost feel the chill of her needle pressed to his skin.

"It's her business card," he uttered, his breath billowing out into the night air.

He turned it over in his hands. It was identical to the one he'd had in his bag in Paris, just more tattered and dog-eared. A list of times had been scribbled on the back, but otherwise it was completely blank except for the Golden Moth etched in gold on the front.

"Not much of a business card," Felix said. "There are no contact details."

"Yeah, I know – strange, huh?"

"Don't suppose those numbers mean anything?" Felix asked.

George thought about his mum and dad in Paris. How they'd looked at Victor's map and read the clues to lead them to La Défense. He turned the card over and read off the times again.

"Maybe phone numbers," he said.

"Or meeting times?" Felix suggested.

The two boys sat staring at the card, each churning the numbers around in their head.

"Map coordinates," George said.

"Or references in a book?" Felix added. "I saw that in a movie too."

George flicked at the tatty corners of the card and stared into the distance as the streetlights started to flicker on. "How would we know, even if we were right?"

"Er, George," Felix said.

"Yeah."

"The card – look at it."

George looked down. Where he'd flicked at the corners, the paper had frayed, revealing a glint of gold beneath the red.

"Hold this," George said, passing Felix the phone. George's fingers felt stiff and cold, but he steadied his hands and slid his fingernail under the lifting edge. Steadily, the paper peeled back, and there, shimmering in the torchlight, was a solid block of gold card.

"Ha!" George exclaimed. "Look at that!"

Etched across the golden card was a set of intricate Chinese characters, each as if they'd been scratched by hand.

"Would be too much to assume that that's her address," Felix said, still holding up the torch.

"Let's hope so," George beamed, gathering up the papers and sliding them back inside the envelope.

"How can we translate that though?" Felix asked, passing George the bullet. "You can barely tell where one character starts and the other ends. You can't exactly type it into a search engine."

"I don't know," George said, leaping up, "but this is exactly what we've been looking for."

"You think you can track down Jin-é based on that?" Felix asked, jumping up to follow him.

"It's a lead," George said, grabbing his bike. "It could help find my mum."

"What are you going to do?"

"I need to show my dad."

"But Dupont said not to show anyone."

George shoved the envelope back inside his jacket and threw his leg over his bike. "I know, but this could tell us where she is, Felix. I have to show him."

"All of it?" Felix asked.

George looked at the bullet in his hand and thought of his dad's reluctance to believe that George's mum was innocent. "Just the card … for now."

Felix nodded. "Fair enough."

George's phoned buzzed. It was home.

Tea!

"I've gotta' go. I'll call you later," George said, pushing off.

"Let me know what he says!" Felix called after him.

"Will do!" George yelled back. "And thanks, Felix! You're a star!"

By the time George pulled into the drive, he had three missed calls from home.

I hope I haven't missed tea.

Sam's van was on the drive.

Yes!

After depositing his bike in the shed, he made for the back door but stopped as he noticed the bulge in his jacket.

For your eyes only.

He undid his zip, grabbed the business card and flattened the envelope back down before re-zipping his jacket.

I can show him this. What harm can it do?

Buzz! His phone went again, so he pulled it out of his pocket.

"I'm here!" he shouted towards the back door, but it wasn't Gran, it was Felix texting.

'Your dad might ask you where you got the business card from!'

"Good point", George mumbled to himself.

'I'll say it was in my mum's old jacket – the one she gave me in Paris,' he texted back, smiling to himself.

Clunk!

The back door was nudging open.

"George!" Sam stood in the doorway, his back-lit silhouette stretching across the lawn.

"Dad," George said, "did I miss tea?"

"Where have you been? I've called you four times!" Sam said, stepping aside to let George in.

"Oh – I thought it was Gran," George said, bounding in through the door and kicking off his shoes.

"So, you still should have answered."

"I was cycling."

"You could have stopped to take the call."

"I'm here now," George said, sniffing the air. "Mmm, smells good."

"George, when I call you four times, it's because I want to speak to you," Sam said, sounding irritated.

"OK, I get it, Dad," George said, burying his head in the fridge. "But I wanted to get home as quickly as possible. I think I might have some really exciting … well, maybe exciting, but still, it could be…"

"George!" Sam bellowed, nearly making George drop the juice carton he'd retrieved from the fridge.

"What the hell, Dad!" he said, slamming the fridge door closed. "You don't need to go mad. It's not even that late." But as soon as he saw Sam's face, he realised that something wasn't right.

"Now I have your attention," Sam said, glaring at George, "I'll ask you again: where have you been?"

All the bounce seemed to drain out of George's legs into a puddle on the floor.

"I … I was with Felix. Gran knew … I … I told her I'd be late."

"And *where* exactly were you and Felix this afternoon?"

George slid the carton of juice onto the counter and folded his arms across his chest.

Oh no!

"In … town."

"Doing what, precisely?"

George could feel the corners of his mum's envelope digging into his chest. He hugged it tighter.

"Not much … why?"

"I had a call from the post office."

George fiddled with his zip and could feel the heat rising up his neck. "Really?"

"Yes, George, really. So, I'll give you one last chance to tell me again. What were you and Felix doing in town?"

George pulled his zip up so high it nearly throttled him.

"Just messing around," he said, trying to smile.

"So, you weren't the scruffy looking boy in a dark jacket and cap using stolen ID to access someone's PO Box?"

"Me?" George squeaked.

"Yes, you and a pale looking kid with braces and glasses."

How can I get out of this one?

"We were just … messing around. It was … just a prank. Felix dared me."

"Really?"

"Yeah – there was no harm in it." George tried to shrug, but his shoulders were already bunching up around his ears.

Sam shook his head. "Stop lying to me, George."

"What? I'm not. I admitted it was me and Felix."

"I know you've been in my room."

What? Gran!

"No … what … I…"

"I know you took my things," Sam said, his eyes burying themselves deeper and deeper beneath his frown. "The lady from the post office said someone turned up pretending to be me! What were you thinking? And more to the point, what were you trying to achieve? I don't even own a PO Box!"

"I … I can explain."

"No! I don't want to hear any more of your lies, George. This is just another example of you losing control!"

"What? No, it's not!" George said. "It's the exact opposite! I'm taking control – I'm actually getting off my backside and focusing my anger on–"

"Exactly! Your anger!"

"No, it's not the same thing!" George shouted. "You never listen to me!"

"I've heard enough!" Sam growled. "You're grounded!"

"What?"

"I can't trust you anymore, George!"

"Trust!" George barked back. "You can hardly talk about trust!"

"Don't push me!"

"Seven years of lies!" George seared.

"Don't you dare throw that at me!"

"Why not?" George spat. "You're allowed to decide which lies you tell, but I'm not?"

"That's enough! Go to your room! I don't want to hear from you again this evening!"

"Fine!" George roared. "That's fine by me!"

From: The Moth
To: The Flame
Re: The Jaybird {Encrypted}

I don't want your money. I want something else.
Something that will cost you a lot less.

Four days and counting.

End.

From: The Flame
To: The Moth
Re: The Jaybird {Encrypted}

Whatever it is, I'll never give it to you.

End.

Chapter 8: Unidentified

George had fallen asleep in his clothes so woke early on Friday morning in a tangled sweat. He glanced over at his alarm clock.

Seven a.m.

Heaving himself onto his back, he peered up at the ceiling. His mind felt empty. Locked in his room, refusing to go downstairs, he'd spent hours last night trying to piece together everything his mother had sent him, and it had left him with such a jumble of thoughts in his brain that he couldn't focus on anything, not even the small spider that was slowly inching its way down from the light shade above his bed. His eyes glazed over and he lost himself in random thoughts as his brain struggled to wake up.

The boiler gurgled to life, and the pipes that ran through the cottage groaned as they were forced to warm up after the chilly night.

Clunk!

George was jolted out of his daze by the sound of a door closing.

Dad!

George pulled his duvet up over his head. He didn't want to speak to his dad or even be in the same room as him.

He wants me to trust him, but he constantly doubts me!

George waited until he heard the front door slam.

I'll prove him wrong!

Throwing back the covers, he sat up and slipped the envelope from his mum out from under his pillow. Flapping the paperwork out onto his duvet, he scrutinised each piece again in turn.

Victor and a mystery man … the guy with one ear … a bloody bullet … Jin-é's business card … and a dead teenager.

"What's the link?" he murmured to himself.

He pulled in his legs and dumped his chin on his knees. Closing his eyes, he tried to see a single thread; a thread that could join all the pieces into a web of a story; something that made sense, but nothing came.

He buried his head deeper between his knees.

Beeeeep!

The alarm clock screamed at him, making him jump.

"Shut up!" he growled, lunging towards his desk and slamming his hand over the snooze button.

Next to his alarm was the box his dad had given him. He pulled out the fistful of photos of him and his mum and flicked through them.

You could have made this easier for me.

Grabbing some tac from his drawer, he carefully stuck them to his bedroom wall, one by one.

One by one, he thought to himself.

He looked down at the paperwork again.

Just look at each piece, one by one.

Unhooking his phone from its charger, he started a new search: Unidentified teenager found dead in French dockyard.

George read all the articles he could find. No one had claimed the body, no parents or relatives had turned up to identify him, and no one had been arrested for his murder. The police were still keen to hear from any witnesses, the last article stated, especially anyone who may have seen a visitor to the boy's grave some two months later.

A visitor?

The boy's body had been buried in a public grave in Calais, and the security system at the site had caught the visitor on camera. George scrolled down and glared at the grainy photo. It looked like one of those pictures you see of wanted criminals – distant and blurry. Most people would shake their heads and comment that it would be impossible to identify anyone from that. But if you knew the person; if you knew their slender frame and poised stance; if you knew the way they walked and how they stood – then you would know for sure. And George knew for sure that the woman standing over the boy's grave was his mother.

Beeep!

His alarm repeated its screech. This time, George hit it so hard, it tumbled across the desk and landed half-wedged between the desk and the radiator.

What has mum got to do with it?

Seeing her there, small and fuzzy on his screen, made him ache.

"Are you up, boy?" Gran called up the stairs.

"Er, yes!" George called back.

He glanced at the upside-down clock and considered bunking school to focus on the case, but not only would it make matters worse with his dad, but there was little more he could do with the things his mother had sent him. He felt lost. He looked up at the pictures of his mum.

What do you want me to do?

"Georgie!"

"I'm coming!"

Slipping out of bed, he picked up the paperwork and slid each piece back into the envelope. He had found out all he could about the dead boy, the other two photos meant little to him, as did the bullet, so the only other lead he had was Jin-é's card. He peeled back the cover again to reveal the hidden characters.

I need to find out what this means.

George had tried several apps on his phone that claimed to translate anything, but the golden etching was so fine and loopy that it could barely be read with the naked eye. Whoever had scrawled the characters across the shiny card had no intention of making it easy to understand.

Opening up his wardrobe, George went to hide everything inside his cricket bag, but stopped.

"Huh," he said to himself, noticing the address on the front of the envelope for the first time.

Mr G Jenkins

She had addressed it to him!

…for my son … think of home

George slapped himself on the forehead.

Of course!

She had meant for him to have it – just him – and whatever it all meant, however it could help, he had to do everything he could to solve the puzzle.

With that thought, he shoved the envelope into his bag, buried it at the bottom of his wardrobe, got ready for school and headed downstairs.

"Have you washed?" Gran asked, as he grabbed a handful of toast and struggled into his coat.

"Er … maybe."

"Well unless you were up with the hens – you haven't been in that bathroom, Georgie. Girls don't like a smelly boy."

"I'm not sure any girls care about how I smell, Gran."

"I'm sure that lovely Lauren does," Gran replied, her eyes twinkling at him over her spectacles. "She won't want to sit next to you on the bus if you stink."

George frowned. "Gran, seriously."

"Suit yourself," she said, shuffling out of the kitchen with Marshall at her heels. "Don't say I didn't warn you!"

George swallowed his toast and sniffed his armpits, before sliding into the bathroom.

"How'd it go with your dad?" Felix asked, as they pushed their way along the corridor to registration. "You didn't call, so I assumed not good."

"Worse than not good," George replied. "The post office called and grassed us up."

"What!" Felix nearly dropped his stack of books. "My folks will kill me! I … I told you we should have worn a disguise."

"Don't stress – she rang Dad because it was his ID we'd used, but I don't think she knew who we were."

"Really?"

"Don't worry, you're safe for now. I, however, am grounded," George said, rolling his eyes.

"Phew – I mean, sorry. How mad was he?"

"Pretty mad, but I said that we were just doing dares."

"So, you didn't show him any of the … stuff?" Felix whispered.

"No," George said under his breath. "It's all hidden in my room."

"So, what's our next move?"

"I need to get that Chinese translated," George said, pushing open the form room door.

"Well, I thought about that," Felix said, striding into the classroom.

"And?" George asked, scampering to keep up.

"That's who you need to ask," Felix said, nodding towards Will and Jess. "They both do Mandarin club."

Chapter 9: A Hard Nut to Crack

George spent all morning chewing over the idea of asking Will and Jess to help him translate Jin-è's card. He knew he'd hit a dead end with everything else his mum had sent him, but he really didn't want to involve more people than he had to.

"I don't see the issue," Felix said, as they wandered into the lunch hall. "Just tell them you had the card in your pocket from Paris. They'll be cool about it."

"I guess," George said, grabbing a tray.

"And anyway, it's not like we've got many other options."

"You went with the baked potato too," Will said, as George and Felix sat down at the table. "Bad choice."

"Why?" Felix asked.

Will walloped his potato with his knife and it rebounded off like a spring. "Stone-baked it should be called."

"Great," Felix said, reaching for the ketchup.

George was pushing his pasta around his plate.

"You alright?" Jess asked.

"Me?" George said, looking up.

"Yeah, you," Jess smiled. "You haven't said much all day."

"Um…"

"He's got something to ask you," Felix said, nudging George's elbow and making him shove half his pasta off his plate.

"Oh yeah?" said Jess.

"Well … I wondered if…"

"He wants to know if you can translate something for us," Felix butted in.

"Translate what?' Will asked.

"Some Chinese," Felix said, nudging George again. "Well, show them."

George put down his fork, plucked the business card out of his pocket and slid it across the table between their trays.

Will and Jess looked down at the Golden Moth.

"Jin-è," Will said, looking up at George, who just nodded.

"Where d'you get this?" Jess asked.

"I had it … from Paris," George replied, checking around for any prying eyes.

A group of year sevens clattered past, so George slid the card under his tray.

"What needs translating?" Jess asked.

"This," George replied, pulling the card back out and revealing the hidden inscription.

"What's that?" Will and Jess both said, leaning in to take a closer look.

"Hopefully her address," Felix said, stabbing at his baked potato.

"We don't know what it is," George said, frowning at Felix again, "but we thought you might be able to tell us what it says."

"Er, I'm not sure about that." Jess said, sitting back. "We do thirty minutes of Mandarin once a week."

"Yeah, just basic vocab," Will added.

"You can't even guess?" George asked, as Felix tried to prise his fork back out of his potato.

"Reading and writing is a whole different ball game, I'm afraid," Will said.

George tucked the card back into his pocket. "Right."

"Great," Felix said, dumping his potato rock back onto his tray, the fork still buried inside it.

"I'm sorry," Jess said, "but you know who you could ask?"

"Who?" George asked.

"Nancy, in year ten."

"Nancy Lewis, the girls rugby captain?"

"Yep, she speaks fluent Mandarin and Cantonese," Will said, grinning. "She's over there."

George looked up. Nancy sat squarely opposite Liam and Jake, almost dwarfing them with her height and width. Not only was she as hard as nails, but she had quite a reputation of losing her cool. George had only ever crossed her path once and that was when he'd foolishly asked her for directions to the boys changing rooms, to which she had grunted, 'How should I know, I'm a girl?' before storming off.

George didn't fancy trying to strike up a conversation with her, especially not when she was sat with two of his worst enemies.

He stared a little too long and caught Liam's eye. "Er, yeah ... I don't think so. Anyone else?"

"Sorry, no one else I know of," Jess said, shrugging.

With that, George spotted the school librarian heading out of the hall.

"No worries," he said, grabbing his tray, scooping up the wayward pasta and shoving his chocolate brownie into his back pocket.

I'm better off doing this on my own.

"Where are you off to?" Will asked.

"I need some fresh air."

George clambered off the bench and scuttled out of the hall, leaving the others to finish wrestling with their potatoes.

Even after an hour of sitting on his backside on the hard, plastic chairs in the school library, George hadn't achieved anything (except managing to squash his brownie). The only relevant book he'd found was 'A Beginner's Guide to Mandarin' and that had made as much sense to him as the Algebra they'd done that morning in maths.

By the time the final bell rang, George was as flat as his brownie. He dragged himself out to the bus stop and slumped down onto the bench to wait for the school bus.

"Hey, how was your afternoon?" Felix asked, coming up behind the bus stop with Josh and Francesca.

"Hi, guys. Yeah, it was just fab. You?"

"I heard you needed some help translating some Mandarin," Francesca said.

"What?" George frowned at Felix who just smiled apologetically.

"I might be able to help," Francesca said, holding out her hand. "Why don't you show me?"

George looked over quizzically at Felix, who just shrugged.

"What have you got to lose?" Josh said.

George sighed.

It's not like I've got any better ideas.

"OK," he said handing over the card.

With that, Francesca spun on her heels and strode away across the drive.

"Wait!" George yelled after her. "Where are you going?"

"To ask Nancy!"

"No!"

But it was too late. Francesca had marched straight over to Nancy, who stood in a huddle with Jake and Jake's older (and even larger) brother, Adam.

George watched Francesca approach the huddle. She looked like a reed amongst boulders. He grimaced as Nancy turned around and peered down at Francesca, but to his complete surprise, the two girls chatted, laughed and then hugged.

"How does she do that?" George asked, shaking his head in disbelief.

"It's the miracle of women," Josh said, knowingly. "They like – actually talk to each other – I don't know – like all the time or something."

"What *are* you talking about?" Jess asked, appearing beside them, with Lauren and Will not far behind.

"Nothing," Josh mumbled.

"What's going on?" Lauren asked.

"Francesca is asking Nancy about Jin-è's card," Felix said, nodding in Francesca's direction.

"Oh good. I knew she'd get it done," Jess said, smiling.

"Did you tell her?" George asked, exasperated.

"You obviously weren't going to do it yourself," Will replied.

George tried to protest, but Francesca was swishing her way back over towards them, her ponytail bobbing along with the rhythm of her stride.

"Well, that was pretty straight forward," she declared.

"Well?" Felix asked.

"She's *so* lovely," Francesca said.

"If you say so," George said, peering back over at Nancy.

"She said it says something like: the triangle has three points but fourteen sides," Francesca said.

"What?" Josh laughed. "Is she having you on?"

"No," Francesca said, scowling at him. "She said it looks like an ancient form of Cantonese and if you want a more precise translation then you should speak to her uncle."

"Her uncle?" George said, flopping back against the bus shelter. "Who the hell is her uncle?"

"He owns the takeaway place in town," Felix said.

"Oh, yeah, the Fat Panda," Josh added.

"The Happy Panda, you idiot," Will snorted.

"It's the Lucky Panda, actually," Jess said, shaking her head at them both.

"OK, I get it," George said. "I know the place."

Felix clapped his hands. "So, we should go there tonight!"

"Yes, we can come with you," Francesca said, excitedly.

"Guys, you really don't have to, I…"

"We want to help," said Lauren, squeezing up onto the bench next to him.

"No, really, it's not necessary."

"We're here to help," Josh said.

"Yeah, we all want to help you find her … your mum," Lauren said, smiling up at him.

George looked around at his friends and could see in their smiles how much they really meant it. Maybe he wasn't going to have to do this alone after all.

"OK, tonight at the Lucky Panda," he said, smiling back at them, but as he trundled home on the bus, he realised that he had no idea how he was going to escape the house and make it into Pendleton when he was supposed to be grounded.

Chapter 10: The Unlucky Panda

By the time George got off the bus, he had mentally discarded over eight useless plans for getting out of the house undetected. He was out of ideas. He couldn't even crawl out of his bedroom window like all those teenagers in those cheesy movies because there was easily a twelve-foot drop from his window to the flower-pot strewn patio below.

With his hood pulled tight around his face, to keep out the October chill, he plodded home. Every step forward seemed to bring with it a step backwards. Even Nancy's translation had only added to his confusion. Nothing was progressing fast enough. As every day passed, he could feel his mum slipping further away from him, and the thought of letting his friends down, when they were trying so hard to help him, made him even more miserable.

I must find a way to get out of the house.

It was darker than usual by the time he reached the front gate, and his mood felt as damp as the fog that was snaking into the village. He desperately needed cheering up so pushed open the front door, hoping that the smell of Gran's cooking would at least go some way to improving his day, but as the door peeled open, the only thing he could smell was burning.

"What the … Gran?"

"Oh, Georgie!" Gran called back. "I'm all in a pickle!"

George hurled down his bag and surged up the hall and into the kitchen, where Gran stood at the sink with a flaming pan in her hands.

"What's going on?" George shouted over the blare from the radio and the squeal of the smoke alarm.

"I was trying something new!" Gran yelled back.

"Shall I call the fire brigade?" George asked, pulling his phone from his pocket.

"No, just grab that old tea towel!"

George dumped his phone on the counter-top, did as he was told and then stood back as she smothered the flames.

"What on earth, Gran?" he said, opening the windows and wafting his arms around under the smoke alarm.

"Serves me right for trying something fancy," Gran said, slumping down onto the bar stool and fanning herself with the charred tea towel.

With that, Marshall streaked out from under the breakfast bar and sprinted out of the kitchen door nearly taking Sam out at the ankles. George froze under the fire alarm, his arms lingering in the air.

What's he doing home?

"What's going on?" Sam asked, covering his mouth and nose.

"It's under control, boy," Gran said. "Just may have to make do with salad for tea."

Salad!

George dropped his arms to his side and thought fast. "Don't worry, Gran. I can get us a takeaway – it's been ages since we had one." He glanced at his dad. "I can go and get it."

Sam dumped his cap onto the counter next to George's phone and went over to the sink to wash his hands.

"You OK?" he asked Gran, practically ignoring George's offer.

"I'm fine. No damage done."

George tried again. "I can pay for it."

"You don't have to do that, Georgie," Gran said, but there was still no response from his dad.

"No, really," George went on. "I … it will be my way of … saying sorry."

Sam turned and looked at him. "Oh, really?"

"Yes," George said, sheepishly. "I know I've been a pain recently and I just thought…"

"You're not a pain, my boy," Gran said, wrapping him in a hug. "We all cope with things in our own way, don't we?" she said, glaring at Sam.

Sam stood at the sink with dripping hands. "Where's the tea towel?"

"Don't we?" Gran repeated.

"Hmm," Sam mumbled.

"So," George said, trying not to sound too eager. "A takeaway then … Chinese OK?"

"Ooh, wonderful," Gran clapped. "I'll get my old chopsticks out of the dresser!"

With that decided, she shuffled out of the kitchen towards the lounge, leaving Sam and George alone.

George tried to break the silence. "Er … how was your day?"

"Not bad," Sam replied, still searching for a towel. "You?"

George thought about Jin-é's card.

Should I tell him?

He knew he really shouldn't keep anything like that from his dad, whatever his mum's note had said, but he couldn't help feeling that this was *his* lead – *his* find. If he told his dad now, it would all be taken away from him and buried somewhere in the depths of MI5, leaving George on the outside again, frustrated and powerless.

He doesn't trust me, so why should I trust him?

He thought of Miss O'Donnell's advice and had to agree that, since he'd had something to focus on, he'd managed to tame his anger.

I'll tell him – just not yet.

"It was OK," George said, passing his dad a new towel from the drawer.

The silence returned.

"I'll go get that takeaway then…" George said, edging towards the door.

"You … want a lift?" Sam asked.

"No," George replied, a little too sharply. "I'll ride … I … need the exercise."

"Hmm, I'll be in my shed," Sam said, reaching for his cap.

Buzz!

George's phone vibrated against the counter-top. Sam picked it up, and George watched his eyes settle on the screen.

"Felix having dinner with us too?" Sam asked, plainly.

"What?"

Sam flipped the phone around. Felix had texted.

'We still on for the Lucky Panda – what time?'

George swallowed. Sam slammed the phone down on the counter. "And there was I thinking that you were genuinely trying to apologise; genuinely trying to get yourself together."

"What? I am!" George said "I just…"

"No," Sam said, holding up his hand. "I don't even want to hear your excuses. Enjoy your dinner!"

With that, Sam stormed out of the back door and marched up to his shed.

George picked up his phone.

Buzz! 'Josh and Francesca can be there at 6pm. You?'

"Goddamn it!"

"George?" Gran had re-appeared. "What happened?"

George tried to explain. "I just wanted to see my friends."

"I know, Georgie. I understand."

"What do I do now?"

"Well, he didn't say how long you were grounded for…" Gran said, smiling.

"You think I should go?"

"I think I need some dinner," she replied, showing him the back door.

"But he'll be mad," George said, as she pressed some cash into the palm of his hand.

"Leave him to me, Georgie. You go get me some noodles … and some of that seaweed!" she called after him as he disappeared up the side path.

The fog swirled and danced in front of George's bike lamp as he wound his way through the back streets towards the Lucky Panda. The others were already waiting outside by the time he arrived.

"It's freezing," Will said, tucking his hands under his armpits.

"Let's get inside then," said Jess.

"Yeah, it smells great," Josh said, sniffing the waft of warm air that escaped from the restaurant as a happy customer bundled his way out with an armful of food cartons.

They all piled in and Lauren pulled the door closed behind them. A couple of other customers stood on one side, waiting for their orders, making it a tight fit.

George had always found the place quite strange. The walls were plastered with pictures of the plates of food that were on offer, including a large picture of a panda eating a bowl of noodles. Mr Lucky (as the locals called him) had large flushed cheeks and tiny sparkly eyes that were buried beneath the folds of skin that framed them. You could just see his cheerful round face above the high counter as he buzzed back and forth.

"Hi," Josh said, leaning his elbows on the counter-top.

"Pick-up?" Mr Lucky asked, smiling so broadly that his eyes completely disappeared under the scrunch of his cheeks.

"No," Josh said, "we haven't ordered yet."

Mr Lucky grabbed a small notepad. "OK – what d'you guys want?"

Josh ordered, followed by George. Mr Lucky turned to the others. "And you?"

"Er, no thanks," Will said, and the others shook their heads.

Mr Lucky scowled. "You come in – you order."

"Um – my mother is cooking for me – I can't," Francesca said.

"You have problem with my food?"

"No, of course not."

"It's best food in Pendleton."

"Yes, I have heard that," Francesca said, smiling politely.

"Then you order or you wait outside," he said, passing the waiting customers their bags of food.

"Um, we actually came to ask you a question," Francesca said, as the door swung closed.

"No order – no warm seat," Mr Lucky insisted, waving his pencil at Will, who had plonked his backside onto one of the random chairs that lined the other wall.

"Nancy sent us," George said, hoping to win him over, but all he did was wave his pencil at them again.

"Ha! No freebies!"

"No, we don't want any more food," Jess said, exasperated. "We just have a question for you."

Mr Lucky turned his back on them and shouted something incoherent through the hatch behind the counter.

"Just order something," Josh whispered.

They emptied out their pockets and gathered together some cash.

"We'll have four packets of prawn crackers," Will said, as Mr Lucky dumped George's bag onto the counter. He screwed up his face and glared at Will.

"And some extra seaweed," George added, forcing a smile. "My gran loves it."

Mr Lucky grinned. "Ha! Of course she does! Now, what's your question?"

George stepped forward and slid Jin-é's card over the counter. Mr Lucky's pinprick eyes opened like saucers.

"Who are you?" he asked, stepping back from the counter. "What do you want?"

"No, no," George said, "we just want to know what it says."

Mr Lucky edged his way back towards the door to the kitchen. He grabbed his mop and jabbed it a them. "I don't want anything to do with that!"

"No, just a translation – that's all," George insisted.

"Nancy told us you knew ancient Cantonese," Francesca added. "She said you could help us understand it."

Mr Lucky slowly lowered his broom. "Why you need to know?"

"Someone close to me … er … I think the person who owns this has something of mine," George said.

Mr Lucky shook his head. "I suggest you let them keep it. You don't want to mess with these people."

"Who are they?" Felix asked.

"This is the sign of the Fourteenth District. They are Triads," Mr Lucky said in a whisper.

"Nancy said something about three points but fourteen sides," Jess said.

"Yes, the sign of the Triads is the three points – Heaven, Earth and Humanity. But the fourteen sides – this refers to the gang and their district. There are many different gangs, each with their own patch."

"And this is the mark of the fourteenth?" George asked.

Mr Lucky nodded. "And they are the worst."

"Where is their district?" Will asked.

"Lucky for me, I don't know and I don't want to know. You even murmur their name and you'll have trouble," he said, coming out from behind his counter. "You need to burn that and never talk of it again." He shoved the card and George's takeaway into his arms and started to herd them out of the door, nudging them with his broom. "You bring me bad luck coming here with that."

"But I need to find them," George said, as they landed outside on the pavement. "Someone must know where they hide out."

"Only one person I know who has history with them, bad history, and she paid the price."

"Who?" George asked, as Mr Lucky tried to push the front door closed.

"Madame Wu," he whispered through the crack in the door.

"Who?"

"The fortune teller – in Margate."

With that, he slammed the door shut, switched off the lights and dropped the blinds, leaving George and his friends standing on the pavement with only half their order.

From: K07
To: J21
Re: Stolen Goods {Encrypted}

Update 1.3

The Rothkos have been mysteriously and anonymously returned to the Louvre.

End.

From: J21
To: K07
Re: Stolen Goods {Encrypted}

Response to Update 1.3

This is an interesting development.
Maybe Angelika had a change of heart?

End.

Chapter 11: Facing Facts

"Doesn't surprise me that Jin-è is part of the Triads," Will said, as they scurried through the back alleys of town.

"Yeah, makes complete sense," Josh added.

"How's that?" George asked, pushing his bike over the cobbles.

"They're pretty full-on," Will replied, grimacing. "I read some stuff about them recently. They're into all sorts of bad stuff."

"Yeah, drugs, smuggling," Josh said.

"People trafficking," Felix added.

"And worse," Will said. "They're properly violent."

George stopped pushing his bike and felt a wave of nausea surge through him.

"OK, guys!" Jess said, tilting her head towards George. "I think we've heard enough."

"Oh, sorry," Josh apologised. "I'm sure this Fourteenth District aren't that bad though."

They had reached the end of the high street and were huddled together under a street lamp, the thin fog hanging in the air around them.

"Yeah, right," George said. "Mr Lucky said they were the worst." Nobody responded. George didn't want to think about the Triads; it only made his mind go to places that were about suffering and pain. "How am I going to find them?"

"Let's ask this Madame Wu," Will said, enthusiastically.

"I think, actually, you need to tell your dad, George," Francesca said, frowning at Will.

"I agree," Lauren said from under her hood.

"But we're in Margate tomorrow night!" Will said. "It's the perfect opportunity."

"You are?" George asked.

"Yeah," Felix said. "It's Fright Night, remember?"

"Halloween," Josh added.

George had completely forgotten. "Of course."

"Boys, I don't think you should encourage him," Francesca said.

"What's the harm in just checking it out?" Josh shrugged.

Jess frowned. "We don't exactly have much luck when we get into these things."

"That's true," Felix said, screwing his face up in agreement.

George sighed and wedged his beanie over his damp hair. He knew they were right.

Time to face Dad.

He slung his leg over his bike and hung the takeaway bag over the handles. "I need to get this food back to my gran before it gets cold."

"You will tell your dad, won't you, George?" Lauren asked, placing her gloved hand over his.

George nodded. "Thanks for coming with me, guys."

"See you tomorrow night," Will said.

"Er, yeah," George said, pushing off.

"Don't forget your fancy dress!" Lauren called after him.

George had mixed feelings as he wound his way back into Chiddingham. He'd managed to find out which gang Jin-é was part of but was still no closer to knowing where his mum might be, and the thought of her being held by a group of brutal gangsters gave him an uncomfortable gripping pain in his chest.

Could it get any worse?

Not wanting to give Gran any cause for concern, he tried to lift his spirits as he entered the kitchen.

"Smells wonderful!" Gran said, as George unloaded the food onto the breakfast bar.

They sat together and slurped down their noodles with the aid of Gran's ancient chopsticks.

"Is there enough for three?" Sam asked, taking them by surprise as he slipped in through the back door.

George sat up and watched his dad pad slowly into the kitchen. He'd spent the whole ride home worrying about what his dad would say about him wriggling out of being grounded and was even more concerned about how he was going to explain his findings at the Lucky Panda.

Gran slid a spare set of chopsticks across the counter and pushed a few cartons of food towards Sam.

"Eat up, boy," she said. "There's plenty."

Sam grabbed a bowl and joined in with the slurping.

Nobody spoke until nearly every last noodle had been sucked up and every last crinkle of seaweed had been plucked from the cartons.

"That was smashing," Gran said.

"Yeah, thanks" Sam mumbled, chasing his last mouthful around his bowl and trying to scoop it into his mouth.

George glanced over at Gran, and she nudged him with her elbow. "Talk to him," she mouthed, silently.

"Er, no problem," George said. "Glad you liked it."

Gran smiled, and Sam peered up over his bowl, locking eyes with George. He opened his mouth to speak, but George beat him to it.

"Look, I'm sorry."

"No, I should have been more understanding," Sam said, his eyes flicking to Gran, who nodded encouragingly.

She'd obviously had a word with Sam while George was out. "I have been too hard on you. You've had a lot to deal with, and I … understand why you might be acting out."

George frowned, as did Gran.

"I wasn't …" George went to say, but Sam tried again.

"I mean, I understand why you may need to let off some steam – with your friends."

"Um, right … but … actually…" *Now's as good a time as any.* "Well, I haven't been totally honest with you, Dad."

"I figured that, but we can move on and–"

"No," George interrupted. "I went to the Lucky Panda tonight because I needed to ask Mr Lucky about something I found – something that might help us find Mum."

Sam lowered his bowl onto the counter. "What?"

"I found Jin-é's business card … um … in the jacket Mum gave me."

"When?"

"A few days ago."

"Why didn't you tell me?" Sam asked, looking confused.

"Well, we weren't exactly…"

"I think he's telling you now," Gran said.

"OK," Sam grunted at Gran. "Do you still have it?"

George slipped it out of his pocket and placed it onto the counter between them.

"I know it doesn't look like much. She gave me one too – in Paris – but what I didn't notice at the time is that the front peels off."

Carefully, Sam picked it up and pulled back the fine red paper.

"What's this?" he asked, seeing the inscription inside.

"Well, that's what I've been trying to find out." George said, standing up and tentatively edging around the counter. "It's the symbol of a gang of Triads called the Fourteenth District."

Sam looked sideways at George. "Are you sure?"

"Mr Lucky seemed pretty sure."

Sam turned it over. "Right."

"Does that mean anything? I mean, it must be a good lead, right?"

"Possibly," Sam said, straightening up.

"So, you're happy?"

"I'm happy that this gets us a step closer, but I'm not happy that you didn't come to me with this straight away."

Gran coughed and tapped her chin with her chopsticks.

Sam sighed. "It's a great lead, George. I just don't want you getting yourself into any trouble again. I want you at school or here at home focusing on being a normal thirteen–"

"Fourteen."

"Yes, fourteen-year-old. The Triads, they make Victor look like your average grumpy uncle. They aren't to be messed with."

"I got that impression from Mr Lucky."

"Well, he's right. You promise me you won't go looking for any more leads. You need to tell me if there's anything that you think is of significance, anything else that you remember from Paris or anything that's occurred to you since."

George thought of the pictures and the bullet hidden upstairs. He didn't think they were any more of a lead than this, he hadn't yet worked out why his mother wanted to keep them a secret, and he wasn't sure that admitting to his dad that he'd gone behind his back would help with his current opinion of him.

"Nothing really," he said. "Although, Mr Lucky said that there's a lady who knows more about this gang. Her name is Madame Wu."

Sam pulled out his phone and made a note. "I'll look into it, but I'm sure we've got enough on the Fourteenth District to be following up on."

"So, you've heard of them?"

"Yes, we know them. I'll get Cate to pull the file and we'll look into it tomorrow, I promise."

Sam popped the card into his pocket and made for the back door. Halfway over the threshold, he stopped and turned to look at George. "Well done, George. This is good work."

George grinned. "So … am I still grounded?" Sam stood in the doorway, contemplating his answer. "It's just … my friends are going to Fright Night tomorrow," George said, bracing himself for the response.

Sam smiled. "Sure, just keep out of trouble."

Sam vanished into the solitude of his shed, and George helped Gran tidy up.

"So, Fright Night, huh?" Gran said, as they crammed all the cartons into the recycling bin.

"You think I should go?" George asked.

"Why wouldn't you?"

"I don't know," George said, looking through the back window towards his dad's shed. "I just feel like I should be here, you know…"

"Georgie," Gran said, coming over and taking him by the chin. "Let your dad do his digging around. If he finds anything out, I'm sure he'll let you know."

"You reckon?" George snorted.

"You've done enough, boy. You go out and try to enjoy yourself. That's what your mum would want."

George sighed. "I guess you're right."

"You just stay out of trouble – you hear me?"

"Yeah, I will. Thanks, Gran, for helping out."

"Oh, I did nothing," Gran said, flipping her charred tea towel over her shoulder. "It was all you, Georgie."

"Hmm, really?"

"I'm always here to help," she winked.

"Ah, on that," George said. "I've got less than twenty-four hours to come up with a Halloween costume."

"I can definitely help with that," Gran beamed. "Leave it to me."

From: J21
To: K07
Re: Stolen Goods {Encrypted}

Update 1.4

We have a new lead. We believe that the Moth is part of the 14D. Let's get everything together that we know about their current activity.

End.

From: K07
To: J21
Re: Stolen Goods {Encrypted}

Response to Update 1.4

This is a great breakthrough and will help us slim down our search.

I'll pull in everything we've got on them and get back to you ASAP.

End.

From: J21
To: K07
Re: Stolen Goods {Encrypted}

Response to Update 1.4

You may have to dig deep. We ran a successful raid not that long ago and arrested quite a few of their top people.

They have been pretty well buried since and seem to disappear into the shadows whenever we get close.

They will see us coming.

End.

From: The Moth
To: The Flame
Re: The Jaybird {Encrypted}

Tick tock – three days and counting.

End.

Chapter 12: Halloween Horrors

After a long satisfying sleep and an over-indulgent lie-in, George spent most of Saturday ploughing through his overdue homework. By the time he made it downstairs, Gran was stooped over her sewing machine with one of Sam's old dust sheets piled at her feet.

George cringed. "A ghost," he said, trying to sound grateful.

He knew that most of the kids that went to Fright Night would go as something truly gory like an axe-murderer or a blood-soaked clown. He wasn't sure he'd seen anyone turn up for Halloween as a ghost since nursery.

"No," Gran said, swivelling around to face him and holding up his costume, "a zombie!"

George laughed. "Awesome – I love it."

Gran had torn up Sam's sheets, stained them various shades of grey and re-made them into a shirt and pants with draping sleeves and extra blood stains for good effect. It was perfect.

"I've got some old face paints you can use," Gran said. "You can wear your clothes underneath it so you won't get cold. You can even pop your beanie on too, if you want. Zombies can wear hats, right?"

"Absolutely!" George chuckled.

With his costume sorted and a stomach full of Gran's homemade soup and bread, he headed for the station to meet the others.

It wasn't a long ride to Margate, but the train was alive with excitement and teenage antics. The array of costumes was eye-popping.

"Some people really go all out," George said, as they shuffled past a group of guys who seemed to be carrying their own heads under their arms.

"Don't suppose they made those themselves though," Francesca tutted.

She and Lauren had come as some sort of demon baby-dolls with their hair in tatty braids, shredded dresses and bloody wounds. They had spent most of the afternoon getting ready and George was impressed.

Somewhat predictably, Will and Jess had come as crazy scientists in their old lab coats. Will had a severed arm hanging out of his pocket, and Jess had goggles on that made her eyes look twice their normal size. She'd even managed to make her mousey hair turn neon blue and stand on end. George barely recognised her.

Slightly less impressive were Josh and Felix's efforts. Josh had come as Frankenstein but really had just drawn some scars on his face, worn his dad's heavy work boots and bought one of those fake neck bolts, and although Felix had made some sort of effort to resemble an alien, George had had to ask him what he had come as, as it wasn't obvious. With tentacles made from his mum's old tights, George reckoned that he looked more like an octopus.

Managing to escape too many attacks from stink bombs and firecrackers, they unloaded from the train and wandered down to the seafront, which was littered with vendors selling roasted chestnuts, candy-floss and fish and chips, amongst other things.

Laughing and screeching, everyone was heading towards the funfair at one end of the beach. George's nose was filled with the chaotic mix of sweet sickly toffee apples, eye-watering vinegar and the sulphuric stink of sparklers. As the sun sank below the horizon, the darkness around him came alive with the neon trails of glow sticks and the joyful rainbow of fairy lights that hung overhead.

By the time they reached the funfair, George could barely hear himself think. Screams and shrieks, music and jingles, and vendors calling out their wares – it was a cacophony of jumbled joy and chaotic clamour. George loved it. He glared up at the Ferris wheel – its silhouette lit up like a Catherine Wheel against the darkening sky – and let out a long sigh. Surrounded by his friends and with his dad looking into the lead on Jin-è, George decided to take the night off and try to enjoy himself. He refilled his lungs and soaked it all up.

"Let's go to the funfair first!" Will shouted over the din.

"Can't we eat first?" Josh called back. "I want a turkey leg before they run out!"

"I want to go to the haunted house before the queue gets too long," Felix said, as they huddled into a group.

"Why don't you guys get into the queue while we grab some supplies," Jess suggested, so they split up, and George and Felix were nominated to stand in the queue.

George had never done the haunted house at Fright Night before, but he'd heard that it was heart-stopping. He wasn't sure that wandering around in the complete dark, while dying and maimed creatures jumped out at you, was his idea of fun, but they joined the queue anyway and shuffled up as it wound its way slowly towards the entrance.

"Don't look now," Felix said, nudging George, "but I'm pretty sure Liam and his gang just joined the back of the queue."

Sliding his beanie further down and hoping that his white face paint and the dark circles around his eyes would disguise him enough, George turned around. "What have they come as?"

They were all in black jeans and jackets and wielding what looked like a collection of axes and knives.

"Nice," Felix said, watching Liam as he tried to intimidate a group of small children that were waiting in front of him.

George grimaced. "Let's try to avoid them tonight."

Just then, the others returned, laden with food and drinks.

"Awesome," Felix said, grabbing a burger from the top of the stack of cartons that Will was carrying.

"You got enough there?" George chuckled at Josh, who was already ripping the meat from one large turkey leg, with two more hanging out of his back pockets.

Josh waved the giant thigh around in the air. "Thought I could use the others as defence when those guys jump out at us in the house."

"Oi!" someone was yelling at them from behind.

Oh no.

"Liam's here," Felix groaned.

"You lot pushed in!" Liam yelled.

"Shut up, Richardson!" Will shouted back. "We got here before you!"

George tried to bury himself within the crowd as Liam, Connor and the Fox twins came striding up the queue towards them, weapons out.

Several people in the queue recoiled at the sight of them. They didn't look like they were out to have fun; just to make trouble. As they got closer, George could see that their weapons weren't real, but in the dark, it was hard to tell.

"You pushed the line," Liam said, pointing his plastic axe at Will.

"So what?" Will said, passing his stack of food to Felix and pulling out his severed arm.

Jess quickly tried to prise her way between the two boys. "George and Felix saved us a space."

"Well, isn't that sweet," Liam snarled. "Shame is, I don't care."

"Yeah, you can all go to the back of the line if you're so desperate to be together," Connor sneered.

"Oh, but they don't let babies in," Hayley Fox said, flicking at the candy dummy that hung around Francesca's neck.

"Yes, you might wet your nappy it's so scary," Annie chuckled.

"Shut up," Josh said.

"What you gonna' do, Frankenstein?" Liam asked. "Club me to death with your turkey leg?"

"Don't tempt me," Josh said, stepping up to Liam and shoving the half-eaten thigh in his face.

With that, Liam swiped his axe at Josh, sending the turkey leg flying from Josh's hand.

"Oi! I paid for that!" Josh steamed.

"Did you pay for these too?" Connor asked, upending the cartons in Felix's arms with his axe; sending baps and burgers cartwheeling across the ground.

"You can pay us what that lot cost!" Will said, shoving past Josh and waving his rubber arm at Liam.

Liam growled and jabbed Will with his plastic axe. "Oh, really?"

"Touch me again and I'll break your toy axe over your numbskull of a head," Will said, grabbing the end of it.

"That's enough!" Jess said, trying to pull Will away.

But Liam was intent on starting a fight. He yanked his axe out of Will's grip and swung it hard, catching Will across the face.

"Stop it!" Lauren squealed, but it was too late. Will was already flying at Liam, and Annie and Hayley were following Liam's lead, swiping their weapons at Lauren and Francesca, whose drinks exploded down the front of their dresses, making Lauren cry and Francesca hurl her cup at Hayley's head.

"Not again," George sighed, dumping his toffee apple on the ground and surging into the rapidly unfolding foray.

By the time he'd prised his way between Hayley and Annie, who had Francesca by the braids, Will and Liam were wrestling on the floor, hammering each other with their respective weapons, and Josh was thumping Connor with his spare turkey leg, while Felix scrabbled around on the floor, trying to retrieve any unsoiled food.

Passers-by looked on in horror. Axes and knives, severed limbs and bloody wounds – it was a sight to behold.

"Police!" someone yelled, making George raise his head.

One of the headless guys from the train was pointing towards the beach road.

"Oh no!" Lauren gasped.

George could just make out the flashing blue lights above all the other colourful chaos.

"Guys!" he shouted, trying to pull at Josh's shoulder. "We need to go!"

"They're coming!" Lauren squealed.

Sure enough, at least six officers were leaping out of what looked like a riot van, accompanied by two hungry-looking dogs.

"Let's go!" shouted Jess, grabbing Will.

Francesca pulled Felix to his feet. "You can have our place in the queue!"

"I really don't need this," George groaned, taking Lauren by the shoulders and pushing her under the railings.

Dad will kill me.

"Come on!' he screamed back at the others, as he glimpsed the officers winding their way through the crowd, directed towards the fight by several by-standers.

"Yeah, run!" Liam yelled after them.

"Run like babies!" Hayley screeched.

As Will retreated backwards, Connor hurled what was left of the turkey leg at him. "You losers!"

Weaving between startled onlookers and dragging Lauren by the hand, George glanced back to see the police breaking through the crowd and coming up behind a smug looking Liam.

Who's the loser now?

But George's amusement was short-lived because two of the officers kept coming, storming towards them with the larger of the two dogs leading the way.

I can't get caught.

"Keep going!" George yelled at the others, as he pulled Lauren towards the Ferris wheel and steamed past the lines of candy stalls.

With Josh and Francesca sprinting to their right and the others coming in from their left, they looked like a herd of startled deer.

"This way," yelled Jess, ducking behind the back of the dodgems.

Taking a sharp left, George followed her call and soon he and Lauren were disappearing into the shadows after her.

"Did we lose them?" Lauren panted, grabbing at her sides.

George stood at the corner, waiting for the others to catch up. As they arrived, one by one, he pulled them into the darkness of the passage and then peeked out, hoping to see no sign of the policemen and their furry companion. He waited, scanning his eyes across the crowd.

"Well?" Josh asked. "Did we give them the slip?"

"I...no!" George gasped. "Look! The dog – it's pulling them this way!"

George turned and shoved Josh, almost making him crash into the fence that ran behind the dodgems. "Go!"

Skipping over cables and shuffling past metal rigging, they made little progress. George kept glancing over his shoulder, desperately hoping not to see the dog appearing in the passageway.

"We need to go faster!" he called from the back of the line, but the bodies in front of him just slowed.

"Oh no!" Lauren squeaked. "It's a dead end!"

The back of the dodgems butted right up to the fence, but Jess wasn't stopping. "Come on!"

George could hear the police dog barking over the screech of the dodgems.

"Where is she going?"

But before anyone could answer, she had disappeared through the fence.

Chapter 13: Dire Destinies

"We can't keep running," Felix puffed, as George wriggled out of the hole in the fence and onto a side street. "I've got a stitch."

George looked around at his friends. Lauren's makeup was smeared down her flushed cheeks, one of Francesca's braids had come loose, Felix had lost a tentacle or two in the chase and Jess had somehow cracked her goggles.

"What do we do now?" Josh asked, pulling off the plastic neck-bolt that was dangling from his collar.

"We need to hide," George said. "That dog will sniff us out."

"Not if it doesn't know our scent," Felix said.

"You wanna' risk that?" Will asked, poking at a graze on his face.

"Here," Felix said, ripping off his remaining tentacles and slinging them down a side alley. "It can follow that scent."

"It can have these too," Jess said, hurling her shattered goggles after them.

"Well, there's no point waiting around here," Josh said. "We can make our way back to the station if we follow the beach road."

"Oh yeah, great idea," Will said. "Back past the police vans."

"Alright, Dr Doom, you got a brighter idea?"

"Stop it!" Jess said. "Let's just get to the end of this parade, then we can look out and see if the police have gone."

"Good idea," said Francesca, taking hold of Lauren's hand and striding up the pavement.

The road curved around and ended at the far end of the beach. They dragged themselves down the road and lingered in the shadows by a small line of shops.

"Any sign?" George asked Jess, who was peering around the corner.

"I can't see the police vans, but there are so many people milling about, it's impossible to tell if we're in the clear."

"So, what do we do now?" Lauren asked, looking over at George.

"We can't risk running into them," George replied.

"Or Liam," Jess added.

"We could take off our costumes," said Will, peeling off his lab coat to reveal his jumper and jeans, "then they won't recognise us."

"That's alright for you," said Francesca, "but Lauren and I don't have anything else to wear."

"We can't just wait here all night," Felix said.

George slumped against the nearest door. "I don't know. I just know I can't afford to run into any trouble. I'm on very thin ice with my dad."

With that, a siren wailed and George jolted, forcing the door behind him to swing open. Tumbling backwards into the darkness, he struggled to stay on his feet, but before he had a chance to regain his balance, the others were piling in around him.

"Guys! What are you–"

"Shhh," Jess hushed, pushing the door closed.

"The police," Will whispered.

They all stood in silence. George could hear the slam of the van doors, the pant of the dogs and the clink of their chain leads. He tried to still his breathing, but something in the air was creeping up his nostrils. Sweet and earthy, and stronger by the second, it caught in his throat.

"What's that smell?" he choked.

"Shh," Jess repeated.

Voices were right outside the door.

"They have to be down this way," one of the officers said.

Frozen still, George watched the shadow of a nose run its way along the gap at the base of the door. Lauren's grip tightened around his arm, and Felix clamped his hands over his mouth and nose. That's when George noticed the fine smoke, curling its way around their huddled bodies and sweeping out of the cracks in the doorway.

Without warning, the dog sneezed, making them all jump, and to George's relief the shadow vanished and the voices moved on.

"That was close," Josh whispered.

"Too close," George said, wafting the pungent haze away from his face.

Lauren was still gripping George's arm. "Have they gone?"

"For now," said Jess.

"So, how long do we wait?" Felix asked.

George looked around at the dimly lit room. The lights were low, and he couldn't make out any windows. Two high-backed chairs stood in one corner, and on the squat table in front of them sat a small jar, smoke snaking up from the sticks that protruded from its neck.

"Incense sticks," Lauren whispered in his ear.

George turned to look at the rest of the room. There were two more internal doorways, but not much else. "Where the hell are we?"

"You are where your destiny brings you," a voice said from behind them.

They all spun around to see a small, stout woman appearing from behind a curtain of beads. She was draped in velvet and countless strings of gems, but what George noticed above everything else was the dark silk patch that covered her right eye.

"Mayling, get out here, girl!" the woman bellowed, her thick, spiralling hair bouncing off her padded shoulders. "We have customers!"

George glared at her as she shimmered in the soft lights. Jewels, gems, beads and lush velvet, it all blurred into a hazy vision.

"Who are you?" Josh asked, with a look of total wonder on his face, but the woman didn't answer. She just flicked a switch behind the curtain of beads making a neon light spring to life above the doorway.

'Welcome to Madame Wu's Parlour of Premonition. Your Destiny Awaits.'

George's jaw flopped open.

"What are the chances?" Will said, scratching his head with his rubber arm.

"Mayling!" the woman screamed again, making them all jump.

A small girl appeared from the shadows at the other end of the room. Shrouded in a sheet, with her glossy black hair tumbling around her deathly white face, she looked like an apparition.

A ghost.

"I'm here," the girl said, her dark gem-like eyes gliding across their faces.

"Where have you been? You are supposed to receive our guests."

"I was just…"

George spied the half-eaten toffee apple that Mayling was trying to hide behind her back. She barely filled the sheet with her tiny frame, yet she was all plump cheeks and cushiony fists.

"Nevermind, you show our guests in," the woman said, vanishing behind the curtain in a clatter of jewels and beads.

"You can't all go in at once," the little girl said, licking at the juice that seeped from her apple.

"We don't want to go in at all," George said, assuming that the others felt the same way.

"We're here now," Will said, shrugging. "Least we could do is ask."

"But we said we wouldn't," Lauren said, squeezing George's arm.

"But we might as well," Will said. "I mean, we're right here."

"I thought we agreed to drop this," Jess said.

The little girl watched the debate bat back and forth over the rim of her toffee crust.

"What have we got to lose?" Will said.

George glanced up at the neon sign.

Maybe I could just … "No, no, I promised my dad. He's got the card. He's looking into it."

"But what if he doesn't find anything?" Josh asked. "Mr Lucky said she knew."

"Boys," Jess whispered, turning her back on Mayling, "don't push him."

George looked at Felix. "What do you think?"

Felix chewed on his cheek. "I mean, I know we said we wouldn't but … we're here now. What harm can it do?"

George frowned. He was relying on Felix to talk some sense into him.

"It only takes two minutes," Mayling piped up, in between mouthfuls. "She doesn't exactly tell you your life story."

"How much is it?" Will asked.

"Tenner each," Mayling replied, holding out her cupped hand. "Or twenty for three of you. That's all she can fit in there at once."

George tried to peer through the curtain, but Mayling slid in front of him. "You have to pay before you go in. No refunds if you don't like what you hear, blah de blah, etcetera."

With that, she took a great chunk out of her apple, spraying George's front with juice.

"We can all chip in," Will said, digging out some left-over cash.

"I guess it won't hurt to ask," George sighed, wriggling his hand beneath his zombie drapes, digging around inside his pocket and pulling out some coins. "Anyone fancy coming in with me?"

"No way," Will said. "Load of mumbo jumbo if you ask me."

"Great," George said. "This was your idea."

"It was Mr Lucky's, actually," Will said, smiling.

"I'll go with you," Francesca said, frowning at Will and stepping up beside George. "I've always wanted to have my fortune read."

"Oh, me too, then," said Lauren, tipping out all the remaining cash from her purse.

"Twenty then," Mayling said, lifting up her ghost sheet and stuffing the cash into her pocket. "Follow me."

George had never imagined himself entering such a place and really had no idea what to expect.

Wrestling their way past the beads, they edged into the small room. Madame Wu sat on a large velvet chair with her one visible eye closed. The room was draped with patterned linens, fairy lights hung from the ceiling and more of the pungent joss sticks occupied each corner. George could feel a tickle in his windpipe, and his head swam.

As they approached the glass table in front of Madame Wu, one of the sets of lights flickered, so she flung out a leg, kicking the mountain of plugs that drooped from the wall, and sparked the lights back to life before re-settling herself and continuing her meditation.

"Sit," Mayling whispered before shuffling out of the room and leaving them in the stifled silence.

They waited. George could hear the hum of a distant fan and the plastic clatter of Madame Wu's gems as she swayed back and forth, breathing in and out, slowly and steadily.

"A-hum," he coughed, trying to speed things up. He didn't want to be in there a minute longer than he had to be. "Hi."

Madame Wu raised her hands in the air and opened her one eye. "I see you have come to ask me about your future. Anything, ask me anything."

"Um … well actually we have a question about something that may have happened in the past," George said.

"Ah, but all questions are about the future," Madame Wu insisted. "Even knowledge of the past will inform your destiny."

"Right," Francesca said, shifting to the front of her seat. "I guess that's true."

"Of course it's true," Madame Wu said, grabbing Francesca by the hand.

George sat as patiently as he could while Madame Wu cooed over Francesca and Lauren, telling them what bright and optimistic futures lay before them, but as usual, his mind wandered. He peered around the room, screwing his nose up at all the dark and dusty trinkets that hung from lampshades and hooks.

What am I doing here?

"You are looking for answers," Madame Wu said, taking him by surprise.

Her eye rested on him and roamed around his face, taking in every detail. "Burning questions – I see them – scorching at your mind – leaving a trail of pain," she wailed.

George grimaced and glanced across at the girls. "Um, I do have a question…" he said.

"Give it here," Madame Wu said, yanking his hand towards her and peering at it with her one intense eye. "You are in pain, boy." She ran her fingers across his palm. "Troubled." Her touch was soft and her skin crumpled like pleated silk, but her fingers were icy cold. He shivered.

"I'm fine," he said, feeling the girls' eyes on him and his cheeks flush. "Really, I just have a question."

"Hush," Madame Wu continued, tracing her fingers down each line in his palm. She closed her eye and breathed deeply. "It will have to be you," she suddenly said, her eye springing open.

"What?" George asked, staring at his palm.

"That is the answer to your question."

"What question?"

"The one you wanted to ask – will it have to be me? And in the end – yes, it will have to be you that finds what you seek. You are the warrior. No one else can do it for you – even though many will try to help – it will have to be you and only you."

George looked over at Francesca and Lauren again, who were both staring intently at him.

"Er ... right, thanks," George said, blinking. "I ... I had another question though."

Madame Wu looked up and her expression changed from a dreamy daze to a flash of anger.

"That will be all," she said, dumping his hand down onto the table.

"What? But–"

"No, no," she said, rising unsteadily to her feet.

"But it's just one question," Francesca said, twisting to look at her as she hobbled around the table.

"No more questions," Madame Wu snapped, shooing them from their seats.

"Then I'll pay," George said, reaching inside his pocket.

"No!" she insisted. "You must leave!"

"But, you said we could ask anything..." Lauren said.

Madame Wu had reached the doorway and pulled back the cascade of beads. She turned and glared at George. "I know what you want to ask me, and no good will come of you knowing the answer."

"Really?" Francesca said, folding her arms. "If you know what he's going to ask – prove it."

Madame Wu growled at her and then turned to George. "You should be careful of what you seek, fierce boy. Even the bravest of warriors will fall in the pursuit of revenge."

"What's that supposed to mean?" Francesca scoffed.

But George had heard those words before. He stood staring at her, eyeballs to eyeball.

"He knows what I mean," she said, poking him in the chest. "You go looking for revenge and you'll fail. There is anger in you, not balance. You go looking for retribution and you will meet an ill fate, boy, and you'll only lose – lose not just what you seek but more – much more."

"But I need to know where they are," George said, as she herded them through the curtain to rejoin the others.

"Mayling! You get them out of here!" Madame Wu bellowed.

"Please," George begged.

"I warn you; anger and revenge will not get you anywhere. They will take it and they will never give it back," she scowled, her eye now burning into George. "They will take from you like they took from me!"

"Took what?" Francesca asked, as Mayling started pushing them out of the front door.

"This!" Madame Wu growled, lifting her eyepatch and revealing a fleshy crater where her eye had once been.

From: K07
To: J21
Re: Stolen Goods {Encrypted}

Update 1.5

We have checked out all know locations on file for 14D, but most of their previous sites are empty, and there have been no reports of recent activity.

Local police in their patch have informed me that things went quiet after the raid, and they believe that the gang has dispersed.

End.

From: J21
To: K07
Re: Stolen Goods {Encrypted}

Response to Update 1.5

This is what I feared.

We will have to dig deeper.

End.

Chapter 14: Triple Trouble

Not stopping to look back, George and his friends raced out onto the beach road and towards the promenade.

"That was horrible!" Lauren squirmed, when they finally slowed at the seafront.

"That poor woman," Francesca said.

"Poor woman? It sounds like she rooked you," Will said. "Did she even tell you where to find Jin-è?"

"We didn't exactly get that far," George said, glumly.

"But she seemed to know what you wanted," Lauren said. "Do you think it was them, who took her eye?"

"That's what she implied," George said, trying to force the image from his mind.

They were striding along the promenade that arched around the bay. A good few hundred feet from the funfair, with only the streetlamps for light, they weren't very visible, but George was on edge.

"We can't just stroll back along the road to the fair," he said. "What if the police are still looking out for us?"

"So, let's cut across the beach," Jess said.

Spying a break in the line of beach huts that ran along the promenade, she leapt down off the beach wall and onto the sand.

"Perfect," Will said, "Come on."

Without hesitating, the others followed her lead, and soon they were all jogging along the beach. George's ankles turned and his trainers quickly filled with sand, but he didn't complain. Anything was better than running into more trouble.

"Let's stick to this side!" Jess called back, as the others started drifting across the sand.

They were hidden from the road by the huts and the beach wall, but George couldn't resist glancing over his shoulder to check for the police. The beach seemed pretty empty.

Wait!

Squinting, he looked again. He swore he saw someone loitering between the huts. Slowing, he turned and peered into the shadows. Someone was definitely ducking in and out of the gaps between the huts, but now he saw, not just one body, but two or even three.

"Er, guys…" he said, catching up with the back of the group. "I think we're being followed."

"The police?" Josh said, snatching a look behind.

"Er, no," George said.

"Is it Liam?" Will asked, spinning around.

They all turned and looked back along the line of huts. Sure enough, there on the beach, a good fifty feet away, and shrouded by the shadows, were three dark figures.

"That doesn't look like Liam," Jess said.

Half the width of Liam but just as tall, they stood with their arms folded, staring right at George and his friends.

"Er, let's just keep walking," Francesca said, slowly turning and starting to walk away. "They're just trying to intimidate us."

"Er, yeah," Felix said, "I think we should try to avoid any more trouble."

George couldn't have agreed more, but as they started to move off, the trio continued to follow.

"They're creeping me out," Lauren said, breaking into a jog.

"Me too," Felix said. "Let's get back to the station. I've had enough of Fright Night."

"Agreed," George said, but as they broke into a run, so did their tormentors.

Stumbling over his own feet, as the sand slid from under him, George tried to keep up. "What do they want?"

"Just run," Josh said from up front. "We're nearly there."

As they pelted past the glare of the funfair, George could feel his heart racing and the stray drapes of his dad's dust sheets tangling themselves around his legs. He tripped and lurched to one side, crashing into Felix and knocking them both off course. "Sorry!"

"Come on, guys!" Jess called back. "We need to get up to the road!"

George regained his balance and tried to up his pace, but it was like running in skates; his feet were moving but he didn't seem to be getting any faster. He glanced back once more.

They're getting closer.

"Where's the ramp?" Lauren screeched.

"How are we supposed to get up to the road?" Francesca said, stumbling to a halt at the bottom of the six-foot beach wall.

"Here!" Will said, leaping on top of a plastic bin and grabbing hold of the lowest railing. With no effort at all, he pulled himself up and over the rim of the wall, rolling underneath the railings and landing on the promenade.

One after another, they followed Will, helping each other by holding the flimsy bin steady, but it soon began to crease and buckle. George was the last. He clambered onto the bin and managed to grip the metal rail, but the bin was caving in beneath him.

"They're coming!" Felix shouted from above, as Will and Josh grabbed George by the arms.

He flailed about with his legs as he was dragged up the face of the wall, scraping his knees against the concrete.

"Hurry!" Felix shouted.

With one last pull, George was yanked up and over the wall, kicking out at the bin, making it topple over completely. He rolled across the pavement and staggered to his feet, only to look down and see the three young men standing on the sand below, staring up at him. He stood for a second and gawped at them.

Triplets!

Identical in every way. Each tall and lithe, each with closely shaved heads, and each carrying a knife – not made of plastic.

Run, George!

This time, he didn't stop to look back. He just put his head down and bombed up the hill towards the station.

"They had knives!" he panted, as they slammed their way through the station turnstiles. "Real ones!"

They pounded up the stairs and crossed over the tracks. "Did we lose them?" Jess asked.

Felix was the first to break out onto the platform. "I hope so."

"Let's just hope the next train is soon," Josh said, looking up at the board above their heads.

Francesca moved down the platform to get a better view of the station entrance. "What if they corner us here?"

"There's a train in four minutes," Felix said.

"Look!" Francesca gasped, making them all turn. "They're here!"

Just visible through the ticket hall window, the triplets were striding in through the station entrance.

"We need to hide!" Jess said. "Come on!"

They ran down the platform and ducked behind a small bike stand. It wasn't much cover, but it would have to do.

"We just need the train to come in," Will said. "Surely they won't follow us onto the train."

"But, what if they do?" Lauren asked, peeking out from behind the bike shelter. "Oh, no," she said, recoiling, "they're on the platform."

"Are they coming this way?" Felix whispered.

"I don't know," Lauren quivered.

George edged out and could see them spreading out along the platform. "We need a better place to hide."

"Er, guys," Josh said from the back of the pack. "Look who it is."

George turned to see a ghostly arm waving at them from a doorway further up the platform.

Mayling?

"Let's go," Jess said. "We can hide in there."

"You trust her?" Will asked.

"You got a better idea?"

With just enough cover from the bike shelter, they shuffled along the wall in single file and slipped into the open door.

"Be quiet," Mayling said, slowly pulling the door to.

George looked around. They were inside a janitor's closet. The smell of bleach stung at his nose.

Mayling stood at the door with her nose just peeking out of the crack. A screaming ghost's mask was pushed up on top of her head, the elastic holding back her cascade of dark hair.

"What are you doing following us?" Will asked.

"Will," Francesca whispered, "she's helping us."

"Oh, really? She just hangs out in here, does she?"

"I said, be quiet!" Mayling snapped.

They waited in silence until Mayling pulled the door fully closed.

"You're lucky I found you first," she said, screwing her nose up at Will. "The triplets get you and you're dead."

"Have they gone?" George asked.

"Not gone, just not outside the door," she said, holding a finger to her lips. "Lucky for you, they are not so smart."

"Who are they?" George whispered.

"They're the Scouts around here. They keep an eye on everyone. Make sure no one breaks the rules," she said, peeking back out of the door. "And now they have their eyes on you for being so dumb."

"How's that?" Josh asked, looking offended.

"You go asking questions about 14D, you're asking for trouble."

"But we didn't even–" George tried to say.

"They followed you from the moment you left my mother's parlour."

"But they couldn't have heard what we said," Francesca said.

"No, but you brought the police to my mother's door and they watch my mother – all the time."

"Why?"

Mayling swiped her grubby ghost sheet across her mouth, wiping away the rest of the toffee that had clung to her lips. "Because she knows their secrets. Why do you think they took her eye? A warning – that's why!"

"Are they with the 14D?" Felix asked, as Mayling peeked out of the door again.

"They work for them, for sure," she replied. "They run this patch, collect debts, recruit new kids. You run into trouble with them, you end up on their list, and you don't want to be on their list."

George looked down at her. A doll of a child, barely nine years old, but she looked like she had seen more things than even him. In her young eyes, he could see wisdom and fragility all at once.

"I'm pretty sure I'm already on their list," he said. "I don't have much choice."

"Why are you looking for the 14D anyway?" Mayling asked.

"They have something of mine," George replied.

Mayling smiled a knowing smile. "Well, I know where you can find them."

"Really?" Will asked, sceptically.

"Yes, but if I tell you, you must do something for me."

"Hmm, there's always a catch," Will grumbled. "What do you want – more toffee apples?"

"No," she scowled. "When you go to get back your thing, I want you to get something back for me."

"Hmm, and what would that be?" Jess asked.

"My brother."

George stared at her. "Your brother?"

"Yes, they have him."

"He was kidnapped?" Francesca asked, horrified.

"No, he was stupid," she spat. "He got into debt with them. When he couldn't pay it off, his only option was to go with them – it was that or they would have taken more than my mother's eye."

"So, he's working for them?" Jess asked.

"Yes, in London, but I want him to come home."

"Guys, the train," Felix said. "We can't miss the train."

The distant crackle of electricity was creeping up the tracks.

"You need to help him get away from them," Mayling continued. "You need to promise."

George looked around at the others.

"I'm not sure you can promise anything," Francesca said.

George looked to the boys, but Will was just shaking his head. "I'm sorry to burst your bubble, but I think your brother needs to get himself out of his own mess. There's nothing we can do for him."

"He can," Mayling said, prodding George in the arm. "My mother called him a warrior. She said he would do it – get back what he seeks, so he can get back my brother too."

"She said I would fail, actually," George said, grimacing.

"No," Mayling said, her lips scrunching up towards her nose. "You weren't listening. She said if you seek revenge you will lose, but if you are a warrior of balance and truth, then you will succeed. That is the ancient Chinese proverb: the warrior who seeks revenge must first dig two graves, but the warrior who seeks balance will succeed."

"What?" Will laughed. "I told you it was a load of mumbo jumbo."

Jin-è's message floated across George's vision.

"That's what she said," he mumbled.

"My mother?" Mayling asked.

"No ... it doesn't matter. I'll do it," he said, locking eyes with Mayling. "I'll do anything I can to help him get home. Just tell me where they are."

Felix was now hopping around near the door. "Guys, the train!" The clatter on the tracks was approaching fast.

"Shake on it," Mayling said, holding out her small, sticky hand.

George shook. "I promise."

"You better," she said, "or I'll give them your name …
Jenkins."

George dropped her hand and glared at her. "How?"

"You better think smarter when you go see them," she
said, pointing at the corner of his torn pants. A strip of his
dad's dust sheet hung down past his knee and there,
printed in Gran's neatest writing, was the word Jenkins.

Screech!

The train was pulling in.

"We've got to go," Felix urged.

"Cece's Deli, Gerrard Street," Mayling said. "Ask for
Julian. Say you're settling a debt."

"Is that your brother?" George asked.

"Yes, you tell him that May says he has to come home."

"We really need to go," Jess said, pushing towards the
door.

"You must go alone," Mayling insisted, grabbing at
George's sleeve. "No adults – it's just kids who pay the
debts. You send an adult in there; they'll see you coming."

"Come on," Jess said, pushing open the door. "We're
going to miss the train!"

"Wait!" Mayling said. "Let me go first."

She slipped out of the door and checked the platform.

Ping!

"The doors!" Felix yelped.

"Go!" Mayling cried.

Halfway between the closet and the closing doors of
the train, George spotted the triplets racing up the
platform, and as the doors sealed closed, he turned to
warn Mayling, but all he could see was a screaming ghost
slipping through a hole in the fence.

Chapter 15: Delinquent Daydreams

George didn't hesitate to call his dad as the train sped away from the coast. He knew he would be in trouble for disobeying his instructions, but he wanted to tell him all about his run-in with Madame Wu and Mayling the second he arrived back in Pendleton.

"Yes, meet me at the station … yeah, I'm fine … I've got loads to tell you … no, I swear I'm fine."

As the train hurtled towards home, George could feel something building inside him. Something that sparked in his chest with a faint glow. Something that began to creep through him, filling him with warmth. Something that felt very much like … hope, and it grew brighter with every new thought. He thought of Madame Wu's prediction, that it would have to be him that saved his mother; he thought of Mayling's words, that he was the warrior who would succeed; he imagined Jin-è hiding in the shadows, unaware that he was coming up behind her and he thought of his mother; still, calm and waiting – waiting for him to bring her home.

"You ok?" Lauren asked, breaking into his daydream.

"Yeah … yeah, I'm fine."

"You're doing the right thing, you know, telling your dad," Felix said, from his seat opposite George.

"I know."

"Your dad will know what to do," Francesca said, re-tying her braids and attempting to hide the evidence of the night's drama.

George ripped off the shreds of dust sheet that hung at his ankles. "I just hope he doesn't ground me again."

"He'll be cool," Josh said. "You've done his job for him."

"Yeah, maybe," George said, but he wasn't sure that his dad would see it that way.

"We're here," Jess said, jumping up.

Will hit the door release and they stumbled from the train. "God, I'm glad to be back in Pendleton."

"Don't often say that," Josh said, smiling.

"Anyone need a lift?" Francesca asked, but George could already see his dad on the other side of the ticket barrier.

"You're earlier than I expected," Sam said, looking them all up and down as they entered the ticket office. "Must have been an … exciting evening."

"It was mental!" Josh said, leaping over the barrier.

"Right," Sam said, attempting a smile.

"See you later," Will said, sticking his thumbs up at George.

The others dispersed, leaving Sam, George and Felix wandering towards the car park.

"You need a lift, Felix?" Sam asked, as they reached Sam's old van.

"Er, is that OK?"

"Of course."

Felix's eyes lit up. He had seen inside Sam's van before and knew what secrets it held.

"So, what are you so desperate to tell me?" Sam asked, as they all jumped up into the van's front cab.

George let Felix squeeze into the middle seat and wedged himself up against the window. "Well … don't get mad but we …"

Sam's hand dropped from the ignition. "What now?" He looked from George to Felix and back to George. "What have you two been up to?"

"We didn't do anything," Felix said, holding up his hands. "It was an accident – I mean we didn't mean to go there … we got chased … I mean."

"Felix," George said, "maybe I should tell it."

"Yes, OK, sorry," Felix said, shrinking back into his seat.

Sam's frown was rapidly forming, so George jumped straight to the point. "We stumbled over Madame Wu's parlour. We didn't intend to go there, but … seeing as we bumped into her, we … kind of asked her about the 14D."

Sam pinched the bridge of his nose. "George, I told you–"

"I know," George interrupted, "but the thing is, we now know where they hang out. It's a deli, in Gerrard Street."

"In London?"

"Yes."

"OK, and this Madame Wu is who?"

"A fortune teller," Felix said, smiling.

Sam frowned fully and looked at George. "Right, and she knows this intel because…"

"They took her …"

"Eye," Felix interrupted.

"Son," George added.

Sam shook his head. "Great."

"Dad, you have to believe us."

"I do, George, trust me, I do. I just wish you didn't have such an appetite for trouble."

George half-smiled. "Can we check it out then, this deli?"

"We?" Sam asked, raising an eyebrow.

"Well, the thing is, the deli, it's a place where the kids take the debts or something."

"A collection rung?"

"A what?" Felix asked.

"The money from trades runs up a ladder," Sam explained. "It never goes direct from buyer to seller. It runs through a debt ladder, usually a bunch of kids who get paid pittance to run the goods and the money. Whether drugs or counterfeit goods or whatever other illegal stuff they deal in, the people at the top keep the deals as far away from themselves as possible. So, if things go wrong, the runners get caught but not the top guys."

"But, what if the kids run off with the money?" Felix asked.

"Or the goods?" George added.

"They don't – or if they do, they don't last," Sam said, gravely.

"Ah," Felix said, getting the picture.

"So, you think the 14D operate out of this deli?" Sam asked.

"Well, we have a contact there. A boy who works for the 14D," George said. "Madame Wu's son."

"OK," Sam said, turning the key and firing up the engine, "Cate and I will look into it."

"Wait though," George said, as they trundled out of the car park. "That's the thing – you can't send adults in."

"What?"

"Mayling said they would see you coming. You'll have to send kids in to ask to speak to Julian. Only kids handle the money and pass it on to him."

"And who exactly do you expect me to send in – you?" Sam laughed.

George bristled. "I can handle it."

Sam pulled the van out onto the main road back to Chiddingham. "I don't think so."

"But…"

"That's a hard no, George."

Sam put his foot down and made a face that suggested that the conversation was over, and it was, at least until they'd dropped Felix off and made it home.

"So, what are you going to do?" George asked, when they finally made it inside.

Sam hadn't said much more in the van, and George could tell that he was brooding over George's constant disobedience, but he didn't want to let it drop. This was the closest they'd come to tracking down Jin-è, and he didn't want to waste any more time.

"I'll talk to Cate," Sam said, dumping his keys and phone on the breakfast bar.

"So, call her now," George said, picking up Sam's phone and thrusting it towards him.

"George, I appreciate that you're excited about this lead, but we can't just rush up there and raid the place. That's not how these things work."

"Why not? She could be there, Dad, right now."

"I doubt that," Sam said, grabbing a glass and filling it with water.

"How do you know?"

Sam downed the drink in one. "Because if this deli is a collection rung, Jin-é is unlikely to want to be anywhere near it. And anyway, we have no evidence to suggest she's even left France."

"But this Julian, he may know more, he may know where she is."

"George, I said I'll talk to Cate and I will. We'll come up with a plan."

"Why not now?" George insisted.

"I'll call her from the shed."

"Why? So, you can cut me out?" George said, curtly.

"What's that supposed to mean?"

"This is my lead. I've got us this far. I want to help, Dad. I don't want to be left in the dark. I want to know that we're doing everything we can to find her."

Sam thudded his glass down onto the counter. "You don't think I'm trying my hardest?"

"No … yes, I mean … what other leads do we have?"

"Well, the Rothkos have been returned."

George sent his eyes to the ceiling. "That's great, but that doesn't get us any closer to mum."

"You're so sure about that, are you?"

"Yeah."

"I've told you before, George, you have to be able to see the whole picture. Until we know everyone's motives..."

"But what if mum is in danger? What if we can find out where they are and get to her before Jin-é does anything–"

"George, we're doing all we can," Sam interrupted.

"But we're not! Not fast enough!"

Sam squeezed his head between his hands. "Listen to me. This intel you've uncovered, it does help, but we can't make any wrong moves. We can't just bring this Julian in and start questioning him. Jin-è would be the first to know about it, and I've told you before, I don't want to force her hand, not until I know where she is and what she's planning."

George leant forward on the breakfast bar and faced his dad. "Exactly! And Julian can help us with that!" George thought of Mayling; her pillowy hand gripping at his arm, pleading with him to bring her brother home. "Maybe if we promise him something, like … protection, he might help us."

"What makes you think he's turnable?" Sam asked.

"His sister said he was taken into the gang, not by his own choice – he was forced."

"Hmm," Sam said, leaning back against the sink, "that's an angle. We can leverage that, I guess."

"Precisely," George said, "and I can do it, Dad."

Sam rubbed at his eyes. "I don't know, George."

"Come on, Dad. How hard can it be? All I have to do is walk into the deli and ask if he's there."

Sam looked up, his eyes red and swollen. "I need to talk to Cate."

George held out his dad's phone again. "Here."

"Jeez, you don't give up," Sam said, grabbing it from George's hand.

Sighing, Sam dialled Cate's number, and George stood as close as he could and listened to every word.

"Apparently so … kids only … no, of course I don't … I guess that's possible … we'd have to get sign off … well, of course it's unprecedented … that could work … OK, pull the ops plan together and we'll look it over in the morning. Thanks Cate."

"Well?" George asked, bouncing up and down on his toes.

"Well, it seems Cate is on your side."

"Really?"

"She's going to pull an ops plan together for you to go into the deli and ask for Julian – but that's it – first contact only."

"Yes!" George said, punching the air.

Sam raised his eyebrows. "Don't get too excited. It's only a proposal. I'll have to get Chief's sign off first, and he'll probably like it as much as I do."

"I can do it, Dad – you know I can – all I have to do is make contact and say that his sister sent me – I'm sure he'll talk to me."

"Hmm – we'll see."

"I'll make him talk."

Sam rubbed at his forehead. "God, you're becoming more and more like her."

"Like who?"

"Your mother," Sam sighed.

"That's a good thing, right?"

"That's scary, that's what that is."

George spent the rest of the evening in a state of flux, seesawing between excited anticipation and overwhelming nerves. Even an exchange of texts with Felix didn't help calm his anxiety.

'You're going alone?'

'I'll have cover and a wire.'

'Wow, like a real mission.'

'Yeah, I know. Mad huh?'

'You're braver than me. What if Julian isn't there or the triplets turn up?'

'I told you, I'll have cover.'

By the time Sam emerged from his shed, George was overflowing with adrenalin-fuelled jitters.

"We're on for tomorrow," Sam said, peering around the bathroom door. "Chief took some convincing, but Cate did a great job reassuring him that the risk level is low."

George was standing at the sink, staring into the mirror, his electric toothbrush buzzing aimlessly in his fist.

"Huh?"

"You OK?" Sam asked, looking concerned.

"Yes," George said, snapping to attention. "Definitely!"

Sam edged further into the bathroom and pushed the door to. "It's not too late to pull out. We can find another way to make contact."

"No, Dad! I'm doing this! If it shortcuts our way to finding Mum, then I'm a hundred percent in."

That night, George struggled to fall asleep. He couldn't stop imagining what his mother would say if it was him that found her. He knew it was stupid, but as they inched closer to finding her, he felt more determined than ever to be the one to bring her home, but when he eventually fell asleep, he dreamt of a three-headed monster: three identical heads but fourteen flailing arms, each wielding a knife, and all he had to defend himself was a half-eaten turkey leg.

From: The Moth
To: The Flame
Re: The Jaybird {Encrypted}

Time is slipping by.
It would be a shame for you to miss out on this one time offer.

Two days and counting.

End.

From: The Flame
To: The Moth
Re: The Jaybird {Encrypted}

I have bigger deals to close.

End.

Chapter 16: Wired

"You look after my grandson up there in the city," Gran said, as Sam and George shovelled down their early breakfast.

"He'll be fine," Sam replied. "You can't be more secure than at MI5 headquarters. He's only shadowing me. Worst thing he'll get is a papercut from all the filing I'm gonna' make him do."

George tried to laugh at Sam's joke but choked on his toast instead. Sam had insisted that they keep the truth of what they were doing from Gran, so George stared at his plate to avoid making eye contact with her.

"Hmm," Gran said, looking up at them over the rim of her tea cup. "You be sure that's all."

The journey to London glided by in a blur, and before he knew it, George was walking beside his dad, along the banks of the Thames, towards the impressive headquarters of the Secret Service.

"Where are we meeting Cate?" George asked.

"We've got a flat, not far from here."

"I suppose I'm not really allowed inside HQ?"

"Sorry," Sam said, shaking his head.

They skirted around the back of Thames House and made their way down a narrow side street.

"Are we late?" Sam asked, as Cate met them at the door.

"No, you're early," she replied, ushering them inside, "and I'm glad you are. We may have some extra stuff to go through."

"Why?" George asked, as they followed her up the carpeted stairs that led to the apartment's front door.

"We've had eyes on the deli and it's been a busy morning."

An antique coat stand greeted them in the hall, and Sam flung his coat onto it like he'd done it a hundred times. "Busy how?"

Warm and musty, the flat smelt like it hadn't been aired out in years. George peeled off his coat and followed his dad into the lounge. He'd imagined a slick, modern hide-out, filled with impressive tech, but it couldn't have been more different. The faded patterned carpets were grubby and thread-bare, the walls were coated in a murky-looking olive paint and the only light in the room was a scrolling, iron chandelier that had only a sprinkling of functioning bulbs. Two sagging corduroy sofas filled one corner of the lounge, and the doorway to a pokey kitchenette could be seen in the other.

"They've been taking deliveries," Cate said, perching on a three-legged stool in front of a computer screen, that sat balanced on a glass coffee table. "Groups of teenagers, coming and going. They come in with plain paper bags and leave with deli bags."

"Deliveries of what?" George asked, standing behind her.

She scrolled back in time through the surveillance footage, and George watched as several teenagers, all in dark jeans and hoodies, came and went from the deli. Cate sped up the feed and he leaned in closer. They looked like clones, every one of them dressed the same way, as if in uniform. He thought of the triplets and had a sudden and disturbing vision: a line of soldiers, hundreds of them, all identical, all carrying knives – streaming in and out of the deli like an army of ants.

"So, what do you think?" Cate asked.

"I'll need to change," George said, looking down at his blue jeans.

Cate laughed. "Yes, good observation, but look again."

"What are they bringing in?" Sam asked, squatting down beside Cate to get a better look.

"I don't know what's inside the boxes, but look closer."

She froze the frame and zoomed in on one of the parcels. It wasn't the clearest of images, but George saw it immediately, stamped on the corner of one of the boxes.

"The Golden Moth!"

"Bingo!" Sam said, grinning up at George.

George tried to force a smile. This was more than he could have hoped for. He should have been over-joyed that his lead was proving to be so fruitful, but it wasn't joy that he felt deep in his stomach, it was trepidation.

"Do we think Jin-é's there?" he asked.

"There's been no sign of her," Cate replied. "We've been watching the shop and there's only one entrance. The old dear that runs it locked up last night and returned this morning, alone."

"You want to rethink?" Sam asked, noticing George's eyes glaze over.

George stared at the frozen image of the moth on Cate's screen. They were whisper close.

"No, this is the closest we've come to tracking her down. We can't sit on it any longer. If Julian is in there, and he's willing to talk, then it has to be worth the risk."

"We won't be taking any risks, George," Sam said, frowning. "You'll walk in, ask for Julian and walk out if he's not there."

"And if he is?"

"Well, that's what we'll spend the next hour going over."

Sitting in the dingy flat, crowded around the coffee table, George, Cate and Sam went through the plans for the approach. George tried his hardest to concentrate when Cate showed him a map of where she and Sam would be running surveillance from, where the deli was and where Dupont and Elías would be stationed.

"Dupont and Elías?" George said, warily.

"We've had to think outside the box, George," Sam said.

"Chief wants us to keep this off the record," Cate added, "so we're using as little MI5 resource as possible."

"And anyway," Sam said, "they were more than happy to help."

"Right," George said, but having two criminals as his backup didn't ease his anxiety. "Why can't you two do it?"

Cate and Sam glanced at each other. "There's a good chance that Jin-é will be expecting us to catch up with her at some point," Sam said. "She's probably circulated our images to every corner of her network. They'd see us coming."

"And they won't see me … or Dupont and Elías?"

"It's very unlikely that anyone will be expecting you and Dupont and Elías will keep their distance. They're just there in case."

"Hmm," George said, still unsure.

"If you see Dupont and Elías, I don't want you to make eye contact. Just pretend they aren't there," Sam said.

George tried to memorise the script that Sam gave him that outlined what he could and couldn't say to Julian.

"No straying from the plan, George. You stick to this script. No improvisation."

And he tried to keep his mind in the room as Cate and Sam debated the best direction to approach the deli from.

"We'll drop you here and you'll have to walk the rest of the way on your own."

But one thought kept distracting him.

What if she's there?

He thought of Jin-é hissing in his ear as she jabbed him with her needle.

"OK, are you happy with everything we've been through?" Sam asked.

George nodded.

He thought of his mum's blood smeared across the back seats of Jin-é's SUV.

"You need any more time to read through the script?" Cate asked.

George shook his head.

He thought of Madame Wu's eye, Mr Lucky's warning, and he thought of the longing in his mother's eyes as she told him that she loved him.

I need to get her out.

George jumped up, rocking the glass table with his knees. "Let's do it."

"OK," Cate said, handing him a carrier bag of clothes. "Go change and I'll get everything ready."

Ducking into the tiny bathroom, George emptied his bladder and changed into the black jeans and hoodie. As he re-entered the lounge, he expected Cate to be busy laying out a collection of wires and gadgets, but she and Sam just stood waiting for him.

"This is your ops pack," she said, pointing towards a plain-white paper bag that sat on the coffee table.

"What's in there?" he asked.

"Cash," Sam said. "You're paying a debt, remember?"

"What about my wire?"

"It's in your zip," Sam said, smiling.

George looked down at his chest and ran his fingers down the length of the zip. "It's in there?"

Cate nodded. "Yes, stitched into the hem. The Microphone is in the zipper, so if you keep it zipped up, we'll be able to hear you loud and clear."

"Right," George said, impressed. "And the tracking device?"

Sam pointed at George's waist. "Your jeans' button."

"Huh, cool."

"So, keep your clothes on and you'll be fine."

George cringed. He didn't want to think of any scenario where he'd lose his clothes.

"Right, the last piece is this," Cate said, coming towards him with a small black pouch.

George had seen one just like it before. In Paris. In his mother's hands.

"Earpiece," he said, as Cate unzipped the pouch.

George picked up the tiny flesh-coloured plug and squeezed it deep into his ear.

"Make sure it's comfy," Sam said. "You don't want to be tempted to fiddle with it."

"It's good," George said.

Cate crossed over to her laptop. "Right, let's run a test. You go into the hallway."

George wandered out into the hallway and Sam closed the lounge door. George stood in the silence, listening to the rumble of his inner ear, until Sam's voice suddenly filled his head. "Can you hear me?"

"Yeah!" George shouted.

"There's no need to raise your voice, George. We can hear you at this end, even if you whisper."

"Sorry."

"Just try to be as natural as possible. Try to forget you've got this stuff on. Just focus on the job. If you think too hard about your wire or the earpiece, you'll give yourself away."

"But how can I ignore the earpiece if you're talking to me?"

"We won't be, unless we absolutely have to, not unless it's an emergency or we need to give you instructions."

"Right."

Sam re-opened the lounge door. "But if I do say something – if I give you an order, you are to do exactly as I say. You understand?"

George plucked the earpiece back out. "No worries."

"I'm serious, George. We'll be watching all the movements outside the deli. If anyone approaches that we don't like the look of, or if you're in there too long, or if we hear anything we're not happy with, we'll pull you out. If I say it's time to leave, you make your excuses and leave. I need you to be crystal clear about that."

"Jeez, Dad, I get it."

"No being a hero."

Cate took off her headphones and came to join them. "The audio is perfect, but you need to know that if you get blocked by any interference, then there may be a delay in us hearing you. I'll need time to change frequency. It's unlikely that anything in the deli will cause interference, but you need to be aware that there are sometimes short blackouts. If you don't get a response from us, try to subtly repeat what you've said."

"I'm sure we won't have those issues," Sam said, trying to reassure George. "More importantly, the code word is noodles."

"What?"

"If you need us to come in or you can't extricate yourself, for any reason, you say the code word and we'll be in there before you can say…"

"Noodles," George said, smiling.

"Exactly."

Cate closed her laptop and slid it into a shoulder bag, gathered up her headphones and gestured to George to pick up the paper bag. "OK, I think we're ready."

"Don't forget that Julian won't be expecting you and they will all be on the lookout for anything out of the ordinary," Sam said, as they made their way back down the stairs and out onto the street. "Things can change very fast in these situations, George – you meet any resistance – see anything odd – you walk out of the door."

"I'll be fine, Dad," George said, as they wandered around the corner and climbed into Cate's car. "I won't screw this up. We're too close to catching Jin-é."

Sam slid into the back seat next to George. "You don't worry about her. You focus on your operational objective: making contact with Julian – that's all. As soon as you mention his sister, he'll either balk or take the bait. You'll know if you've hooked him. It's usually obvious."

"What if I can't get him alone?" George asked.

"If he wants to talk to you, he'll find a way to get you alone. The important thing is not to spook him. Stick to the script and you'll be fine."

"I've got it."

"Don't be brave, George. If he doesn't bite, we'll find another way – you just walk away."

George nodded, but as they snaked their way towards Chinatown, George knew he would stop at nothing to get Julian on side, whatever it took, he had to make him talk.

From: H09
To: K07
CC: J21
Re: Stolen Goods {Encrypted}

Update 1.6

Surveillance update from MI6.

The Billionaire left his villa by helicopter this morning. The border team at Lydd Airport have confirmed that he and two others cleared customs in the UK at 08:02.

Let us know our orders.

End.

From: J21
To: H09
CC: K07
Re: Stolen Goods {Encrypted}

Response to Update 1.6

Now he is on UK soil, we can increase our surveillance efforts. Wherever he is staying, I want the place bugged. No blank spots. I want to hear every conversation he's having.

End.

Chapter 17: Dead-end Deli

"We're here," Sam said, slowing his pace.

He and George had left Cate's car at Charing Cross and walked as far as Leicester Square. Early November mist filled the air and clung to George's hair. He pulled up his hood, checked the earpiece and readjusted the zip at his chest.

"Just head directly to Gerrard Street. You remember the directions?" Sam asked.

George looked out over the busy square. Pedestrians buzzed past him from every angle, but he looked right past them, scanning the far side of the square for the streets he knew from the map.

"I know the route."

Sam nodded. "OK, if at any point you lose your nerve…"

"I won't," George insisted, shaking out his chilled fingers. "Can we just get on with it?"

Sam stepped in front of him. "No risks."

"Dad, I'm not Mum."

"So, prove it to me."

"Seriously?"

"I mean it, George. I can see it in your eyes. You think you can bring her home all by yourself, like no one else can help you, but it's not your responsibility and that's not how these things work. It's teamwork, George, and sticking to the plan, that's what brings in the results."

"What, like in Paris?" George said, smirking.

Sam frowned. "I'll be on comms, just around the corner. You do exactly as you've been briefed. No deviations – not for anything."

"I get it."

"Time to go." Cate was in George's ear. "Dupont and Elías are in place."

George filled his chest and took one last look at his dad. "I'll be fine."

"I'm proud of you, whatever the result," Sam said.

"I know," George smiled, before striding off across the square.

George had never been to Chinatown, but he tried to hide his amazement when, after crossing the bustling square and sliding down several drab, grey side streets, he was spat out into a bubble of oriental colour and culinary chaos.

Every other shop front was gilded in gold and red, displaying a festival of exotic looking foods, and filled with trinkets of unfamiliar wonder. George tried not to gawp at the windows full of naked hanging ducks, the washing lines of lanterns and the images of far-off places, but what he noticed more than anything else was the sudden quiet. Marooned in its own mini-world, Chinatown was almost empty. It was Sunday and it was early. Restaurants were closed, blinds were drawn and only the odd shopkeeper shuffled in and out of their doorways, taking in deliveries.

Deliveries!

Someone was coming his way. Someone in a dark hoodie. Aware that he was standing alone in the middle of the brick-lined street, George ducked to one side and watched the stranger approach. Sixteen, maybe seventeen, he sauntered down the street clutching a deli bag. He glanced up at George and nodded, his eyes flicking to George's bag. George stood frozen still.

I've been clocked.

"You've stopped," his dad said in his ear, making George jump.

"Jeez, Dad!"

"Don't talk. Just keep walking if everything's OK."

George wrapped his arms around his paper bag and continued down the street, but he hadn't gone very far before another dark figure was coming directly at him. George tried to lower his gaze, but couldn't resist glancing up. Tall and rigid, wrapped in a shabby fur coat and mustard scarf, and wearing a purple bobble hat, the woman crossed the street and slipped into a noodle bar that had just opened its doors. George glared at her through the glass window as she plonked herself onto a stool and opened up her newspaper. Drifting past the window, he tried to look away, but she looked so odd bundled up in her cocoon of autumn colours, like some giant caterpillar. He was so used to her pale and drawn-out look, but he couldn't mistake the beak of a nose poking out of the gap between her scarf and her hat.

Dupont!

She didn't lift her eyes from her paper, but somehow, he felt like she was watching him.

Gerrard Street.

The sign above his head told him that he had almost arrived. Staring up at it, and unaware of what was at his feet, he almost tripped over a bundle of clothes that was spilling out of a doorway. To his horror, the bundle groaned.

"I … I'm so sorry," George spluttered, jumping aside, but the man just readjusted his position and pulled his stash of blankets higher up over his head.

God, George, concentrate!

With that, someone chuckled and George spun around to see who it was. A young boy's face peered out from a doorway opposite.

"What you lookin' at?" the boy asked.

George tried to look away, but an older girl had appeared at the boy's side, and George couldn't help noticing the scar just above her eye. It made him think of the pictures his mum had sent him.

The dead boy.

George rubbed his eyes.

"You keep walking," the girl said, glancing at his bag, "that way."

Just get this done!

Taking long steady breaths, George zigzagged around the piles of rubbish that lay blocking the pavement and tried to appear relaxed as he scuttled down Gerrard Street, but no sooner had he calmed his nerves, when he suddenly became aware of footsteps behind him; not just one but several, and they were coming at pace.

They're onto me.

Desperately trying not to look back, he lengthened his stride, but the deli was fast approaching and he had to make a choice.

Stick or twist?

He knew he'd been seen and he guessed that they were closing in, but he was so close. He didn't want to pull out. He didn't want to fail. Breaking into a jog, he grabbed at his zip, ready to say the codeword, but before he could decide whether to bail or not, someone was calling his name.

"George!"

George nearly crashed into a pile of bin bags in his effort to spin around. There, charging towards him, were his friends.

"Fancy seeing you here!" Josh said, as they all came skidding to a halt in front of George.

George stood with his eyes out on stalks. "Er … guys … what are you doing?"

"It's half-term," Jess said, shrugging, "and we fancied a trip to London."

"Yeah, because we had so much fun last time we were here," Will grumbled.

George was speechless. "But…"

"Felix told us what you were doing," Lauren whispered, "and we couldn't let you do it alone."

"But," George repeated, looking at Felix.

"What's going on?" Sam asked in George's ear.

"Er … my friends are here," George said, a little too loudly. Sam didn't say anything, but George could hear the frustration in his groan.

"Who are you talking to?" Josh asked.

"My dad," George whispered, tapping his zip. "He can hear us."

They all looked impressed. "Cool."

Sam's voice entered his ear again. "George, you're within sight of the deli; you are probably being watched."

"We'll come with you," Lauren chirped.

"Yeah, we told you we wanted to help," Francesca said.

George peered down the street. He could see a few bodies loitering outside a shop front, and it wouldn't be long before they noticed the unusual gathering.

"Wow, guys, thanks, but I'm not sure that's a good idea."

Sam was in his ear again. "George, we're wasting time. We're losing any advantage of surprise. You need to go in before they start checking you out."

"OK."

"Excellent!" Felix said.

"Er, no – not you," George said. "I was talking to my dad."

Felix visibly deflated.

George knew they meant well, and he definitely felt less vulnerable with them there, but he couldn't help feeling thrown off course. "You guys need to stay here," he said, trying to recompose himself. "I need to go in alone."

"We'll be right here," Lauren said, "waiting for you."

George forced a smile and pulled his zip up even higher, before turning and making his way the last twenty paces to the deli.

As he approached, the group of teenagers who were hanging around outside turned to look at him. Swallowing hard, he dropped the bag to his side and tried to swing his arms, as if he hadn't a care in the world. In an attempt to look like he knew what he was doing, he nodded towards them, like the boy in the street had done to him, and although he tried not to let his eyes linger on their faces, he couldn't help noticing the same scar above one of the boys' eyes.

The door jingled cheerfully as he pushed it open and squealed softly as it slowly closed behind him, leaving George alone in the deli with the gang of youths loitering at the door like guard dogs. Foods of every variety lined each wall, were stuffed into the chilled counter and even hung from the ceiling above George's head. The smell reminded him of the Lucky Panda, but it was crisper, fresher and zestier. Fruits and vegetables, that George had never seen before, erupted from overladen crates; meats and fish, that seemed almost alive, peered up at him from their beds of ice and three golden cats, with cartoon eyes, sat on the sagging shelves, waving at him, as he stood and stared in wonder.

"Hello," someone said from behind the counter.

Squinting at him from between the prostrate ducks and limp eels was a squat, round-faced woman. She was wrapped up in a dress of finely embroidered silks that was partially covered by a blood-splattered apron.

"Hi," George said, maneuvering his head to see her more clearly.

"What you after?" she asked, picking up a large cleaver and decapitating a fish in one brutal blow.

George cleared his throat. "I've come to see – I mean, I wondered if Julian was here … today … please."

She lifted her cleaver to behead her next victim, but paused midair. "Julian?"

George nodded but was aware that his head was moving up and down far too quickly. "Yup – Julian. Is he here?"

"Why you asking?" she said, glancing past him.

George followed her gaze. The youths from outside had spread out in front of the window, blocking his view of the street.

"I owe him some money," George said, trying to flatten out the tremor in his voice.

He could feel his palms getting damp and the paper bag softening in his grasp.

"He's not working today. You can leave it here. I'll pass it on to him." She nodded towards the corner of the shop where a small metal hatch was buried in the wall. "You can take some fortune cookies with you on your way out."

George looked at the stack of deli bags next to the hatch. He got it. The debt collectors dumped their cash in the hatch and took a bag of cookies to make it look like they had just been in to pick up some groceries. He knew that this was what she expected him to do, but he didn't want to leave with only a bag of cookies.

"Um … I'd rather give it directly to Julian, if that's OK."

"Take some cookies," she snarled, before picking up her cleaver and sliding the next fish onto the chopping board.

"Um, I really–" George started.

"That's it, George," his dad said, barging into the conversation through George's earpiece. "Give her the cash and walk out."

"But…"

"But what?" the lady said, glaring at him.

"But nothing," Sam said in his ear. "You tried. It's over."

George could feel his frustration bubbling up.

"Can you at least tell me where Julian is? I need to speak to him and–"

"George," Sam growled, "get out!"

George stared at the woman, who had returned to her butchering. She lifted her gaze for a second, chuckled and pointed towards the door.

"Take some cookies, kid!"

He wanted to wipe the smug smile off her face. She knew where Julian was, yet she just stood there, like a bouncer not letting him into the club. He wanted to leap over her counter and…

"Time to go!" The bells jingled again as one of the boys from outside flung open the door.

George went over to the hatch, and with his back turned on the woman, he slipped his hand into the bag, took the fistful of cash and slid it into his pocket before dumping the empty bag into the hatch and watching it slide down a chute.

Have that! he thought, before snatching up a bag of cookies.

"You can take some for your friends too," the woman said, snidely.

George looked out of the window. The crowd had vanished, but now his friends stood outside, rounded up like a flock of sheep and guarded by the girl with the scar.

Gripping the deli bag in his fist, George strode out of the door, convinced that the cats' eyes followed him as he went.

Chapter 18: Nine Lives

"I dunno' why Julian told you to meet him here, but I wouldn't come back if I were you," the girl with the scar said, but as George looked at her, he realised it wasn't a scar at all. In fact, it was a tattoo, arching along the curve of her eyebrow – a tiny inscription, too small to read without leaning in closer.

George unzipped his hoodie and clasped the zipper in his fist. "I need to speak to him."

The girl shook her head and slipped her hand into her pocket. George looked down as she jutted her jacket towards him, and he could see the point of something sharp.

"It's OK, we're leaving now," Francesca said, taking George by the arm. "Have a great day!"

As quickly as they could, George and his friends scurried back down Gerrard Street. George didn't even bother to look up as Dupont stepped out onto the pavement. He was embarrassed. All that effort, for nothing. He had failed. The one thing he'd tried to achieve had fallen completely flat, and he knew he was so close – so close he could almost feel Jin-é breathing down his neck, her needle in his ear. So close he could hear his mother's voice, whispering to him in the woods. So close he wanted to scream at them all. Steaming around the corner, he kicked out at a pile of kerb-side boxes, sending rubbish flying across the street.

"George!" Lauren cried. "What's wrong?"

"It was a complete waste of time!"

"Calm down," Sam said in his ear. "You did exactly what we asked of you. There was always a chance–"

"Julian's here! I know it! And now we have nothing!" George roared.

"At least you tried," Felix said, dodging another flying box as George lashed out again.

"George, it's OK," Lauren said, reaching out towards him, but he pulled away.

"It's pointless! That was our only lead!"

"Pull it together," Sam ordered. "Get yourself to Leicester Square – all of you – I'll meet you there."

George ripped out the earpiece. "Whatever!"

His friends cautiously gathered around him.

"We'll find another way," Francesca said, stacking some of the boxes back onto the pavement. "It's not a dead end."

"Yeah," Felix said, "we know who they are now. I'm sure your dad will–"

"Er, guys," Will interrupted. "I think we have company."

Standing on the corner, half-hidden behind the trellised archway that marked the entrance to Chinatown, was the laughing boy from the doorway. He waved and beckoned them over.

"What does he want?" Will grunted.

Subtly, George slid the earpiece into his pocket. "He's one of them."

"I think we should just leave," Lauren said, checking the side streets around them. "They weren't particularly friendly."

"You guys can stay here," George said. "I'm going to see what he wants."

The boys looked at each other. "We'll come with you," Will said.

"Oh, and leave us here," Jess said, frowning. "Not likely."

With that, they all wandered towards the archway.

"What do you want?" Josh asked, towering over the boy. He was awkward-looking; all arms and legs; halfway between child and teen, like he'd been stretched out but not yet filled out.

"You after Julian?" he said, shifting around from one foot to the other.

"Maybe," George said, glancing down the street from where they'd come. "You alone?"

The boy nodded. "I know where he is."

"Really?" Will said. "And why would you tell us?"

The boy fidgeted with the frayed ends of his sleeves. "Money."

Will laughed. "Ha! No surprise there."

"You got any?" the boy said, looking at George.

George nodded.

"George," Lauren said, tugging at his arm. "You sure about this?"

"Yeah, he could be lying," Will added.

"You wanna' see him or not?" the boy said, looking over his shoulder.

George pulled the cash out of his pocket.

"Whoa!" Josh exclaimed. "Don't give him all that."

Seeing the wodge of cash in George's hands, the boy's eyes lit up. "I'll take you there … personally."

"Half now and half when we get there," George said.

The boy stuck out his hand and took half the cash. "Deal." Then without giving it another thought, he crossed the street and ducked down a narrow path that delved between the buildings.

"George," Felix said, as they raced to keep up, "is this a good idea?"

"If we can find Julian, the mission's not a complete failure," George replied.

"And you think this kid really knows where he's going?" Will asked.

"This way," the boy called back, turning sharply into another cut-through.

George could feel the closeness of the walls bare down on him and started to wonder if Will was right, but the boy kept going, and soon they were climbing over bags of rotting fruit and crates of discarded vegetables at the back doors of Chinatown's eateries.

"Did we really have to come this way?" Francesca asked, turning her nose up at the smell.

The boy laughed at her. "If you want to avoid the eyes, you go where no one else wants to go."

"Yeah, only the rats come down here," Will scoffed.

Francesca groaned and sped up, but it wasn't long until they stumbled out of the end of the alleyway, almost colliding with a homeless man who was loitering in the shadows.

"Get outta' here!" the boy said, trying to push past, but the scruffy stranger stood solid as a rock.

Wrapped in blankets and dragging his feet, he looked harmless enough, but George saw something in his stance. His broad shoulders gave him away, and the speckled beard that escaped from beneath his tattered hood.

Elías!

"Hey!" the boy spat, flicking a pocket-knife from inside his sleeve. "I said, get out of the way!"

George locked eyes with Elías and shook his head.

Not now!

"Yeah, old man," George grunted, "move aside!"

Elías' eyes hardened and he stepped aside, growling at them as they passed. George tried not to look back as they scurried around the corner but knew that Elías wouldn't be far behind them.

The tracker! Dad!

George hadn't stopped to think that his dad must be going crazy. He could probably hear everything that was being said and could see George's blinking dot on Cate's laptop screen disappearing further and further away from Leicester Square. He needed to tell him to back down; that he was going to find Julian, but what would his dad say? Would he tell him to stop, to turn around and come back?

The earpiece!

Wriggling his hand into his pocket, George tried to locate the tiny plastic plug, but just as he felt it brush his fingertips, the boy up front stopped abruptly and spun around to look at George.

"We're here," he said, sticking out his hand. "You owe me the rest of the cash."

George glanced up and down the littered alleyway. There was no one else to be seen, and all the back doors that led out into the alley were firmly closed.

"Funny," Will said, "I don't see Julian."

"He's inside," the boy sneered.

"So, get him out here," Jess said, eyeing up the set of doors nearest them.

The boy scowled and stamped his foot.

"There's no need to have a tantrum," Francesca tutted, but to all their surprise, the thump echoed back up at them from a metal plate beneath the boy's feet.

Bang! Bang! He repeated the action and the plate flew open, making him topple backwards.

"You're supposed to knock back first!" he complained at the head that appeared from under the plate.

"It's Clem!" the head announced to the depths below.

"What does he want?" someone shouted back.

The boy climbed up another step and popped his shoulders above the pavement, lowering the plate to the ground. He squinted at George and his friends from behind a pair of thick glasses, before looking up at Clem. "Who are they?"

"They're here to see Julian," Clem replied.

The boy flicked his glasses up onto the top of his head to get a better look at them. "You his friends?"

George peered down at him. "I need to talk to him."

"He expecting you?"

"Probably not."

"They've got money," Clem said, bouncing around and pulling up his hood.

The boy in the hole sighed and shook his head, making his glasses flop back down onto his nose. "How many times have I told you, Clem?"

"Is Julian there or not?" Will said, losing his patience.

George glared at Will before looking back down at the boy in the hole. "It's OK, we can wait for him to come out."

"You're not waiting out there," the boy said. "You're not exactly an inconspicuous bunch. Get down here."

He stepped back down the stairs and waited at the bottom.

"I'm not sure we should go down there," Lauren said, but before anyone else could add their opinion, someone was shouting from below.

"Get off the street! We've got Scouts coming!"

"Go on!" Clem said, pushing George.

George stood his ground and looked both ways down the street but couldn't see another soul.

"You get down here or you scarper. Either's fine by me," the boy shouted from below. "But you get me into trouble with the Scouts and I'll hang you up like a duck."

George looked at Clem. He hadn't pulled his pocketknife on them; no one was forcing them. If Julian was down there, then this was their best chance.

Come on, George!

With that, George barrelled down the metal steps and leapt off onto the concrete floor. The others swung down after him, and soon they were all standing in the dingy basement. Clem was the last. He slammed the trapdoor shut, and the screech of metal bounced around the basement as he turned the lock.

Clem smiled up at George. "Cash?"

"Where's Julian?" George said, not smiling back.

"I dunno'. Ask Mac," Clem said, shrugging, but the other boy had disappeared behind a bank of shelves.

George ventured further into the basement with the others at his back.

"I don't like this," Francesca said, to his right.

"Let's just find Julian and get out of here," Jess whispered.

Dimly lit and cluttered, the basement looked like an overpacked garage. Chinese tapestries hung from the walls, and a narrow passage divided the lines of shelves and piles of boxes in two. George could see a dozen kids, buried behind the shelves, sat on upturned boxes and stuffing something into tiny parcels. None of them looked up at him. Only the collection of waving cats seemed to acknowledge the newcomers.

"Those cats freak me out," Felix whispered.

"Me too," Lauren said, sticking to George's side.

"No further," a voice said from behind one of the shelves. It was Mac. He'd reappeared, dragging a large box; a large box just like the ones George had seen on Cate's laptop; a large box carrying the mark of the Golden Moth.

"George," Felix squeaked at his shoulder.

George dug his elbow into Felix's ribs to shut him up. "Where's Julian?"

"He's in a meeting," Mac said, flicking open a box-cutter and slitting open one of the boxes. "Here, make yourselves useful."

George stared down at the tiny packets that filled the box.

Fortune cookies.

He looked at the deli bag in his hand and then at the kids that were busy stuffing the cookies. Fast fingered and barely stopping in their stride, they stuffed each cookie with a tiny plastic bag, re-wrapped them and threw them into a deli bag.

"Drugs," Will murmured.

George stood gaping.

Mac laughed. "You really are newbies. Where did Julian find you?"

But as George tried to think of an answer, one of the tapestries at the far end of the room was drawn aside and a girl appeared from behind it, slurping on a can of drink. Spotting the gathering ahead of her, she crushed the can against the wall, flung it into an open bin and grabbed what looked like a baseball bat from the nearest shelf. "Who the hell are you?"

Mac straightened up, and Clem sank behind one of the rows of shelves.

"They're here to see Julian," Mac said.

The girl stood filling the space between the shelves. Tall and square, she reminded George of Nancy, except Nancy had hair, where this girl had a head of stubble. "Why?"

Mac threw Clem a look.

"They were asking for him at the deli," Clem said from the safety of the shadows.

"Right," the girl mocked, "and you thought – oh, why not bring total strangers down to the den – what a stroke of genius, Clem!"

Clem shrunk further into his hiding place. "I'm sorry, Lu, I just thought…"

"Shut up!" She stormed up the passageway and stopped inches from George with her bat slung over her shoulder. "What are you here for?"

George rocked onto the balls of his feet and tried his hardest to meet her hard stare. Her eyebrows were too close together, giving her a look of perpetual menace, but this close, he could read the tattoo above her eye. A tiny inscription, ancient Cantonese, undoubtedly recognisable because he'd seen it before.

14D!

He tried not to stare, and despite his trembling hands, he slowly pulled the zip back up on his hoodie. "We're here to see Julian."

"Friends of his, are you?" she asked, looking them up and down.

George could smell the sugar on her breath. "We've got business with him."

"What patch are you from?" she asked, scanning their faces.

George realised what she was looking for.

The tattoo.

It was obviously a sign of membership, maybe even status, and they certainly didn't belong.

Lu lifted her bat and prodded at George's coat. "You paying up?"

"I've got money," he said reaching for his pocket, but she swotted at his hand with her bat.

"Oi," Will said, "there's no need for that!"

"You're in my den; I'll do what I like," she said, turning her bat towards Will and swirling it in circles around his face.

George tried to think fast. He knew Will wouldn't be able to ignore the bait, and he knew that if he let Will erupt, it would all end in chaos, but before he could do anything, Will had swiped the bat out of Lu's hands, sending it crashing into the metal shelves. *Clang!*

No!

This wasn't some school-yard squabble, this was the real thing. This was the 14D, and George needed to step in and fast.

"We really don't mean to…"

But his words were lost in the scrape and clatter of a dozen stools as every one of the packers rose to their feet and came out into the passageway, their box-cutters in their hands. Falling into ranks behind Lu, they filled every last void in the narrow space between the shelves.

George tried again. "Th… there's really no need to…"

But Lu had retrieved her weapon, and was coming at him. "It's time to leave!"

George staggered backwards and slammed into the others. With Mac and Clem at their backs and Lu and her army at their front, they had nowhere to go.

George thought of Elías outside and Dupont just streets away. He thought of his dad, listening through the wire, and he thought of the code word.

Noodles.

But before the word could leave his lips, someone else was erupting out from behind the tapestry at the end of the passageway. "What's going on?"

George just stared as the enemy turned and their ranks split. There, standing at the end of the room, was a tall, scrawny boy – a thin, floppy fringe hanging over his forehead – and as he tilted his head to one side, the fringe fell away, revealing Mayling's dark eyes.

Julian!

But George faltered. Everything he knew he had to say – the whole script – just melted from his memory, because there, standing at Julian's side, thinner and frailer, and with his dark braids twisted up into a knot, was JP.

Chapter 19: On and Off the Hook

Confusion and uncertainty seeped from George's friends.
He's alive!

Francesca was at George's side, her lips parted as if she was about to speak, but no words came, and JP was just as silent. Rooted to the door's threshold, he just stared at George, his eyes open wide in warning. George stared back. Lanky and sharp-edged, where before he'd been lean and smooth, JP looked like a whittled stick, worn down and brittle – a shadow of the figure they'd left in the catacombs of Paris.

The silence in the room was only broken by the shuffle of feet as Julian strode towards them and the packers scuttled aside, getting out of his way. Even Lu stood to attention as Julian stepped into the light and pushed his fringe to one side. He certainly had his sisters eyes: young and alert but shrouded. In what? Anger, sadness, fear? George couldn't tell. All he knew was that he had to speak first. He had to get Julian on side. He clawed at his brain for the words of his script and wished that he had his dad in his ear. If Julian exposed him, the dogs wouldn't stay at bay.

"We're here to pay Mayling's debt," George said, knowing that her name should send enough of a message, but a message that hopefully only Julian would comprehend.

George watched Julian's eyes, dark like oil, glide around the room. Was he waiting to see if anyone flinched? Would anyone in the room know his sister's name?

"I can get rid of them," Lu said, in a milder tone than she'd used with George.

Julian was in charge here and that was clear. He held up his hand and took another step forward. "Who are you?"

George tried again. "We're friends of Mayling's. She sent us to pay–"

"Yes, so you said."

Julian's face stuck rigid. George couldn't read him. He had no clue whether the hook had stuck. Should he re-cast the line with a different bait or start to reel him in?

"Maybe we could talk alone. She wanted us to … give you some important information." George was now thinking on his feet. If Julian was reluctant to trust a stranger wielding his sister's name, maybe he could be convinced with a warning. "She said it was urgent."

Julian's expression finally flickered. A crease of an eyebrow. Was it confusion? Fear for his sister's well-being? That was the angle. However reluctant he may have been to show anything other than strength in front of his underlings, he must still hold a desire to protect his family. Isn't that why he had left in the first place? To protect his mother and sister from any more pain? "She said we weren't to leave until you agreed to speak with us."

Lu stood, bat in hand, waiting on Julian's word, but impatience got the better of her. "Who's Mayling?"

Julian's nostrils flared. "Get in there!" he said, pointing towards the door at the back of the room. "We'll talk alright."

George began to move, and his friends glued themselves to his sides, shuffling together, moving as one and keeping all their eyes on the surrounding enemy.

"No, just you!" Julian growled, pointing at George.

George looked at his friends and nodded. He could tell from the look on their faces that they feared that Julian had not bitten, but George thought of his dad's words.

If he wants to talk to you, he'll find a way to get you alone.

Sweeping past the line of packers, he tried to show no fear.

"Back to work!" Julian bellowed, and they scurried into the shadows like startled rats, except for Lu who stood her ground and scowled at George as he passed.

Reaching the door, George peered inside. It was set out like an office. A desk stood at one end, more heavy tapestries hung from the walls, and a solid wooden table sat in the centre, surrounded by chairs. Lu shoved him in the back. "Get in!"

"I'm going," he said, glimpsing up at JP, who only let his eyes lift for a second, but in that second George saw the warning again.

George stumbled over the threshold with Lu at his back, but Julian stopped her. "Go check outside. Make sure they haven't attracted any trouble." She opened her mouth to object, but Julian snatched the bat from her grip and pointed it towards the steps that led to the street above. "Go! I'll deal with them!"

George felt calmer with Lu gone and hopeful that Julian had taken the bait, but as the door closed behind them, he was slammed against the wall, the bat at his throat.

"Don't you dare come in here using my sister's name," Julian hissed in his ear.

"But she's … the one … that sent us," George croaked. "She wanted us to … give you a message."

"I don't care. You use her name; they start asking questions; questions I've spent too long avoiding."

George could barely breathe. "I know … she told us…"

"Be quiet," Julian whispered. "They will have seen you come in. They have eyes everywhere. Even in here. Always watching us, always ready to punish us for stepping out of line." He pushed harder and George could feel his windpipe collapsing. "You shouldn't have come because now I have to show them that I'm getting rid of you; that I'm dealing with you, or they'll be in here before you can say…"

"Noo…dl…es," George tried to say, but the broken syllables puffed out of him like a dying man's final breath.

"Raid!" someone yelled from outside the door, and before Julian could react, the door burst open and JP stormed in with George's friends at his tail. He yanked them through the doorway, pulled the tapestry down over the hole in the wall and slammed the door shut, dropping a heavy bar across its middle.

Jess was the first to spot George. "Get off him!" she screeched, lunging at Julian.

Julian pinned George with his right arm and swung the bat towards Jess with his left, but Will was at her side and raised his elbow in time to block the blow. "Drop it!"

"That's enough!" JP said, barging between them and almost knocking Jess off her feet. "We need to get out of here!"

"This is your fault!" Julian spat at George, backing up and readjusting his bat. "And now the Scouts will punish us all!"

"I don't think it's Scouts," JP said, holding his finger to his lips. "Listen."

Julian stood, confused, listening to the deep muffled voices that seeped from behind the heavy door. His eyes widened. "Who have your brought here?"

"Just go," JP whispered.

"Go where?" Josh whispered back, but they didn't have to wait long to find out, because Julian was already snatching up his satchel, ripping back one of the hanging tapestries and sliding into a small hole in the wall.

"Follow him," JP whispered, standing guard by the other door.

"In there?" George asked.

"That's where they all went," Felix said, "all the others."

"Into the walls," Lauren added, "like rats."

George glanced back at the door. Who was out there? Was it Dupont and Elías? Had his dad heard the codeword? Or was it Scouts? The others stood waiting for him to make the first move.

"You don't want to get caught down here," JP whispered. "Scouts or anyone else. You've seen what they're doing down here."

George looked down at the deli bag in his hand. *Drugs!*

He dropped the bag and looked up at JP.

"You'll get serious time," JP said.

George suddenly realised that JP had no idea who George really was. He didn't know he was Jay's son, or the son of an MI5 officer. All JP knew was that they had owed Victor's gang a debt; a debt hefty enough to get them kidnapped in Paris; a debt similar to the one he had been forced to pay off for his father.

"What shall we do?" Francesca asked, peering down the hole through which Julian had vanished.

George looked at JP. "Can you make Julian talk to us? Will he trust us?"

"Depends what you're offering him in return," JP said.

Bang! Something thudded against the door, making JP jump. *Bang!*

"They've found the door," Lauren squealed.

George clutched at his zip and prayed that his dad was still listening. "We're following Julian. We've come too far not to go all the way. We'll get him to talk."

And without stopping to check whether the others were on board, he crawled through the hole and into the darkness.

Chapter 20: The Rat-run

George felt like a rodent, on all fours, scurrying through the dank darkness, sniffing at the stench of discarded food, desperate for a whiff of fresh air.

Where the hell are we?

The scratching and scurrying of his fellow rats scampered up the tunnel and drifted past him.

"How much further?" Lauren squeaked from close behind.

"I can't see a thing!" Felix said from further back.

JP's voice was the most distant. "It's not far."

George could feel the rough concrete scraping at his knees, but he pushed on, feeling his way, one arm's length at a time until he saw the light.

Jumping down out of the hole, he found himself inside another basement. It too was lined with shelves, and things hung from the walls, but not tapestries and boxes of cookies. Instead, the shelves were lined with jars filled with swollen creatures, bulging eyes, pale and frozen in time; skins hung from the walls, exotic and rare; shelves of electronics; a tiger's head, stuffed and still baring its teeth; crates of weapons and a rack of artwork, lined up like books on a shelf.

"What is all this stuff?" Lauren breathed at his side.

"A smuggler's hoard," JP replied.

"So, where's Julian gone?" Will asked, striding towards the stack of electronics.

"He won't be waiting for us," JP said. "We'll have to hurry if you want to catch him."

"But," Josh said, "where's he…"

"Over here," Jess called from behind a set of shelves that were slightly shifted away from the wall.

"Not another hole," Francesca groaned.

"It's not so bad," Jess said. "Look."

She nudged the racking another inch back to reveal a brick archway.

"What are these passages?" Felix asked.

"They stink," Lauren added.

"Victorian sewers," JP said. "They're usually fouled up with all the grease that's been running out of Chinatown for decades. Lucky for you they've been recently cleaned or we'd be wading through a river of fat."

"Oh great!" said Francesca, peering into the dark.

"Come on," George said, "we're losing him."

"Wait!" said Will, grinning. "Sure no one will mind if we borrow these." He shoved past JP and handed out a stash of brand-new flashlights. "You're welcome."

George grabbed one and powered it up. "Perfect. Let's go!"

George let JP take the lead as they ran through the tunnel, trying to close the gap on Julian. The tunnel was dry but the grease appeared in patches, catching George out and making him lose his footing. He could smell it, and it reminded him of the fish shop that he went to with his dad.

Dad!

With Julian out of sight, George dug around in his pocket, pulled out the earpiece and rammed it into his ear.

"We're beneath Chinatown," he said, as clearly as he could between his heavy breaths. He could hear static. He tapped on the plug and pushed it in further. "Can you hear me?"

Something came back; broken and distant.

Damn!

"What's that noise?" Jess asked from halfway up the line.

They all stopped. Footsteps were splashing in the distance. Voices leaked from the bricks. It felt like they were surrounded.

"It's the others," JP said, "in another tunnel. They must be heading towards the exit."

"Where?" George called from the back.

"I don't know," JP called back. "I've never been this far."

"So, you have no idea where this leads to?" Jess said, standing beside JP and shining her light into the gloom.

"There's a split in the tunnel up ahead, I think," JP said.

"You think?" said Will.

"Great!" Josh said. "Why on earth did we trust you?"

"Yeah, like we did in Paris!" Will added.

George pushed forwards. "Guys, come on. There's no time to argue." But as he wandered towards the fork, Julian appeared from the darkness, grabbed George around the neck and pressed a knife to his throat.

"Why are you following me?"

"We need to talk!" George said, his feet sliding across the greasy stones. He clenched his toes, trying to get a better grip.

Jess was the closest. She shone her light into Julian's eyes. "Put him down!"

"No!" he spat back at them. "Everything was fine until you turned up. You tipped them off, and now I'll get the blame."

JP had got as far as Jess. "Julian, let him go. It wasn't him."

"How do you know?"

"Because I know him – I know them all."

Julian's arm tightened around George's neck. "How?"

"We … worked together … on a job in Paris," JP said.

Julian readjusted his grip on the knife. "What job? Which gang?"

"No gang," George spluttered.

"They're like us," JP said. "They had no choice. They don't want to be here. They've been forced."

Julian's grip slackened. "How do I know you're telling me the truth?"

"It's true," Jess said, inching closer. "I've got the scar to prove it." She lifted her t-shirt and shone her light on the remnants of the gash across her stomach.

"And me," Josh added, pulling at his jacket and revealing the pit in his shoulder that the bullet had made.

Will pointed to the scar on the palm of his hand, and George thought of the small mark on his neck where Victor had pierced his skin. It was true. They all had scars. Inside and out.

"We didn't want to be part of this," George said. "But we are, whether we like it or not, and now we want to put an end to it."

Julian released his grip on George and shoved him back towards JP, his knife held out in front of him. "How d'you know my sister?"

George rubbed at his neck. "I was looking for someone, and the trail led me to Margate."

"Margate?" Julian said, his rigid jaw loosening.

George nodded. "That's where we met your sister."

"Did anyone see you go there?"

George paused. He hated lying but needed to keep Julian right where he had him. "Your sister is pretty smart. She's safe."

"I need her to stay that way. If I put one foot wrong, they'll…"

"Take your mother's other eye?" Josh said.

Julian's eyes flamed.

"We saw her," Francesca said, stepping towards him. "She was scared, Julian. Scared for her life, scared for your sister, but most of all, scared for you."

"They want you to come home," George said. "Mayling begged for me to find you and tell you to come home."

"I can't," he said, his eyes glistening in the torchlight. "This is it for me. I'll never get out."

George stepped closer still. "I can help you."

Julian laughed. "You have no idea who these people are. The Scouts, that's the least of my worries. They'll punish me, for sure. Maybe just a beating, or maybe they'll make me beat someone else, one of the kids, to prove my loyalty. But I try and run…" He shook his head. "It won't be the Scouts; it will be the Dragon's Head. She'll kill me – but not before she drags my family out in front of me and makes them pay first."

"Jin-é?" George said, before thinking.

Julian locked eyes with him, but said nothing.

George didn't push. He needed to seal the deal first. He tried to remember his lines. What could he offer him? "I can get you protection – all three of you."

"You?" Julian scoffed.

"Yes, the people I … work for … they can help you."

Julian slammed his fist against the bricks. "Ha! I knew it! Who sent you? Which gang? You gonna' promise me some big promotion so I rat this lot in – give up their secrets? That only gets me dead either way. I've seen it happen. I snitch, I'm always a rat – no one will trust me again. No one trusts a rat! And the 14D would hunt me down … you can't offer me anything!"

"No," said George, "I can't, but MI5 can."

His words hung in the tunnel before dissipating into the still air.

"What did you say?" Julian's knife was still in his hand, clenched tight and pointing towards George.

George had to reveal his cards now. He had nothing left to hide behind. "The reason I went to Margate is that the 14D took someone – someone that MI5 are looking for." He let that sink in before pushing on. He knew he was off script. He knew he'd already revealed too much, but surely honesty would win through. "Someone that means to me what your mother and Mayling mean to you. And MI5 are willing to offer you and your family complete protection if … if you help us locate the … Dragon's Head."

Julian's gaze sank within itself.

"It's a way out," Francesca whispered. "A future – away from all of this."

"You can go back to them," Lauren added.

"Did you know?" Julian said, looking at JP, but JP just stared at George, a furrow of concentration across his forehead. Was he just working it out?

"He didn't know in Paris, and he didn't know we were coming today," George said.

"We thought he was dead," Josh added.

Julian stepped up to George and rasied his knife towards George's face. It hovered just an inch from George's eye, and all George could think of was Madame Wu. "Even if what you say is true, why should I trust MI5?"

George tried to steady his breathing and focus on Julian's face. With his fringe sticking to his forehead in strands, George could now see the tattoo above his eye. He knew that Julian was one of them: official, loyal, part of the tribe. But was he in so deep that he couldn't be turned? "Because you want your family back together as much as I do … and honestly, what better options do you have?"

Julian's knife fell away and George knew then that the hook had caught its fish.

"Are you in?" Will asked.

"I don't seem to have a choice," Julian said. "If you really are with MI5, then I've just led you right into the Dragon's den, and she won't let me live, regardless of whether I take your deal or not."

"It's a good deal," George said. "I promise you; we'll get you out of here. I'll take you directly to the officers who can make it happen."

Julian sighed. "That's if we can get out of here alive."

Chapter 21: An Icy Reception

"It's just a little further," Julian said, as they scurried through another stretch of old sewer that joined the basements of Chinatown.

"How do you know which tunnel to come out of?" Jess asked, shining her light at the brick walls, trying to spot the exit.

Julian stopped. "Here, this one."

George shone his light at the hole. Scratched into the rough bricks was an X or was it a moth? Either way, it was the exit.

"What's on the other side?" Josh asked, peering into the hole.

"The deli basement," Julian said, climbing in. "Just keep your voices down until we're sure it's empty."

Head first, he quickly disappeared from view, leaving the others to squirm their way through the short, narrow tube. By the time George landed on the other side, the others had moved away from the hole and were spread out amongst the mountains of clutter that filled the deli's basement: barrels filled with stale baguettes; buckets of softening onions; broken jars, spilling out a rainbow of spices; wilting greenery hanging over the edges of crates like sodden seaweed. The room smelt like the school bins in the middle of summer. George tried to close his nose.

"All this wasted food," Francesca grimaced, covering her mouth with her sleeve. "Such a waste of money."

Josh grabbed a couple of the stale baguettes. They were as hard as rocks. "It's not like she needs the money."

"No," said Will, from the other side of the room. "Not when she's got all this." He lifted up a large wicker basket and tipped its contents onto the floor. Bundles of cash; some wrapped in plastic, some just tied up in string.

George spied his empty bag at the end of the chute.

"I'd leave that where you found it if I were you," JP said. "You don't want anything to do with that money. It's dirty."

As tempting as it was to grab a handful, Will replaced the basket and joined the others.

"How do we get out of here?" Jess asked.

"We need to go up and out through the shop," Julian said, pointing to a ladder at the back of the room.

"And what can we expect when we get out there?" Will asked.

"I imagine the others have already passed through," Julian said, swinging his satchel off his shoulder. "So, she'll be expecting us."

"Who?" Felix asked.

"Old Celia," Julian replied. "She'll probably be out front of shop. She'll know that the den has been compromised, and she won't want to draw attention to the deli, so she'll make us leave in small groups."

"That's easy enough," said Josh, spinning his batons of bread like swords.

Julian was rummaging in his satchel. "She won't flinch when she sees me," he said, pulling out another knife.

"What's that for?" Lauren asked, taking a step back.

"You lot are unfamiliar faces, and she won't like that, especially if Lu has had anything to say about your visit to the den."

"Er, actually, I think she'll recognise me," George said, "and she definitely won't be happy to see me."

Julian screwed up his face. "Even more reason to arm ourselves."

"Let her try me," Josh said, wielding his crusted batons.

"Seriously?" George said. "She's got a cleaver."

"I don't need a weapon; I've got these," Will said, holding up his fists and winking.

"How's this?" Felix asked, appearing from behind a stack of crates, carrying a large glass jar of something pink and glutinous.

George just shook his head. "What even is that?"

Felix shrugged. "No idea but it's heavy."

"Great," Jess said, "you go with that."

"Come on, guys," Francesca said, making for the ladder. "The sooner we get out of here the better."

They filed towards the back of the room and slowly climbed up towards the trapdoor. Julian nudged it open with his head, and an icy mist twisted down from above.

"What's that?" Lauren whispered from the rungs below, but Julian just signalled for them to be silent.

Slowly, he inched upwards, sliding the trapdoor aside until his body was engulfed in a waterfall of ice. The cold air bathed the others as they waited for his signal.

"Clear!"

One by one they shimmied up the ladder and into the cold. The frozen air clung to their hair and crystallized in tiny beads on their jackets.

"It's f…freezing," Felix chattered.

"It's her deep freeze," Julian said, trying to squeeze his way to the door.

It was a tight fit for nine bodies: a small narrow space amongst the heaving shelves. They were packed in like penguins. George peered through the mist only to see eyes peering back at him – fish eyes. Bulbous and swollen and creepily unblinking, they made him shiver. Lauren was at his side, and he could feel her shaking.

"I just need to unlatch the door," Julian whispered, "but once I do, we'll be out in the open. Our best hope is to take her by surprise. Once I give the signal, we'll leave the freezer as quickly and quietly as we can, then we charge – around the counter, straight for the door."

"You really think that will work?" Jess asked

"It's our best option – trust me. The minute she sees you lot, she'll swing that cleaver. She won't care whose head she takes off."

"Just m...make it q...quick," Felix stammered. "I can't f...feel my t...toes."

George could feel his muscles jump and twitch; his jaw tighten.

Hurry up!

Julian shoved at the lock. "It's stuck. Someone help me."

Josh was closest.

"P...please h...hurry," Francesca said.

Hiss!

The solid door cracked open and the warm air rushed in.

"Now," whispered Julian.

But the doorway was narrow and the shelves were tight on either side. As they jostled in their attempt to dash from the freezer, Felix bumped into George, who stumbled and nudged Lauren, who crashed into the nearest shelf, knocking it sideways. It teetered and nudged its neighbour, making the layers of fish slowly slide along the shelves, their expressions unchanging.

"Oh no," Lauren squeaked.

"Go!" George said, but it was too late, the momentum of the gliding fish had started an avalanche. George dived for the door, Lauren's hand in his, but as the ocean of frozen bodies came cascading down, her hand slipped from his and they both crashed to the floor.

"Arghhhh!"

Finding his hands and knees, George pushed himself out from beneath the debris and turned to look for Lauren. There she sat, half way across the pile of bodies, with a head in her lap – not a fish head – a human head; it's features magnified and distorted, squashed up against the sides of its flimsy plastic bag.

"Get it off me!" she squealed.

George lunged back through the doorway and scrabbled over the pile of carcasses. He kicked out at the head, sending it bouncing over the frozen mountain and rolling across the floor, before disappearing through the hole in the ground. The thud of its impact on the basement floor below sent a tremor through them both.

"Come on!" he said, hooking his hands beneath Lauren's armpits and pulling her towards the door.

They slipped and slid in their effort to get back on their feet, and by the time they had made it out into the deli, all hell had let loose.

The crash of the fish and Lauren's squeals had been more than enough to move old Celia into action. All element of surprise was lost, and Celia was slashing her cleaver at anyone who dared to come close. George could see her broad shoulders heaving from left to right as she swung her weapon at Josh, who had somehow made it to the other side of the counter with Will, Jess and Julian, but the others were still trapped.

Josh tried to cushion Celia's blows with his baguettes as Will and Jess hurled onions from a crate near the door, but Celia easily severed Josh's baguettes in half, leaving him unarmed.

"Do something!" Francesca screamed at JP.

"Over the counter!" he bellowed, leaping up onto Celia's chopping block and swinging his leg over the glass display, but Celia saw them and turned, swinging her cleaver towards the counter, missing Francesca's thigh by barely an inch.

"No!" Josh screamed, slinging half a leg of ham at Celia and knocking her backwards.

I need to do something!

George searched the behind the counter for any form of weapon. Knives of every description hung from the wall.

I can't.

"Here!" Lauren said, shoving a broom into his hand.

Celia had regained her balance and was jabbing her weapon at Will, who was on his toes, ducking and diving, dodging every blow. Gripping the broom tightly, George crept towards Celia's back. She grunted, deflected a flying pineapple with her shoulder and then swung at Will again. Another miss.

Now!

As she raised her arms one more time, George charged at her from behind, catching her right between the shoulder blades with the butt of the broom handle and making her buckle. She lurched forwards, but before George, Felix and Lauren could get over the counter, she was turning and coming at George, her cleaver raised.

Back up!

George thought fast. He scurried backwards towards the freezer, drawing her past the counter; opening up a route of escape. Felix was halfway across the counter now, straddled over the glass with his heavy jar still in his arms, but Lauren was still stranded on the wrong side.

"George!" she cried, as Celia pushed him further back towards the freezer, slashing at him and splintering his broom handle as he tried to deflect each rageful blow.

"You!" Celia spat, slashing again. "I'll take your head and add it to my collection!"

"No!" Lauren screamed, but the path was now clear.

"Go!" George shouted, and JP skittered around the counter and dragged Lauren out towards the door, leaving George as the only one left to escape.

"Help him!" Lauren screamed.

Julian surged back towards Celia, his knife in his hand, but she saw him coming in the reflection of the freezer door. She turned.

Clash!

Cleaver met knife, and Julian's weapon flew from his hand. He stumbled, lost his footing and tumbled to the floor. Scrabbling backwards across the tiles, he tried to get out of her reach, but she was on him, lifting her arms; ready to strike. With only half a splintered broom handle left in his grasp, George righted himself and charged. He swiped at her ankles, knocking her completely off balance, and she crashed to the floor, the cleaver spinning from her grip.

"Get out!" he yelled at the others as he leapt over her flailing body, but no sooner had he landed on the other side, than his friends were screaming at him. "Behind you!"

George spun around. There, coming at him from the depths of the freezer was Lu. With her shaved head and steam flying from her nostrils, she looked like a raging bull, charging at him at full tilt, and without breaking her stride, she snatched a knife from the wall and dived over Celia in one fearsome leap.

"Go! Go!" screamed JP, holding the door open as the others raced out.

Felix and George lunged for the door, but Lu was barely feet behind them.

"Run!" George screamed at Felix, but in one last ditch effort to slow Lu down, Felix hurled his jar at her feet and the glutinous jelly oozed across the tiled floor, making her hit the deck – hard.

From: The Postman
To: J21
Re: The Golden Moth {Encrypted}

Urgent.

I have a potential sighting of the Moth. A source of mine claims that there was an incident this morning on the beach at Deal. Several migrants were heaved out of the water.

They claim that two women transferred to another vessel just before they hit land, leaving them to fend for themselves.

I can't get any closer to the details but you may be able to.

End.

Chapter 22: Mopping Up

Nobody spoke, they just ran. They ran down Gerrard Street. No eyes on their backs. No Scouts. No on-lookers. All had vanished into the brickwork. They raced across Leicester Square, dodging startled pedestrians and trying to put as much space between themselves and the deli.

George took the lead and tore ahead down the side streets towards Charing Cross. He refused to let them all slow until the cushion and camouflage of bustling London had put him at ease.

"Don't think we'll ever be welcome back there again," Josh said, as they gathered on a street corner, catching their breath.

"I don't want to ever come to London again," Lauren said, her face still white and her hands still shaking.

"You OK?" George asked.

But she just buried her face beneath her hood, so he drew her in and tried to comfort her. "It's over," he said, but he could feel her sobs against his chest.

"What's the plan?" Julian asked. "Don't mean to rush you, but you made me a promise and…"

"Yes," George said, "I know and I intend to keep it. I just need to contact my dad."

"Huh," JP said, like something had just occurred to him.

George looked at him. With just shirt sleeves and jeans on, his teeth chattered against the November chill.

"You want my hoodie?" George asked.

JP's eyes narrowed. "I don't want anything from you."

"What's that supposed to mean?" Will asked, scowling.

"It all makes sense now," JP said, shaking his head. "Your dad, MI5; Jin-è kidnapping you; a debt to repay …

oh, and I suppose the person you're trying to track down is … what – your mum?"

George let go of Lauren and turned to face JP. "Something like that."

"And to think, I tried to help you in Paris."

"Hey!" Will said. "We helped *you*. We dragged your half-dead butt through those stinking catacombs."

"That means nothing!" JP snapped. "If it wasn't for his mother, I wouldn't have been in that hole in the first place!"

"W... what?" George said.

"No offence," Julian interrupted, "but I'm now on the run and–"

"Get used to it!" JP sneered. "I've been on the run for months – thanks to his mother!"

"Guys!" Jess said. "Is it really necessary to do this now? We're drawing attention to ourselves."

Several passers-by were stopping and staring as JP raised his voice further. "Your mother will get what she deserves!"

"Hey!" Francesca said, taking JP by the arm. "There's no need for that!"

He yanked his arm away and glared at George. "You don't even know who it is you're trying to save, do you?"

"She's my mother," George said, bluntly. "No, I don't know her, but I know that everyone deserves a second chance."

"Yeah, well my father didn't get that chance and that's thanks to her!"

"Guys!" Jess repeated.

Several small groups had gathered, and George could see a group of hooded teenagers loitering a few metres away. "We need to move on."

"Do not move!" George jumped as his dad's voice suddenly erupted in his ear. "Stay right where you are – all of you!"

"Dad, I…" but George didn't have time to finish because a large van was screeching to a halt at the kerb beside them, and before they could even think about running, the side door was thrown open, and there, standing in the darkness with his cap pulled down low, was Sam. George couldn't see his eyes but could make out the lines on his face, and he knew that he wasn't smiling. "Get in!"

Without hesitating, they all clambered in, except JP, who stood on the pavement staring at Sam.

Sam jumped down from the van and turned his back on the onlookers. "I'm not arresting you," he said, "but I'd strongly encourage you to get in."

"Why should I?"

"Because your father is desperate to see you."

JP's eyes opened wide. "How?"

"We promised we'd inform him the minute you reappeared. We knew after Paris that you'd gone into hiding. We just didn't know where."

JP seemed to wobble at the knees. "Where is he?"

"On his way."

JP glanced at George who was peering out from the van. George nodded and reluctantly JP jumped in.

Cate drove them all back to the flat and then left to retrieve Dupont and Elías.

"Make yourselves comfortable," Sam said, as they entered the lounge. "There's something to eat and drink on the table. I'll be two minutes."

George's friends grabbed some snacks and crammed themselves onto the couches. JP was pacing back and forth by the window, and George decided to keep his distance, so he made for the coffee table, but Julian was soon at his side. "When will they get my mum and sister? They need to do it now. If word gets down to Margate…"

"Don't worry," George said, "that's probably what my dad is doing right now."

"Probably?"

With that, Sam came back in with an armful of paperwork. "Ling Jun," he said, not looking up. "Or Julian, is that correct?"

"Yes," Julian replied, glancing at George for reassurance.

"Your mother, Wu Mai and sister, Ling May. Correct?" Julian nodded. "This is their address?" Sam asked, coming closer and holding out a piece of paper.

"Are they OK?"

"We've got a team with them now," Sam said. "Your mother doesn't seem keen to leave her parlour, but we've sent officers to their flat to get their belongings. They will be held at a local police office until we can relocate them, but they'll be safe there."

"And no one will know…"

"Not a soul – not even me. Their new names and location will be classified."

Julian's body sagged in relief. "When can I see them?"

"We've got a bit of work to get through first. After all the … commotion at the deli today, we've had to send in a team to mop up. There will be arrests and that will send ripples up the chain to the Dragon's Head, as you call her."

Sam was frowning which made George frown in return. *Why isn't he happy?*

George had done what they'd asked of him. He'd brought Julian in.

"We will have to see what ramifications that has," Sam continued. "We were hoping to get you on board without causing a stir." He raised an eyebrow and looked at George.

George felt his jaw bulge. "I did the job."

Sam smiled a terse smile. "Take a seat, Julian. I need a word with George."

George rolled his eyes and followed his dad out into the hallway.

"Dad, I know what you're going to say, but we–"

"Do you?" Sam said, ripping off his cap. "Do you know how it feels to sit by and watch your son throw himself into danger even when you've put every mechanism in place to protect him?"

George flexed his shoulders. "I stuck to the objective."

"Risking lives, George – your friends' lives – that's what you did – that's exactly what I feared, and you only proved me right."

"I just went with my gut! I knew Julian was there; I knew I could bring him in!"

Sam slapped his cap against the palm of his hand. "George, you're fourteen for God's sake! I told you to leave and you completely ignored me! And worse than that, you removed your earpiece!"

"I didn't know! I thought it was over!" George said, yanking the plug from his ear. "I didn't realise we'd get a second shot and then it was too late!"

"But I gave you an instruction! An order!"

"Yes, you told me to get Julian and I did!"

Sam buried his face in his hands.

"And anyway," George continued, "when I did put the earpiece back in, there was nothing."

Sam grabbed the earpiece from George. "That's because you'd gone and buried yourself beneath the street, George. Cate tried everything to get you back on frequency but…" Sam sighed. "You know what, it doesn't matter. What's done is done."

George knew he'd taken risks, but being there, in the heat of it all, he'd felt that the risks were measured, and he just wished that his dad could see it that way too. He opened his mouth to try to explain, but angry voices were drifting up the stairwell.

Clunk!

The front door crashed open and rebounded off the returning wall. "Dios Mío!" Elías cursed, as he stormed into the hallway and stopped dead in front of George. He swiped off his hat and dumped an armful of blankets on the floor at George's feet. "You speak to me again like that…" He bunched up his fist and growled at George.

George stepped backwards.

"That's enough ranting," Cate said, closing the door behind the three of them.

Dupont shirked off her thick fur coat, returning herself to her usual bean-pole stature, and pulled off her ridiculous bobble hat. She waved it at George. "I'm not sure what your mother would have made of that circus act!"

"OK, OK," Sam said, trying to calm everyone down. "It didn't exactly go to plan. We can all agree on that."

"Huh!" Dupont huffed. "You're not the one who had to crawl through those rat holes."

"And this," Elías said, pulling down his collar to reveal a nasty scratch at his neck. "That monster of a child who attacked me at the trapdoor. See what she did!"

George thought of Elías and Lu, hand to hand in combat and had to try hard to contain his amusement. Two titans in a tussle, thrashing it out. At least they were an equal match.

"Yes, yes," Sam said, "I'm sure you've had worse."

Dupont snarled at Sam and threw her hat at him. "You said this would be a low-key approach. You said we would do nothing to spook Jin-é. Well, now, thanks to your son, everyone and their aunt will know we're coming. The CCTV footage from the deli will be circulated to every corner of the 14D network. We have lost any advantage we had!"

"It's true," Elías said. "I knew it was a bad idea to rely on him."

"You're all incompetent, just like Jay said!" Dupont went on.

"I think that's enough!" Cate tried to say, but Dupont turned on her.

"And you were supposed to be running comms!"

"I did, you just didn't listen to me!" Cate insisted.

George stood staring at them all squabbling and lost his patience. "Shut up! All of you! We have Julian! He's in there and he's ready to talk, so why don't you stop laying into each other and focus on what we've achieved! I thought we were supposed to be a team!"

They all stood blank-faced, except Sam who smiled. "Absolutely. We have Julian and we also have JP."

"JP!' Dupont gasped. "Here?"

Sam nodded. "In there."

"Why didn't you tell me?" she scowled, dumping her fur coat in Cate's arms and rushing into the lounge.

Cate followed Dupont and Elías, and George was left in the hall with his dad.

"I know it wasn't perfect…" he said.

"It's OK," Sam said. "It's my fault for agreeing to let you go in the first place. I should have known it was unlikely to go smoothly."

By the time George made it back into the lounge, his friends were sat crammed in on the couch, munching through the snacks; Julian was standing anxiously in one corner of the room; Cate was on the phone; Elías had disappeared into the kitchen to look for more food and JP and Dupont were deep in conversation, gabbling to each other in French.

"How do they know each other?" George asked his dad.

"Dupont worked with JP's father, Marcel, before he started working with Victor. There's a long history."

"Dad," George said, pulling Sam aside, "JP said that Mum had something to do with the debt he owed Victor."

"Hmm, afraid so."

"What do you mean?"

"Marcel is under our protection but he's no angel. He's a fraudster, just like the rest of them. He got himself into trouble by leaking intel about Victor to your mother."

"Ah!" George said, glancing over at JP. "So, he's right. No wonder he hates me."

"Hate's a strong word, George. Don't forget you pretty much saved him in Paris, and thanks to you, he'll be reunited with his father in less than an hour. I'm sure he'll come around."

George nodded, but as he locked eyes with JP over Dupont's shoulder, he wasn't sure that the ice would ever melt.

"Right," Cate said, ending her call, "we've tidied up at the deli."

"That was quick," George said.

"Wasn't difficult. The lady who owned the place and the young girl–"

"Lu?"

"Yes, we apprehended them just after you left them at the deli. Dupont and Elías flushed out most of the kids in the tunnels. We've stripped the CCTV and found the feed, so that should limit any chance of footage leaking. It will be eye-witness reports only."

"That's amazing!"

"Well, yes, we might be able to keep your identity under wraps, but it won't be enough to stop word spreading of the raid. Jin-é will hear what's happened, you can be sure of that."

"So, we need to act fast," George said. "Julian must know something that will tell us where she is."

Sam put a hand on George's shoulder. "Slow down. We'll get Julian to talk through what he knows, but first I need to get your friends home, and we've got some other leads to follow up on."

"We have?" Cate asked, surprised.

"I need to contact Border Force."

"Movement?"

"Possible."

George shrugged his dad's hand off his shoulder. "You wanna' tell me what you're talking about?"

Sam massaged the back of his neck. "Jin-é and your mother may have crossed the Channel this morning."

George felt something skip inside him. A sighting. "So, she's alive?"

"We haven't confirmed identities yet. It's only a tip-off; someone Eddie knows at the port."

"Do we know where they've gone?"

"Not yet," Sam said. "We need to speak to Border Force."

"I'll get onto it," Cate said, taking her phone back out of her pocket and disappearing out of the door.

George could feel his heart fluttering inside his chest. *She's here.*

"We need to know where they're going. We need to …"

"George, we're on it," Sam reassured him.

"But Julian must know. He must know all their hideouts. We need to get him to talk."

"Agreed," Sam said, pushing open the lounge door, "but first of all, we need to get this lot out of here."

George looked at his friends huddled up together on the couch and grimaced. "Go gentle on them. They were only trying to help."

"Hmm," Sam grumbled.

Chapter 23: Silence is Golden

George joined his friends while Sam arranged for them to be chaperoned on the train back to Pendleton. He tried to focus on the conversation but couldn't take his eyes off Julian, who sat curled up in the corner, staring out of the window.

"Is your dad mad?" Francesca asked, as they scooched up to make space for George on the couch.

"No, I promise," George said.

Julian glanced over at George and then shuffled around to turn his back on him.

"He seemed pretty mad to me," Will said, raising both eyebrows. "Trust me, I've seen that look on my dad's face."

"He always looks like that," George shrugged.

George shifted his position and tried to see the side of Julian's face. He seemed to be mumbling to himself.

"Have we ruined everything?" Felix asked, looking at George sideways. "George?"

"Huh?" George shook his head. "No … it was good … to have you with me."

"Yeah, always saving your butt," Will said, slapping George on the back.

"Do you think Julian knows where Jin-é is?" Jess asked.

George glanced back towards him. He felt sorry for him, curled up in the corner, alone. He tried to imagine how it must feel to be trapped in a world full of fear, never knowing if you'll ever see your family again. He felt a familiar pain in his chest. The pain that reminded him that his mother was still out there somewhere; still at Jin-é's mercy. He glanced towards the door. Cate and his dad were still outside. "Maybe I should go and speak to him."

Francesca nodded. "He looks lost."

"And hungry," Lauren said.

"I'll come with you," Felix said, grabbing some of the left-over snacks.

George heaved himself from the couch and they made their way across the lounge. Half way across the room, George looked towards the kitchen where Elías, JP and Dupont sat deep in conversation.

What are they talking about?

JP looked up and glared at George, so George turned away.

Just focus on Julian.

Julian had his nose pressed up against the window, his eyes tracking the pedestrians that passed by on the street below.

"You hungry?" Felix asked, offering him a packet of crisps.

Julian grabbed it and grunted his thanks without shifting his gaze. George squatted down beside him; his back against the windowsill. "Everything's gonna' be OK."

"Really?" Julian huffed, his breath misting up the glass. "A life in hiding – that's all I've got to look forward to."

"It won't be like that," George said.

"At least you'll be back with your family," Felix added.

Julian leaned his forehead against the glass. "They'll never stop looking for me. They make it their mission to punish disloyalty. They'll make an example of me. They won't let it go. I've seen what they do to people who break the code."

"What code?" Felix asked.

"The code of silence," Julian replied. "It's the first thing she makes you do. Swear to it – on your life." He lifted his fringe to reveal the tattoo. "That's how you get one of these – you've passed the test of loyalty."

"What do you have to do to pass?" Felix asked.

Julian dropped his fringe back over his eyes. "You don't want to know. She makes you do things; things that only the most loyal will do."

"She," George said. "Do you mean Jin-é?"

Julian drew his gaze away from the street below. "I've never heard that name," he said. "Whatever you want to call her; what does it matter?"

George lowered himself completely to the floor. "But the boxes you were packing … in the den."

Julian looked at his feet. "It's not like I wanted to get involved with that stuff."

"No, no, I know. Mayling told us. It's OK." George didn't want Julian to feel like he was in trouble. "I get it … there's stuff I've done that I wish I hadn't, but sometimes…"

"You have no choice," Julian said, dumping his chin onto the windowsill.

"It's just, I noticed that the boxes had the sign of the Moth on … the Golden Moth."

Julian lifted his chin and pursed his lips. "Yeah, that's her, the Dragon's Head."

George glanced up at Felix, who nodded in encouragement.

George shuffled closer to Julian. "Have you ever met her?"

Julian narrowed his eyes. "Once."

"Did she come to the deli?"

Julian shook his head. "No, she never comes to us."

George waited, hoping that Julian would go on, but he didn't. "So, where does she … like hang out?"

Julian sat upright. "I…"

"Don't say anything!" JP had appeared at Felix's side.

"Hey," Felix said, "who asked you?"

JP ignored him and pushed his way in beside Julian. "If you're gonna' make a rat of yourself, you make sure they're keeping their promises first."

George looked up. "We've already taken his mum and sister to a safe place. We're not trying to–"

"That means nothing. Your mum promised my dad protection. She said she'd look after him, protect him from the people who he'd ratted on."

George pushed himself to his feet. "I'm sure she'd have meant it."

JP snorted. "What do you know? My father led her to their hideout and then she scarpered. Left him to run for his life."

Julian lifted himself to his feet too. "JP's right. Maybe I shouldn't talk until…"

"No!" George said, a little too abruptly.

"I should wait," Julian said, "until I see my family."

"But we had a deal," George said, trying to wedge himself between JP and Julian.

"You shook on it," Felix said.

Julian looked from JP, to George and back again. "I…"

"Don't you say a thing!" JP said, elbowing George out of the way.

"Hey!" Felix snapped. "There's no need to be like that!"

George tried to shuffle back in front of Julian. "If we work together, we can bring them all down … then it will all be over. None of us will have to run. We'll all be safe."

JP grabbed George by the arm and tried to push him aside. "Don't let him sweet talk you – he can't guarantee that!"

"Oi!" Will and the others were up from the couch. "What's going on?"

"This is none of your business!" JP spat.

"Oh, I think you'll find it is," Will growled back. "Get your hands off George!"

JP released George's arm and turned to face Will. "You need to sit back down!"

"You gonna' make me?"

Slam!

Sam flung the door closed behind him as he re-entered the lounge. "You're all going to sit back down!" He pointed to a chair in the corner of the room. "JP, I suggest you take that seat. Julian, stay there by the window, and you lot…" Sam glared at George's friends. "Mr Steckler will meet you at Pendleton and drive you all home." He looked at his watch. "You've got ten minutes to get to Charing Cross. Cate will escort you to the station and an undercover officer will accompany you on the train. Your daytrip is over. Move out."

George followed his friends as they slunk across the lounge, heads hanging.

Sam stood at the open door, his cap in his hand, counting George's friends out. George looked up at his dad as he reached the doorway. "I thought you were going to go easy on them."

"This is going easy."

"Nice one," George huffed.

He went to follow his friends, but Sam tapped him on the head with his cap. "Not you. You're staying here."

"But I just…"

"I'm not letting you out of my sight."

George rolled his eyes. "Seriously, Dad."

Sam plonked his cap onto George's head. "And anyway, I might need your help."

"Really?"

"I think Julian is much more likely to talk to someone his own age."

"I'm not sure about that," George said, glancing back towards JP.

"Don't worry," Sam said, following George's line of sight. "I've got a solution to that problem."

"Like what?"

"His father."

With that, the door flew open and a dark flustered figure surged into the hallway with Cate at his heels. "Where is he?"

Marcel Perron was the spitting image of his son: dark skin, syrupy eyes. The only difference was that Marcel had a light fuzz of greying hair where JP had a full head of braids.

"He's in here," Sam replied, "but I need a word with you first."

Marcel stared at George and his friends. "What are you running here, a school?"

"It's a long story," Sam replied. "Cate, can you take this lot to the station?"

"Can I at least see them out?" George asked.

Sam nodded, and George stumbled down the stairs after his friends.

"You gonna' be OK?" Lauren asked as they all stepped out onto the pavement.

"Yeah," George replied, tightening the back of his dad's cap.

"Give us a call," Felix said, "when you get home."

His friends huddled around him. "Let us know what happens," Josh said, squeezing George's shoulder.

George smiled. "Thanks, guys. Thanks for coming."

"No worries," Will said. "We love a bit of excitement."

"Hmm," Jess said, pushing Will towards Cate's van, "a bit too much."

Lauren was the last to jump into the van. As George went to slide the van door shut, she leant out. "Be safe, George."

"I will."

"I hope you find her."

With that, Cate started the engine, and George watched the van pull off and dissolve into the London traffic.

He stood for a moment, alone on the pavement, and looked up at the darkening clouds that were gathering above the city. He felt a tightness in his chest; a weight that pulled down on his shoulders and cramped his lungs. The clouds distorted as they grew, swelling and shifting, like a giant slowly rising up from its sleep. He felt its restlessness and something brewed inside him. Fear. Impatience. Anxiety. His mother was on the move. Moving beneath the same rippling sky. Somewhere out there – moving on a path hidden from him – a path that he needed to uncover – before it was too late.

From: H09
To: K07
Re: Stolen Goods {Encrypted}

Update 1.7

Urgent: The surveillance team have hacked into an email account from an IP address within the hotel that the Billionaire is staying at.

I thought you'd want immediate visibility. Call me ASAP.

End.

Chapter 24: Give and Take

With the afternoon sun shrouded in cloud, the light in the flat had dulled, as had the atmosphere. George's friends were on their way home, leaving him with a room full of criminals – none of whom seemed to trust or like each other very much.

He loitered in the hallway and listened to the jumble of voices that drifted out from behind the lounge door. He could hear JP's voice above the rest, arguing with someone in his native tongue. George sighed and pushed the door open, nearly knocking Dupont off her feet.

"Er, sorry." He looked up at her, wondering whether he should steal the chance to ask her about his mother's envelope, but she had already turned her attention back to her paper.

"Right!" Sam said, slamming a small stool down onto the floor in front of the coffee table and making everyone flinch. "We have some work to do!"

Everyone in the room turned their attention towards Sam, except Julian who was chewing at the collar of his t-shirt and still peering out of the window.

I need to get him to open up.

"As you may all now be aware, myself and Officer Cate Knowles are heading up the task force that is looking into the fallout from the Paris attack." He paused and glided his eyes around the room. "And you lot are, from this moment on, our extended team."

George followed his dad's gaze. They were an unlikely bunch. A French con-artist and her burly Spanish sidekick, an ageing Frenchman and his brooding son, and a nervous wreck of a boy, cowering in the corner, desperate to go home. Was this really who they were relying on to find his mum and bring her home?

JP perched on the edge of one of the sofas. "Why should we help you?"

Marcel frowned at his son, but Sam didn't hesitate to answer the question.

"All of you have been informed of the deal you'll get if you help. None of you are innocent. You've all committed crimes that we could detain you for. I shouldn't need to remind you of that. The UK government will clear you of any charges and offer you protection and anonymity but only if you pull your weight and are completely transparent. That's the deal."

George folded his arms and leant up against the wall as a heady mix of emotions swirled around the room. Dupont and Elías had already shown their intention to help, Marcel looked keen, even if his son seemed defiant, but Julian just buried himself deeper into the corner of the room.

Surely, he wants to take the deal?

"What's our task?" Marcel asked, squatting on the sofa next to JP.

Sam perched on the small stool and flipped open his laptop. "We had four objectives originally: recovering the stolen Rothkos, which have now been returned; apprehending Angelika Volkov, who is still in hiding; locating the weapon that Victor stole, which we believe he has already sold; and tracking down Jin-é and our missing officer."

"Your wife," JP grunted.

Sam didn't react. "With the Rothkos returned, Angelika still missing, and the buyer for the weapon still unknown to us, our main focus is on tracking down Jin-é." Sam paused and cracked his knuckles. "JP has worked with Jin-é, Julian has inside knowledge of the 14D and Dupont and Elías were the last to see … Jay. Between us, we should be able to flesh out some ideas as to where they are likely to be and what they are planning to do."

"What about Victor?" Marcel asked. "Surely he knows more than the rest of us put together."

"Most probably," Sam said, readjusting himself on the stool, "but he doesn't seem inclined to help."

"Even if he did talk," Dupont snorted, "we couldn't rely on any of it being factual."

"So, what *are* the facts?" Marcel asked.

Sam squinted at the laptop and pulled up some files onto the screen. "The facts are this: Jin-é and Jay are already back on UK soil." Sam glanced at George for just a second, but George registered the look of concern. "We've just had eye-witness reports back from a group of migrants who made land this morning from France. Their description of the two women that made the crossing with them was pretty conclusive."

George tried not to let his expression change.

It's definitely her – she's here.

"So," Dupont said, "what are you waiting for?"

Sam rolled his shoulders. "We don't have their location. They passed through the border undetected."

Dupont threw her hands in the air. "Why does that not surprise me?"

"We got the report *after* they'd hit land," Sam said, tersely.

"So, where is she headed?" Elías asked, stepping closer to the table.

"We don't know."

George watched Julian. He had turned his head slightly towards Sam but his eyes didn't stray from the window.

He knows.

"Does MI5 know *anything*?" JP sneered.

With that, the lounge door flew open and Cate charged in. "We know…" she panted.

"We know what?" Sam asked.

"Motive," she said, holding up her phone. "We've got motive."

George pushed himself away from the wall and Sam was already on his feet. "Who's motive?"

Cate took several deep breaths and recomposed herself.

"You two," she said, pointing at Sam and George, "in the hall. We need to talk."

George stared at his dad.

"Well, let's go," Sam said, scooping up his laptop and steering George towards the lounge door.

George looked back over his shoulder, and all eyes were on him, even Julian's.

"What's this about?" Sam asked, pulling the door tightly closed behind them.

They stood huddled together in the cramped hall, crowded out by the overloaded coat stand and tangled up in the pile of Elías' discarded blankets.

"I've just got off the phone with MI6," Cate said, kicking some of the blankets aside.

"And?" Sam asked.

"We know Jin-é's motive for taking your wife."

"What? What is it?" George asked, struggling to keep the impatience out of his voice.

Cate's eyes skimmed over George and settled on Sam.

"There's a … bounty on your wife's head."

"A what?" George asked, but no one replied.

"How much?" Sam asked, his eyes widening.

"A lot."

"Do we know who?"

Cate nodded. "Our favourite billionaire, Ivan Pozhar, or should I say 'The Flame' as he apparently calls himself."

"Who?" George asked, but still he got no response.

"Since when?" Sam asked.

"We're not sure," Cate replied, looking down at her phone, "but the comms we intercepted suggest that Jin-é has already been in touch with Pozhar and that she is pretty keen to make the trade."

"Trade what?" George asked, ripping his dad's cap off his head.

"When?" Sam asked.

"We–"

"Hey!" George bellowed. "Will someone tell me what the hell is going on?"

Sam straightened up and looked at George. "Someone wants your mother and is willing to … pay for her."

George screwed up his face. "To like … buy her?"

"More like they want her…" Sam said glancing at Cate, "because of something she's done."

"Or something she knows," Cate added.

"And they have offered … a ransom of sorts … to anyone who brings her in," Sam concluded.

George leant back against the bundle of coats. "Why … why would they want…"

"We don't know," Cate said, "but Pozhar is currently holed up in a hotel on the south coast, and Jin-é has just crossed the channel. She's making her move."

Cate and Sam's words drifted out of George's consciousness. All he could hear was his own mind as it spiralled away into a whirlwind of chaotic thoughts.

Why would someone want to offer a ransom? Why would they want her? What would they do with her?

He thought of his mother's words. *There are things I've done.* And he thought of her desperate need to make things right.

Has she done something to make someone mad? Do they want her dead?

"We have to stop her!" he blurted out, storming back into the conversation without warning. "We need to stop the trade! We need to stop Jin-é from reaching this guy! We need to get to Jin-é first! We need to–"

Sam laid his hand on George's shoulder. "George, calm down."

"Calm down? Dad, they could want her dead!"

"We don't know that, and anyway, we have Pozhar under surveillance. Jin-é won't get anywhere near him without us knowing."

"What like how you caught her crossing the channel?"

Sam frowned. "George, don't start."

"I'm serious, Dad! We need to intercept her. We know Mum's alive now, but we have no idea what this guy will do to her if he gets his hands on her!"

"You're jumping to conclusions," Sam said. "There are plenty of reasons why he might want your mother."

"Like what?" George asked. "Do you even know anything about him?"

"Yes," Cate replied, "he was the owner of the Rothkos, the ones Victor stole."

"But Mum had nothing to do with that," George said, confused.

"No, but he's a very rich and influential man, maybe he–"

"Wait!" George said, stopping Sam mid-sentence. "What does he look like?"

"Why?" Cate asked.

Sam had his laptop wedged under his arm. George nodded his chin towards it. "You got a picture of him?"

"Yes," Sam replied, sliding the laptop out and flipping it open. "Why?"

George's mouth suddenly felt very dry. "Er, I just … can I see it?"

Sam flicked through a few files and pulled up a set of photos taken outside a foreign villa. George peered down at them. Sure enough, his instincts were spot on. There, climbing out of an expensive looking sports car, was the man from his mother's photos. The watch, the rings, the slicked back, golden hair.

"What is it, George?" Sam asked, grabbing at George's shoulder again.

George stared at the photo, unsure of what it meant; unsure of why his mother would want to keep it quiet. There was something that connected her to this man; something that she didn't want anyone to know.

"George," Sam repeated, "if you know something…"

George felt his hesitation wrangle at his insides. Where did his allegiances lie? Should he ignore his mum's request? Should his honesty to his dad be his priority?

The objective is to get her home, whatever it takes.

He looked up at his dad. "Mum knows him, and I think she knows something about him, maybe something he has done."

Sam stood with the laptop balancing on his open palm. "And you know this because…"

"Please don't be mad," George pleaded.

Sam took a deep breath. "I'm trying not to be."

Cate laid her hand on Sam's arm. "George, we're a team and we have the same objective. No one is going to get mad. We just want to solve this and get everyone safely back home."

George blew out his cheeks. "She sent me something."

"Your mother?" Sam choked.

George nodded.

"When?" Cate asked.

George thought of the card from Dupont, the key and the single, white envelope. "It's a long story, but I think she posted it to me while she was in Paris, before she was taken."

George watched Sam's expression as his words sank in.

"The PO box," Sam said.

"Er, yeah – sorry, Dad."

"Why didn't you tell me?"

"She asked me not to tell anyone."

Sam covered his face with his free hand and squeezed his temples.

"It's OK," Cate said, slowly taking the laptop from Sam's unsteady grasp. "It doesn't matter. Now we know, we need to understand what it was she sent you."

"This guy," George said, pointing at the photo of Ivan Pozhar.

"Yes," Cate said.

"Mum has a photo of him shaking hands with Victor."

Sam uncovered his face. "Victor and Ivan?"

"Yes," George said, "it looks like Mum took the photo in Turkey, back in August."

Sam looked at Cate. "That's our link."

"The buyer," Cate grinned.

Sam's face lit up. "Victor sold Ivan the weapon!"

"Makes sense," Cate said. "Although, why would Victor then steal his art?"

George thought back to the hangar in Paris. He could see his mother, tied to her chair, goading Victor. *"I knew he'd double cross you."*

"Ivan did something," George said. "He double crossed Victor!"

"So, Victor took revenge," Cate added.

George could feel a buzz pulse around the stuffy room, like someone had turned up the electricity and it had no way of escaping.

"This starts to make sense," Sam said.

"So, Ivan wants Jay because she can prove that he's been buying stolen weapons from Victor," Cate said.

"But is that enough?" Sam said, as if asking himself the question. "Jay can link Ivan to Victor, so what? Is that enough to make him hunt her down?"

"Maybe she knows more," Cate said.

George squirmed. "Ah, there may be some other stuff she sent me…"

Cate and Sam both looked at him.

"Like?" Sam said, bluntly.

"Er … another photo … it was of Ivan with another guy."

"Can you be more specific?" Cate asked.

"He had one ear," George offered.

Sam took the laptop back from Cate and opened up a spreadsheet. "We've got details of all of Ivan's business associates here. Can you remember anything else?"

George shook his head. "Not really, he was kinda' skinny and, I don't know, mean looking."

Sam frowned.

"I'm trying my best," George insisted.

"It's OK," Cate said, "we can run those details. Something might come up. Anything else?"

"There was an article about a dead Chinese boy, found in Calais."

Cate and Sam exchanged looks.

"What?" George asked.

"Nothing," Sam said. "Was that all?"

George scratched at his neck. "No, she also sent me … a bullet."

"A bullet?" Sam repeated. "Your mother sent you a bullet?"

"Yeah, and it looked like it had been … used."

Sam lifted his eyes to the ceiling.

"It must be evidence," Cate said. "But why send it to George?"

Sam's brow creased. "She doesn't trust *me*, that's why!"

Trust.

George let the word circle around inside his head.

Trust.

He should have trusted his dad, he knew that now. By lying to him, he had let his mother's distrust infect him too. His head drooped and he stared at the cap in his hand.

"Was there anything else?" Cate asked.

"Nothing, that was it," George replied. "Oh, and Jin-é's business card."

Sam looked more disappointed than George had ever seen. "You told me–"

"I know, I'm sorry, but I didn't know why she wanted me to keep it a secret. What else could I do?"

"I would like to think that you could have trusted me … even if she can't."

"I'm sorry, Dad," George said, handing back the screwed-up cap. "You just … don't always…"

Sam sighed. He took the cap from George's grasp, flapped it out and wriggled it back down over George's head. "Well … at least we know you're good at keeping secrets."

George hid beneath the peak of the cap. "I screwed up."

Sam tipped up the cap's peak, lifting George's gaze from the floor. "Your mother shouldn't have put you in that position. The important thing is that we now know the facts and the picture is starting to come together."

"So … what do we do now?" George asked, glumly.

"Well," Sam said, smoothing his beard. "Jin-é has Jay… Ivan wants Jay because of what she knows … Ivan may have the weapon … all our targets are linked."

"So?" George asked.

"I guess we sit it out and wait to see who makes the first move."

"Ah," Cate said, chewing at her lip.

Sam rolled his eyes. "Let me guess – there's something else you need to tell us."

Cate's teeth dug deeper into her lip.

"Cate?" Sam said, his eyes unblinking.

"The comms we intercepted…" Cate started.

"Yes?" Sam and George both said together.

"Well, it seems that Ivan isn't exactly playing ball. He's refusing to meet Jin-é's demands."

"I don't blame him," George said. "He must know she was involved in stealing his Rothkos."

"Good point," said Sam, "but if he wants Jay badly enough, surely he'll make the trade."

"Hmm, he seems pretty reluctant, and the problem is: Jin-é seems to suggest that if Ivan doesn't meet with her to make the trade, she will … dispose of Jay herself."

George fell back against the coats again, this time nearly burying himself completely.

"But if Jin-é kills her," Sam said. "Ivan's problems are over. Jay can't rat him in."

"No," Cate said, "but George can."

"Because Jay sent him the evidence," Sam said, shaking his head in disbelief.

George could see it now. His mum knew the risks in the game she was playing, and she knew that the evidence she had against Ivan was her one 'get out of jail' card.

"Surely he'll want to make the trade then," Sam said.

"I'm sure he does," Cate said, "just not with Jin-é."

"So, we have a stand-off," Sam said.

"And either way, Mum dies," George added.

Sam closed his laptop. "How long do we have?"

"Less than twenty-four hours," Cate replied.

George looked at his watch. It was already early evening, and Jin-é was already there somewhere – there in the UK, holding his mother captive, preparing to sell her like livestock to the slaughterhouse, or kill her herself.

"What are our options?" Sam asked.

"We can't force Ivan's hand," Cate replied, "so our best option is to get to Jin-é first."

"Julian!" George said, fighting his way out of the coats. "We need to get Julian to talk. He must know where Jin-é is likely to be hiding. She has to stay somewhere tonight."

"OK," Sam said, shoving his laptop back under his arm. "Let's see what Julian knows."

"Oh, great idea!" George said, mockingly.

Sam raised an eyebrow. "Yes, I know. I'm full of them."

"I'm not sure he's going to open up that easily," George warned. "JP has got into his head."

Sam put his hand on the door handle but stalled. "Do you trust me, George?"

"Huh?"

"We can't force Julian to talk…"

"Why not? You're MI5."

"That's not how we work," Sam said, "especially with someone so young."

"So, what do we do?" George asked.

"So, we need to … coerce him."

"OK," George said, unsure of the difference.

"You've got a plan?" Cate asked.

"Well, the best way to get an asset to open up is to find the thing they want the most and make them desperate for it. And what does Julian want most?" Sam asked, looking at George.

"To get back to his family," George said.

"So, we make him feel like that isn't going to happen."

"How?" George asked, confused.

"I suggest we go in there and act like he isn't important to us at all. Like we don't need his information and he has nothing valuable to offer us. Then he may start to panic. Without giving us something, we don't need to give him anything in return."

"Huh," George said, impressed, "I get it."

"That could work," Cate agreed.

"So, follow my lead," Sam said, "and maybe we'll get something useful out of him before the night is over."

"Less than twenty-four hours," Cate reminded him.

"It could be a long night," Sam warned.

George readjusted his cap. "I'm in."

Chapter 25: Playing the Room

Sam addressed the room and informed them all of the latest intel. George watched the gathered faces as the information sank in. Focusing his attention on the adults in the room, Sam practically turned his back on Julian, but George watched him like a hawk. The more Sam revealed about what they already knew, the more Julian fidgeted.

"We know who has offered the bounty," Sam said, "and we have eyes on him, so if the Moth makes her move, we'll be there to take her in."

"Who's offering the bounty?" JP asked, now balancing on the very edge of the couch.

"He's a Russian businessman by the name of Ivan Pozhar," Sam replied.

"Ivan Pozhar?" Marcel said. "The Mob?"

Sam twisted to look at Marcel. "You think he has links with the Russian Mob?"

"Ha!" Marcel laughed. "He *is* the Russian Mob! Nothing gets moved between Moscow and London without his say so."

"You've got proof?" Cate asked.

Marcel laughed even harder. "Proof? No one has anything on him. He's untouchable! Backed by the Russian government, protected by the Security Service. You won't get near him, and if he wants your wife, there must be a pretty good reason … and I dread to think what he'll do to her if—"

"Yes, thank you," Sam said, cutting him off.

"We're watching him," Cate reminded them, "Jin-é won't get near him without us knowing."

George looked at Julian again. He had shuffled closer; his chin resting on his shoulder.

He's listening.

"Jin-é?" Marcel said, pulling himself from the sofa. "Pozhar won't trade with the 14D."

"Why not?" Cate asked.

"They hate each other. I don't know all the details, but they have a longstanding feud."

"The Mob and the Triads," Dupont said, nodding. "It's true. They battle over territories, ambush each other's deals…"

"Wait," JP said, "wasn't it the Mob who tipped off the police and got those Triad guys arrested?"

Marcel was nodding too. "Yes, Victor found it very amusing. Something about a raid. They lost millions."

"OK, we get it," Sam said, trying to get back in control of the conversation.

"So, there's some bad blood," Elías said, shrugging. "Didn't stop me from working with Jay."

Sam forced a smile. "Exactly. Some things are obviously worth burying the hatchet for."

Cate and George glanced at each other. Sam was trying his hardest to conceal his concern over Ivan's reluctance to trade. He needed Julian to think that MI5 could pull this off without him.

"I don't know," Marcel said, frowning. "I can't think of anything that Pozhar would want badly enough…"

"And what does Jin-é get out of it? Money?" Dupont asked.

"Yes, and lots of it," Sam said.

"Something doesn't feel right," Marcel said. "I can't see Jin-é going cap in hand to Ivan, even if she has got your wife. There's plenty of other things she can do to earn that money."

Julian was breathing condensation onto the window and tracing his finger through it in spirals.

We're losing him.

"It's a lot of money," Sam repeated, "and anyway, we have evidence that supports the theory."

"Like what, exactly?" Dupont pushed.

George could see the tension in his dad's jaw. "E-mails between Ivan and Jin-é."

"Saying they're going to meet to do the trade," Cate lied.

Marcel flopped back onto the couch. "Right, so, you don't really need us after all."

Bingo!

"Well," Sam said, stretching out his legs under the coffee table and leaning his head back into the cradle of his hands. "It seems we have most of the intel we need … so now we just sit and wait."

Julian's finger had stopped its circuit and was hovering mid-air.

"So, you might as well let us go then," JP said, smugly.

"Er, no," said Sam, rocking back towards the coffee table. "No one leaves until we have all three targets secured."

George couldn't help smiling. He coughed into his fist, trying to conceal his amusement because Julian was now staring right at Sam, a look of despair on his face.

"But of course," Sam went on, "those of you who have shown your willingness to help will be fairly rewarded, as was promised."

Bam!

Julian opened his mouth to speak. "You're wrong."

His voice drifted out from the corner of the room, and everyone turned to look at him.

"Sorry," Sam said, so casually that George almost choked. "Wrong about what?"

"Everything," Julian replied.

Sam swivelled around on his stool. "So, why don't you enlighten us … Julian."

Julian looked around the room and his eyes loitered in JP's direction, but JP just lowered his gaze to the couch and fiddled with the rib of the corduroy.

All other eyes were on Julian. "I know you think I know where to find her, but I don't."

"Really?" Sam said, unconvinced.

"I only met her once."

"Where exactly?"

"It doesn't matter. She won't go back there. When she comes to London, she doesn't stop moving; never stays anywhere for long; never returns to any place more than once."

Sam folded his arms. "That's convenient."

"It's true," Julian insisted.

Sam turned back towards the table. "So, you're no use to us then."

"Wait!"

"Yes?" Sam said, fiddling with his laptop.

"I don't know where she is, but I know what she wants."

Sam peered at him over his shoulder. "What do you mean?"

"She doesn't want the money."

"Why would she not want the money?" Dupont asked.

"She's got plenty," Julian replied.

"So has Ivan," Cate said, "but that doesn't stop him from dealing with crooks."

"She won't trade your wife's life unless she sees Ivan face to face."

"And why is that?" Sam asked, turning around completely and leaning so far forward on his stool that its back two legs lifted off the floor.

"I … want to see my family," Julian said.

Sam's stool slammed back to the floor and his shoulder's slumped, but George wasn't ready to give up.

"So do I," George said, edging towards Julian, "and we both can, if we get this right."

Julian turned back towards his window, but George edged closer still. "You help us and you'll see them, and this nightmare will be over."

Julian sighed, fogging up the window again.

"Go on," Sam mouthed at George.

George crouched down at Julian's side. "Why is Jin-é bothering to trade my mum's life if she doesn't need the money?"

Julian stared out of the window. "Same reason she teamed up with that Russian guy and stole Ivan's art."

Everyone in the room seemed to lean in closer.

"Do you mean Victor?" Cate asked.

Julian nodded.

"And what reason would that be?" Sam asked.

Julian traced a large R into the condensation on the glass. "Revenge."

George blinked and saw the message that Jin-è had written to him.

The warrior who seeks revenge…

"Revenge for what?" George asked.

Julian tilted his head and peered out at George from beneath his fringe. "Revenge for her son's murder."

George looked at Julian but all he could see was the face of the dead boy: drawn out, scared, the same tattoo above his eye.

He looked at his dad. "The Chinese boy."

Sam paused for a second. "In Calais."

"Hang on," Elías said, "if Ivan killed Jin-é's son, there's no way he's letting her get anywhere near him. She'll be out for blood and he'll know it."

"He'd have to be mad," Dupont said.

"Or desperate," Marcel added.

"Is he really that desperate to get his hands on Jay that he'd risk facing Jin-é?" Dupont asked. "She'll want him dead."

George could see everything slipping away in front of his eyes. If they didn't know where Jin-é was, and Ivan refused to do the trade, there was no way of getting to his mum before the deadline. He looked down at Julian and was surprised to see him peering back up at him.

"I'm sorry," Julian whispered. "I really would help you find her … if I knew."

George didn't know what to say. Was he telling the truth? Surely, there was no need for him to hold back now. He couldn't go back to the 14D. His only option was to take the deal. All George knew was that his mum was doomed. Without the trade, Jin-é would kill her.

"What can we do?" Cate asked.

George's thoughts floated from the room. He could hear the voices bounce around him, but his mind exploded into a storm of panic.

How can I get to her?

"Arrest Ivan," Elías said.

There must be something we can do.

"I knew we should have gone out there ourselves," Dupont said. "Elías and I could have flushed Jin-é out."

Flush Jin-é out.

"Ivan's lawyers would be on me before I could secure the cuffs," Sam argued.

Ivan in cuffs.

"Unless we catch him doing the trade," Cate added.

The trade.

George could hear his own voice in his head.

That's it! The only way to save Mum and catch them all is to draw them all out into the open!

"We need to force the trade!" he shouted above all the other voices.

Everyone stopped and stared at him.

"What?" Sam asked.

"We need to find a way," George said, "I mean … there has to be something that will draw Ivan out … something he couldn't resist. Somehow, we need to force him to meet with Jin-é."

George looked at the faces that were scattered around the room. No one seemed to see it.

"Elías said it," George said, moving to the centre of the room, "some things are worth burying the hatchet for. Some things are worth taking the risk for."

"O…K," Sam said, "but we have no idea what Ivan wants that badly."

"Badly enough that he'd take the risk of standing in a room with his fiercest enemy," Dupont added.

"There must be something," George said. "You're all criminals. What would make you take the risk?"

Dupont frowned at him. "We may have a history with the wrong side of the law, but we're not crazy."

George looked around at their misfit of a team.

"Come on. He doesn't need money, but he obviously wants to get his hands on my mum, or he wouldn't have offered the bounty, so what else is there that can tip the balance? What else can we put out there that would make him take the risk?"

The room fell silent and George could feel the small glimmer of hope that was left alight inside him start to fizzle out.

"I don't know what Ivan wants," Marcel said, breaking the silence, "but I bet I know someone who might."

"Who?" George, Cate and Sam all asked at once.

"Victor."

"Why would he know?" Cate asked.

"He knew Ivan," Marcel explained. "He idolised him; studied his every deal; worshipped him. Victor modelled himself on Ivan. All he wanted was his acceptance; his blessing. If anyone knows him, Victor does."

Sam turned to Cate. "I think it's time we recruited our last team member."

"Victor?" Cate asked, astounded.

"If he knows something, anything that can help, now's the time to make him talk."

"But … you want him … here?"

"Why not?" Sam replied. "If a room full of his enemies won't encourage his ego to blab, nothing will."

Chapter 26: The Dealer's Hand

It took several hours for Cate to get clearance and arrange for Victor to be escorted from his cell beneath the MI5 headquarters.

Sam tried his best to keep the mood in the flat calm. He ordered pizza and raided the sparse fridge for more drinks, but it seemed that, even though the room was filled with crooks, no one relished the thought of sharing it with Victor, least of all George. By the time Cate reappeared at the lounge door, the air in the room had turned to ice; the kind of ice that could shatter with a heartbeat.

"Well … well … well, so nice to be invited to the party."

George nearly gagged on his last mouthful of pizza as Victor Sokolov shuffled into the room, sandwiched between two armed guards and shackled at the wrists and ankles.

It had been several weeks since George had tasered him to the ground in the hangar in Paris, but he hadn't changed a bit. If anything, he looked more arrogant and obnoxious than ever before, and George hated it. He hated being near him, he hated the way the air changed when he walked into the room and he hated having to rely on him to bring his mum home. Nothing about him was modest or subdued. Even in his prison overalls and handcuffs, he still looked around the room as if he was the guest of honour at a dinner party. Every smirk, every chuckle, showed that he knew he had an audience, an audience that resented him and revered him, but also needed him.

"So many familiar faces," Victor chortled. "How lovely to see you all again."

Dupont and Elías had eaten in the kitchen, but were now loitering in the kitchen doorway. Elías had his arms folded; his sleeves rolled up revealing his bulging forearms. Dupont stood straight as a board, her eyes burning into Victor. The hatred pulsed across the room.

"The feeling isn't mutual," Elías grunted.

George thought back to the hangar in Paris: Elías on the floor, grabbing at his bleeding shoulder; Dupont staggering from the woods, her shirt soaked with blood. The injuries may not have been inflicted by Victor's hands, but he had led the team that pulled the trigger and stabbed the needle.

"I'm actually surprised to see you alive," Victor said. "Shame Jin-é didn't kill you both."

"That's enough!" Sam said, as he and Cate took Victor each by an arm and forced him down into the sofa, making Marcel and JP leap up from their seats and abandon the rest of their meal.

Victor turned his head and smirked at Marcel, who seemed to shrink in his presence. "I see they found the hole you were hiding in," Victor growled. "Lucky for you I didn't find you first."

Marcel took JP by the arm and they rounded the couch and dived into the kitchen.

"Oh, don't you want to introduce me to your son?" Victor shouted over his shoulder.

"I said, that's enough," Sam said, clearing the pizza boxes from the couch. "You're here to answer questions, not ask them."

Julian was the only one who didn't seem to care for their new flat mate. He stayed rooted to his corner, staring out of the window.

"Do you really think that bringing me here to your den of thieves and con artists will intimidate me?" Victor asked. "What makes you think I've changed my mind about talking?"

"We think you might be interested in our recent findings," Sam said, grabbing his stool and repositioning it in front of Victor.

With his hands and feet bound, Victor struggled to stay upright, the undulations of the sofa throwing him off balance. Wriggling and shuffling, he righted himself and faced Sam. "I doubt there's anything MI5 have uncovered that I don't already know."

Sam leant his elbows on his knees and clasped his hands together. "Let's see shall we?"

George loitered by the lounge door. Victor had walked right past him as he entered, and George had been more than happy to stay out of his way. He edged along the wall, trying to get a better view, whilst managing to stay out of Victor's peripheral vision. The longer he could go without making eye contact, the better. Even the sight of the falcon tattoo that covered half of Victor's shaved head made George boil. Everything that had happened, had happened because of him. The years without his mother, the hatred between his parents, the pain and torment that his friends had gone through, and worst of all the despair George had felt when Gran had been taken – it was all Victor's fault.

Even now, even with Victor in custody, George's life, his very happiness, was on the cusp of destruction, all because of Victor. With his mother about to be handed to the Russian Mob, George knew he needed to focus on the operation. He knew that Victor might hold the key to bringing her home, but he couldn't help but let his hatred sear through him, chewing at his gut and willing him to lash out. He wanted to see Victor pay, not in prison, but really pay – for all the pain he'd caused. He thought of his mother, standing over Victor, her rifle in her hands.

Crunch! The sound of the barrel as it crushed Victor's nose.

Revenge.

George shrank further behind the door.

"Let me lay out the facts," Sam said, pulling his stool closer to the couch.

"I tell you what," Victor said, leaning back into the dip of the sofa. "Why don't I guess." He stared around the room, just missing George. "From the collection of bodies in this room, I'm guessing there's something you need to know. Some piece of the puzzle that you just can't put your finger on, and you've gathered this pathetic ensemble together and offered them … what? Immunity? Protection? … in return for the missing piece." Several of the bodies in the room shifted uncomfortably. "And by the looks of things," Victor continued, "none of them have been successful. Maybe they don't know," he said, his eyes drifting to Elías and Dupont. "Or maybe they do know but don't believe your empty promises." His eyes glided towards Julian. "Or maybe they've been stung before and simply don't trust anyone," he said, looking towards the kitchen, where JP and Marcel were cowering behind Elías. Victor looked back at Sam. "And let's face it … who would blame them? You don't exactly have a history of honesty, do you, Sam? I mean, I should know."

"You didn't deserve our protection then and you still don't now," Sam said. "We're only keeping you fed and watered for the sake of human rights. As soon as we get a good enough offer for you, we'll trade you in, don't you worry."

George smirked to himself. There was something satisfying about watching his dad at work.

"Go ahead," Victor said. "Trade me. Then I'll never be able to give you the missing piece and poor George over there, hiding behind the door, will never see his mother again."

George felt his face flush.

"Oh, don't think I didn't see you there, George," Victor said, inspecting the cuffs at his wrists. "I could smell your teenage angst as I came up the stairs."

"Shut it," Sam said. "I won't hesitate to dump you back in your hole."

"Oh, Officer Jenkins, you know I can tell when you're lying," Victor teased. "You do it far too often. You need me. In fact, I think you're out of other options."

Cate was back from seeing the officers out. She slammed the lounge door, exposing George fully, and then leaned down to whisper something in Sam's ear.

"Right," Sam said, "we don't have time to mess about."

"Hmm, time sensitive is it?" Victor asked, lifting his cuffed feet up onto the coffee table and exposing a chunky tracking bracelet at his ankle. "Never a better time to negotiate than when your opposition are desperate. Let me guess, Jin-é has given you a deadline."

"Not so much *us*," Sam said.

George could see Victor's head tilt to one side and the skin on his head crease into leathery folds.

"Who then?" Victor asked.

"Ivan Pozhar," Sam stated.

Victor stretched out his neck. "I wouldn't waste your time talking to him."

"Oh, it's not me talking to him, it's Jin-é," Sam said.

Victor's head straightened. "Now I know you're lying."

Sam laughed through his nose. "I thought there was nothing we knew that you didn't."

"There's no way those two are talking about anything – other than plotting to kill each other."

"So we heard," Cate said, perching on the sofa beside Victor.

George crept closer to the couch. He could see Victor's fingers, clamped together; his thumbs rubbing at the back of his scarred hands.

"Hmm," Cate said. "now what could they possibly have to talk about? Two sworn enemies, drawn towards each other by what?"

"Oh, I don't know," Sam said, "maybe one of them has something that the other one wants."

"The Jaybird," Victor said. "Jin-é has your wife and Ivan wants her."

"Wow!" Sam said. "You really do catch on quick."

"It's not new news, you know," Victor sneered. "Ivan's wanted to get his hands on your wife for quite some time."

"Oh, really?"

"She's upset him several times. In fact, I'm surprised he hasn't sent his snipers after her sooner."

"For what?" Sam asked.

"You'll have to ask him that," Victor grinned, mockingly, "or her – if she survives."

George grated his teeth together. He hated how much fun Victor was having, toying with them. He knew the answers and he obviously loved the power it gave him.

"It doesn't really matter why he wants her," Sam said, ignoring Victor's gloating. "The point is–"

"Jin-é wants to trade," Victor interrupted.

"Spot on," Cate said.

"But Ivan won't – not with her," Victor said.

"Yes," Sam said, "and we know that Jin-é doesn't want the money – she wants revenge."

"Revenge is probably too soft a word for it," Victor said. "She wants blood."

"We know that too," Sam said, "but the thing is, we're quite keen for the trade to go ahead."

"Hate your wife that much, do you?" Victor chuckled.

Sam ignored him. "We just need to give Ivan a little nudge."

"I see," Victor said, plonking his hands into his lap, "you think you'll be able to catch them at it."

"That's the plan," Sam stated.

"Brave choice," Victor said, "or should I say, only choice."

"It's our operational decision," Sam said, flexing his fingers.

Victor smiled. "And you thought I'd be able to help you with that, did you? What did my friend Marcel say? Did he put this idea in your head?"

Marcel shrank further into the kitchen.

"Does it matter?" Cate asked.

Victor sighed and snuggled himself into the softness of the couch. "What's in it for me, exactly?"

"A cell with a window," Sam said with a dead-pan face.

"You'll have to try harder than that, Officer Jenkins."

"Why should I?" Sam snarled.

"Because from what I can tell, your wife's life depends on it." Victor leant forwards. "So, tell me again, Sam, what's in it for me?"

Sam sat upright. "A private cell in an A-Grade prison."

George frowned.

Don't give him anything!

"You'll have to do better, Sam," Victor sang.

"House arrest – that's the best I can offer."

No!

George looked around the room, looking for any reaction from the gathered faces. Surely, no one in the room wanted to see Victor get away with what he'd done.

You can't offer him any freedom! You can't let him off the hook!

"Pah!" Victor said. "Tied to an MI5 hovel, constantly suppressed. What kind of offer is that?"

"It's better than anything the Russian Security Service would offer you for your treason," Sam spat.

"So, sell me back to the Russians. I'd happily go back home and see you suffer *again*. You know, Sam, this feels a little like deja-vu. Wouldn't you agree? Two opportunities to save your wife; two times she'll end up dead."

George clenched his fists. Marcel and JP had edged up to the kitchen doorway, and Dupont and Elías had ventured out into the lounge. They all waited.

"You know my government won't let you off for what you've done. You know I can't go any lower," Sam said.

"I can help you, Sam. I know what Ivan wants. You want to save your wife, don't you?" Victor smiled.

Sam looked at Cate, but she lowered her eyes to the floor. "Electronic tagging, a UK residence and limited geographical freedom. That's my final offer," Sam said through gritted teeth.

George's jaw flopped open. "Dad! No!"

Victor sniggered and relaxed back into the couch again. "Well, even your son knows a good deal when he hears one. I'll take it, but this time I want it in writing, with the signature of your chief."

Sam nodded at Cate and she leapt up and dashed past George and out of the door. George watched her go; his mouth still hanging open.

What just happened?

Dupont stormed back into the kitchen, shoving past Marcel and JP, who looked like they were ready to kill Sam, but Sam just steadily rose to his feet and padded around the couch.

"Jay won't like this one bit," Dupont said to Sam, as he slipped into the kitchen to get a glass of water.

"She'll like it even less if she's dead," he replied, curtly.

George followed his dad and squeezed into the kitchen, next to JP. "Dad, you can't let him off the hook."

"If you give him this much freedom," Marcel whispered, "there's nothing stopping him from sending someone after us. We won't be safe. You promised me safety."

"Empty promises," JP grumbled.

Sam drained his water in four large gulps and placed the glass in the sink. "Close the door, George."

George, peered over his shoulder at the back of Victor's head. Victor was whistling to himself and rocking his feet back and forth on the coffee table.

God, he's loving this. He's got exactly what he wanted.

"We all have reasons to want him behind bars, I know that," Sam said, "but listen. He may have made a deal with us, but he hasn't made a deal with the French, and they still want him to stand trial for what he did in Paris."

George's eyes lit up. "So, they could…"

"I can promise him a comfy sentence here, but I can't promise him anything in France," Sam said.

JP was shaking his head. "So, you're lying."

"I'm making the best of an impossible situation," Sam frowned.

"And you expect us to trust you?" JP scoffed.

"It's best for us," Marcel said, laying a hand on JP's arm.

"And how's that?"

"If you keep your end of the deal and help us, you'll get your freedom, and Victor will be out of the picture," Sam said. "If he really knows something that will draw Ivan out, we've got every chance of succeeding in this operation, and we should all get what we want."

Dupont said something in French and Marcel responded. JP propped himself against the radiator and begrudgingly listened to his father.

"I'm happy," Elías said.

Marcel seemed appeased. "You better be true to your word. I don't want to spend the rest of my life looking over my shoulder."

"You have my word," Sam said.

Slam! Cate was back. Sam made for the kitchen door, but George stopped him in his tracks. "Dad, are you sure about this?"

"Do you want your mother home?"

"Of course."

"Then just trust me."

As they re-entered the lounge, Cate was handing Victor the signed paperwork.

"Happy?" she said, with a look on her face that seemed to suggest she wasn't.

"Delighted," Victor beamed.

"So," Sam said, retaking his place on the stool, "what does Ivan want?"

"Me," Victor grinned. "Oh, and he'd love to get his hands on that weapon."

Chapter 27: A Team Game

"You're lying," Sam said, pacing back and forth. "We know that you met with Ivan in August. Why else would you meet with him?"

"We've got proof," Cate said.

Victor slid his feet off the table.

"Oh, I met him alright. There's no denying that. He promised me everything – money, inclusion, a seat at the table – all he wanted was to get his hands on that weapon."

"And you're trying to convince us that you didn't give it to him," Sam said.

"Oh, I was going to, trust me. I was sorely tempted, but then a little bird song floated in on the breeze," Victor said, fluttering his fingers through the air. "A little Jaybird song in fact."

Sam stopped pacing. "What?"

"Your wife scuppered the deal. Didn't she tell you?"

George thought back to the hangar in Paris.

She knew Victor still had the weapon. Why else would she have come to Paris?

"Lucky for me," Victor continued, "she got wind of Ivan's intentions to double cross me and that wind blew its way across the channel just as I reached land."

"You abandoned the deal based on a rumour?" Sam asked, sceptically. "You're a fool."

"No, I wouldn't say abandoned. I left him something, just not what he was looking for."

"What did you leave him?" Cate asked, intrigued.

"A box full of water-filled vials," Victor chuckled. "He was going to take the weapon back to the Russian government, and sell me out at the same time. It's Ivan who's the fool. He took that crate of seawater from the boatyard in France and ran back to his Russian friends with nothing but egg on his face!"

Sam and Cate glared at each other.

"You served him a dummy?" Sam asked, his forehead concertinaed in confusion.

"Of course … and then I stole his Rothkos to teach him that no one double crosses the Falcon and gets away with it."

Victor sat smug and proud on the couch as everyone else in the room looked on bemused.

"No wonder he hates you," Elías said, from the kitchen doorway.

"I'm surprised he hasn't put a bounty on *your* head," Dupont said.

"Oh, he probably would if I wasn't comfortably wrapped up in the basement of MI5," Victor grinned.

"So," George said, sliding around the side of the couch, "you still have it."

"Ha! The only brains in the room," Victor said, smirking. "Yes, Master Jenkins, I still have it."

"And you didn't think to tell us this before?" Sam asked.

"As I told your wife in Paris, Sam, I always have something left in my hand, something to bargain with. You should know that. And I always keep my winning card until the very end."

George looked towards his dad. "Great, that's what we'll use as the bait, then. We'll offer Ivan the weapon."

Victor raised an eyebrow. "What makes you think I'll give it to *you*?"

"Because if you don't," Sam said, "Ivan will go free while you sit in jail and rot."

"You've made me a promise," Victor scowled.

"Only if you cooperate," Sam reminded him.

Dupont and Elías had come out of the kitchen.

"Why not give him Victor too?" Elías smirked. "That's sure to tip the balance."

Good idea, George thought.

"You're very funny when you're not being annoying," Victor jibed back.

"This is all fine and well," Dupont said, coming around the side of the couch, "but how do we set this up? Ivan may want the weapon, but the objective is to draw Jin-é out."

"Yeah, we can't exactly leave the weapon at Jin-é's front door and ask her to add it to the trade," Cate agreed.

Sam looked miles away. "We need a way to add it to the deal."

"That's what I just said," Cate frowned.

The room fell silent and George looked from one face to the next. Everyone stood littered around the couch, Victor in the centre, Julian on the outskirts.

George looked at Victor.

Ivan wants Victor and the weapon.

And then back at Julian.

Julian is our only link to Jin-é.

"We'll set up a sting," George said, breaking the silence.

Sam snapped out of his daze. "What?"

George strode around to stand beside his dad and pointed at Victor. "We put Victor and the weapon out in the open." He turned towards Julian. "Julian can then leak the intel back to Jin-é." And then he turned back to his dad. "And Jin-é will surely turn up to grab Victor and the weapon so she can offer it all to Ivan."

Victor laughed. "And how exactly am I supposed to put myself and the weapon out in the open when I'm in MI5 custody?"

George shrugged. "You'll escape."

Everyone in the room seemed to gasp at once, except Victor who just smiled. "Just like your mother," he said. "Willing to take any risk to get what you want."

George looked over at Sam. "Well?"

"You want me to release Victor?" Sam asked, looking shocked.

When he said it like that, it sent a shiver of fear down George's spine, but something about it felt right. Victor was the one who had started all this and now he had a chance to finish it.

Balance over revenge.

"He's tagged," George said, pointing at the black band at Victor's ankle. "We'll stage an escape." He looked towards the kitchen. "JP can do it. We can say that he got a tip off from Marcel and they are trying to repay their debt to Victor."

JP laughed nervously, but Sam's look of disbelief seemed to dissolve as George ploughed on.

"No one knows that JP's cooperating with MI5. Ivan won't know. Jin-é won't be any wiser."

Everyone in the room was standing gaping at George, including Julian.

"And you think Jin-é will risk ambushing JP to snatch Victor?" Dupont asked, unconvinced.

"If she knows that Victor is going to go straight to the weapon," George replied.

"And that Ivan is desperate to get his hands on both," Cate added.

"She wouldn't let an opportunity like that pass," Elías agreed.

"Yes, and if what Victor says is true, Ivan won't be able to resist such a large bounty. Everything he wants in one clean sweep," George said, feeling an energy skate around his veins.

"And you think we can use Julian to leak this intel?" Sam asked, looking towards the corner, where Julian now stood a few paces closer to the rest of the team.

"No one knows it was MI5 that took him in," George replied. "You've got Lu and Celia in custody. All Jin-é will know is that the deli was raided. Julian can leak the message back into the 14D. He'll say that JP approached him about helping break Victor out, and he can tell her where JP intends to take him."

"Somewhere that we can stake out," Sam said, slowly nodding.

"We can be waiting," Cate added.

"Exactly," George said. "Then, bam, we've got her."

"That's fine, as long as Jin-é brings Jay with her," Dupont said.

"Why wouldn't she?" George asked.

"Even if she doesn't bring her then," Sam said, "she'll definitely take her to the trade."

"Agreed," Dupont said.

"And if Jin-é has Victor, Jay and the weapon, Ivan is sure to show his face," Elías said.

"So, we'll tail her as she makes her way towards Ivan," Sam said.

"And then we can snare them all!" George grinned.

Sam smiled down at George. "That's one hell of a sting."

"A lot of things will have to go to plan for us to pull it off," Cate warned.

"And everyone will have to play their part," Sam added.

George looked around the room. Dupont and Elías seemed to be in agreement, but all the other players looked unsure.

"You really expect me to break Victor out single-handedly?" JP asked. "That's ridiculous!"

"Dupont and Elías can help," Sam said.

"Oh, great," Elías huffed.

"It'll be staged," Sam said, "you won't have to break a sweat."

"And what happens when Jin-é turns up at the intercept point?" JP asked, concerned. "She won't need me. She'll only want Victor. She won't hesitate to skewer me with that needle of hers."

Sam scratched at the stubble on his neck. "You're right. You, Dupont and Elías will have to pull back. Victor will have to approach the site alone."

"Oh, really? And what protection do I get?" Victor demanded.

"We won't be far away," Sam said, "and you'll be tagged."

"That's the first thing she'll look for."

"I'm not sending you in untagged. That's non-negotiable. We'll make it subtle. We'll hide several trackers in your overalls."

"We can mess up your ankle," Cate said. "We'll make it look like JP hacked off your tracking bracelet. She won't look further than that."

"Oh, nice," Victor said. "I look forward to that!"

"Stop complaining," Sam frowned.

"Are we all in agreement?" Cate asked the room.

There were several reluctant nods.

"All I have to do is make a call?" a voice from the corner asked. It was Julian.

"Yes," George said, "just a call." He walked over to stand in front of him. "Do you know who you can call? Someone that will feed the intel straight up to Jin-é."

Julian nodded. "And if I do this … I'll get to see my family … you'll keep your promises?"

"Absolutely," Sam said from the other side of the room.

"OK," Julian said, tucking his fringe behind his ear, "I'll do it."

"Looks like everyone knows what they have to do," Sam said, looking at his watch. "We've got fifteen hours to make it happen."

Chapter 28: Well-laid Plans

The following few hours dissolved in a flurry of activity. Cate and Sam came and went from the room, on and off their phones, in and out of the kitchen, briefing individuals on their roles in the play as the details cemented themselves into a concrete plan. They rolled out maps and penned driving routes, they printed out a script for Julian and debated when and where he should instruct Jin-é to intercept Victor.

"Once JP, Dupont and Elías have Victor on board," Sam said, as they all huddled around the coffee table, "they will deliver Victor to this car park, here, before falling back."

"Victor will then be alone," Cate reminded them.

"This is the location that you will relay to your contact as the point of interception," Sam said to Julian, who had finally torn himself from his corner. "Jin-é must grab Victor here."

"And where will you be?" Victor asked.

"We'll be here, in this building, waiting for her to arrive. You'll have your trackers on and we'll be watching."

"How very reassuring," Victor said.

"You focus on your role," Sam said, "and we'll focus on ours."

"I'm sure you'll have no trouble convincing Jin-é to keep you alive," Cate said, folding up the large map. "You've worked together before, and you have what she needs."

"The weapon," George said.

"Yes," Cate went on, "and you must lead her to it as quickly as you can so that she can get to her rendezvous with Ivan before the deadline."

"And how will we know if Ivan has accepted the offer?" Dupont asked.

"We won't," Sam replied. "We'll follow Victor and Jin-é from a distance as they approach the meeting point, and we'll be ready to dive in as soon as Ivan arrives."

"And if he doesn't?" Elías said.

"We'll at least have Jin-é, the weapon and hopefully Jay," Sam said.

"No, no, no," Victor said, shaking his head. "He has to be taken out. That's the deal: you get the weapon, and I get to watch you slap the cuffs on him."

"That will be our intention," Sam said. "If he takes the bait and turns up for the trade, we'll be there to catch him red-handed."

"We may already have enough on him to arrest him anyway," Cate said, "but catching him at it will make our job a lot easier."

"You know what else would make our job a lot easier?" Sam said. "Knowing the weapon's location up front."

Victor shook his head again. "I've told you it's in Dover; that's all you're getting. I'll do my bit and lead Jin-é to it, but I'm not giving away my last bargaining chip until I absolutely have to."

"You don't get to decide that," Sam said.

"Yes, I do, and if you want my help at all, this is how it goes," Victor replied. "I know you, Sam. I give you that weapon and suddenly I'm expendable."

Before long, the flat began to empty out. Marcel was taken back to his safe house and Dupont, Elías and JP were taken by Cate for their briefing. For over an hour, George was left in the flat with Victor, Julian and two armed guards.

George curled up on the sofa as far away from Victor as he could. Trying to ease the tension between him and Julian, he offered him a place to rest his head too, but it was obvious that Julian wasn't going to relax at all until he got what was promised to him, so he retreated to his corner and wrapped himself in a blanket.

"I wouldn't waste your time," Victor said. "He doesn't want to be your friend."

"I don't need him to be my friend," George grumbled.

Victor sighed an over-the-top sigh. "Ah, we all need friends, George."

"Who's your friend?" George sneered.

"Oh, I have friends, George, don't you worry."

"Yeah, right, seems to me you upset everyone you come in contact with."

"Just because I've upset them, doesn't mean they aren't useful to me."

"That's not friendship," George said, rolling his eyes.

"What use is a friend if they can't help you out?"

"Whatever," George replied, turning his back on Victor.

"I'm just saying, you shouldn't trust him."

"What do you know about trust?" George mumbled into the couch cushions, before closing his eyes.

Before long, Sam burst back into the lounge with a new set of overalls for Victor. "These are tagged. It's subtle but they have full range."

"So, you're removing my bracelet now?" Victor asked, lifting his legs in the air.

"Not yet. Cate will switch it for the dummy when you arrive back at HQ. Your journey will start from there, but I want you to change now … under the supervision of the guards outside."

"What happened to privacy?"

"You don't get any," Sam replied, "and I legally have to warn you that if you try anything funny, we will shoot you on the spot. We'll aim to incapacitate you, not to kill, but if you try to pull a fast one on us, I won't hesitate to put a bullet where it hurts."

"Lovely," Victor said.

Sam dragged Victor off the couch and escorted him to the door. "You can change in the hall. Before JP attacks your convoy, Cate will stain your ankle to make it look bruised. JP will do the rest."

Sam closed the door on Victor and turned back into the room. He looked flustered and exhausted.

"This is going to work, isn't it?" George asked.

Sam perched on the couch next to him. "We'll make it work."

"But … it could go wrong?"

Sam smiled. "Every op has its risks. I've been involved in more risky ones than this, trust me. The worst thing that could happen is that Jin-é doesn't take the bait, but if she shows up, we'll have her and hopefully your mum too. The rest is a bonus."

"And you think Victor will do his bit?"

"Dupont and Elías will be with him until the very last moment. Worst case scenario, we have him tagged. I'll be waiting at the intercept point. We won't lose sight of him from there, and anyway, there's no benefit to him in running."

"But he did before."

"Yes, but this time I'll be five paces behind him."

"What can I do?" George asked, sitting up.

"You can go home."

George frowned. "But I want to be useful."

"I can't ask you to be part of this, George. You've done your bit. You've got us this far. This op is your making. You got the intel on the deli, you got Julian on side, you came up with the sting – that's enough for one day."

Sam looked at his watch. "It's time for Julian to make the call. We need the message to filter up to Jin-é as quickly as possible."

George nodded, and stared over at Julian who was struggling to stay awake. His eyelids drooped and his head lolled about, jerking back up as he desperately tried to fight the sleep.

"Dad, where will Julian go?" George whispered.

Sam lifted himself from the couch.

"I'll have to find him a cell."

"He's a kid, Dad. He's only a few years older than me."

"He's a criminal," Sam said, sternly, "and I can't leave him here."

George frowned. "Can't he go back to his mum?"

"Not until this is over. I can't trust him to keep his end of the bargain if I don't hold back my end. We'll take him to join her when this is all over."

"But we said all he had to do was make the call. We promised him," George said. "I promised him."

"And what if he runs?"

"Why would he? He just wants to get back to his family. He'll have done what we asked of him, and he knows that the 14D will be after him the minute it becomes obvious that he's set Jin-é up."

Sam sighed. "I guess your right. If we need him, we'll know where to find him."

"So, he can go back to his mum?"

"Yes," Sam said, "although I'm not sure how quickly I can arrange his escort."

George looked over at Julian again and his head had finally found a resting place on the windowsill. He thought of Mayling, begging with him to bring Julian home.

"He can share my escort," George said. "The officer that drops me off can take him on to meet his mum."

"I guess that can't hurt," Sam said. "Let's get this phone call over with, then you can both go and get some proper sleep."

George gently shook Julian's shoulder. "Hey."

He startled, and fear shot across his face. Disorientated and groggy, he reminded George of himself when he woke from one of his bizarre dreams. "What time is it?"

"Time to make the call," Sam said. "You've studied the script I gave you?"

Julian pulled the crumpled paper from beneath his blanket. "I know it."

"OK," Sam nodded, "get yourself together and we'll dial when you're ready."

Julian uncurled himself, and the blanket fell to the ground as he shook out his legs and stretched his neck. "I'm ready."

Sam handed him the phone. "Keep your voice as steady and even as you can."

Julian took the phone and looked at George. "I hope this works out for you. I hope you get your mum back."

George smiled. "You too."

Tap, tap. Julian dialled a number. *Ring, ring, ring.* It rang three times.

"Nǐ hǎo," Julian said, tentatively.

George looked at his dad, but Sam's eyes didn't shift from Julian.

There was a greeting from the other end of the phone, and Julian exploded into a monologue of Chinese, barely breaking to breathe.

Leaning in closer, Sam tried to make out what noises were coming from the other end, but there was no response until Julian finally stopped.

George and Sam held their breaths. "Yǐ shōu dào," the person on the other end said, and then hung up.

Julian passed the phone back to Sam. "It's done."

"And?" Sam said.

Julian shrugged. "They said they understood the message."

"OK then," Sam said, "let's get you two out of here."

"Where are we going?" Julian asked.

"George has kindly convinced me to let you go back to your mum. Once George has been dropped off, the escort will take you directly to the police station where your mother and sister are. They'll know to expect you."

Julian smiled and George could see Mayling's eyes again. "Thank you."

Sam saw them down to the street and locked up the flat. A car was waiting for them on the corner.

"You will call me," George said, as his dad opened the car door, "as soon as you have Mum."

"You'll be the first person I call."

George let Julian duck into the back seat first. "I won't be able to sleep."

"I know," Sam said, "but if you do, just think, by the time you wake up, all this will be over."

"I hope so," George said, climbing into the back seat next to Julian.

"You made this happen," Sam said, smiling. "Now I'll finish it."

Julian slept the whole way back to Chiddingham, but George couldn't calm his mind. He kept thinking of all the things that could go wrong. By the time they pulled up outside his cottage, George's stomach was in knots. He looked over at Julian and wondered how he was managing to stay so relaxed.

"Hey," George said, nudging him, "this is my stop."

Julian opened his eyes and looked down at his watch. "Good timing."

With that, everything around George exploded. Glass shattered, his body was thrown sideways, his head smashed against the remnants of the window and the outside world spun out of control. He could feel the pound of his head, the warm blood running down his cheek, and he could hear the groans of the officer up front as he reached for his gun, but it was too late. *Thud!* The officer was down, his body tumbling from the car.

No!

George couldn't tell whether the spinning of the car or the impact to his head had left him dizzy, but when he eventually managed to focus on the faces that surrounded him, he could see three of them, three identical faces.

The Triplets!

With panic rising up his throat and choking his voice, George failed to scream. He lunged for the door handle, but the door fell away, leaving him with nothing but pavement to break his fall, and before he could raise his head, someone had him by the arms and was dragging him across the tarmac. Swimming and throbbing, his head struggled to focus, but as he was thrown into the back of the van, he could just make out the glow of Gran's bedroom light as it flicked to life.

From: The Moth
To: The Flame
Re: The Jaybird {Encrypted}

Ten hours to go, and I have something that may sweeten the deal. Something you won't be able to resist.

End.

From: The Flame
To: The Moth
Re: The Jaybird {Encrypted}

What could you possibly offer me that I couldn't refuse?

End.

From: The Moth
To: The Flame
Re: The Jaybird {Encrypted}

Something that will get you off the hook with your friends back home and something that will make your revenge on the Jaybird even more satisfying.

I'll send you the coordinates of the meeting point. I suggest you make it there before the deadline.

End.

Chapter 29: The Malice of the Moth

George drifted in and out of consciousness as the van rumbled out of Chiddingham. With no sense of time and not a shred of light to see by, he became more and more disorientated. Bruised, bleeding and shivering against the cold metal floor, he felt like death itself. By the time the van came to a halt, the most George could do was try to concentrate on the noises around him: slamming doors, terse voices, the echo of something heavy clanging against metal.

Where am I?

"I still can't believe you rammed us side on," a muffled voice said from somewhere outside the van. "You could have killed me."

"Shame I didn't," another voice mumbled back.

The voices were edging their way down George's left side and heading towards his feet. He strained his eyes, trying to work out what was where, but before he could make head or tail of his surroundings, the back doors flew open and light flooded in, forcing his eyes closed again.

"Get up!" someone yelled at him.

George raised his hands against the light and felt a shooting pain run down his side. Wincing, he tried to lift himself onto his elbows, but the van rocked as someone jumped up to join him. "I said, get up!"

George's hands found the floor, and pain seared through his palms.

Glass!

Fragments of the car's window had sliced at his hands. The pain made his head spin, and he almost collapsed back to the floor.

"Help him," someone said from outside.

George recognised the voice.

Julian!

Hands were on him, yanking at his arms, dragging him towards the light. His knees slid across the metal floor of the van, and he fell shoulder first to the ground.

You need to get up, George.

Gritting his teeth, he clenched his fists and tried to ignore the pain as he pushed himself up with his knuckles and staggered to his feet, but no sooner had he found his balance, than he was being shoved from behind.

"Move!"

George glanced around from under the peak of his dad's cap. He was surrounded. Knives out and still head to toe in black, the triplets looked like a band of assassins. George lurched forwards, struggling to walk in a straight line, but as the blood started pumping around his limbs, his head started to straighten and he began to see more clearly. They were inside a warehouse: high ceilings, bare walls, a smooth concrete floor and empty shelves.

Abandoned.

They weaved their way between the shelves and made it to the other side, where a small office occupied one corner. A dull light came from inside, and a shadow moved across the misted windows. George swallowed hard. He could see her childlike frame, her closely bobbed hair, and he could hear the *tap, tap, tap* of her tiny feet.

"Ah, fierce boy," she said, as she slid into view. "I thought I told you to be careful of what you seek."

There she stood with her back to her desk, her bleached blonde hair capped with a dark parting of roots. On the run, moving under the radar, there had been no time for personal grooming, yet her blood-red bow still sat proudly on top of her head, like a cherry on a cupcake.

Seeing her again left George searing: her overly chirpy chatter, her broken English, her ability to make all the evil things she did seem like a game. Being there with her did nothing but remind George of how much pain she'd caused him, but strangely, standing in front of her also sent a ripple of hope through his veins. During all those sleepless nights, wondering where his mother was, picturing her torn and bleeding on the back seats of Jin-é's SUV, imagining her tied up and tormented, not knowing whether he'd ever see her again, only one thing had occupied his mind: finding Jin-é. And there she was, right in front of him, which only meant one thing.

Mum must be somewhere near.

George flashed his eyes around the office: empty cabinets, a single lamp, a collection of wooden crates.

Is she here?

He could feel the adrenalin fill his head and sharpen his vision.

"Where's my mother?"

Jin-é tapped her needle against her chin. "Who?"

George could feel his muscles tighten. He knew he was surrounded by enemies, but all he could think of was unleashing his monster and throwing himself at Jin-é with all his rage.

"I'll kill you," he growled.

"Ha!" Jin-é scoffed. "You need revenge. I know this need. And I know it has a dark face. I warn you: no good will come of it."

Two of the triplets had George by the shoulders. They pushed him further into the office and then shoved him down into a chair.

"Tie him up," Jin-é ordered.

Buzz!

Somewhere, a phone went off.

"I'll get it," one of the triplets said, disappearing towards the back of the office.

Julian was the last to enter the room. He slunk around the door frame and slipped in behind one of the triplets.

"You did good," Jin-é said.

"My mother?" Julian said, his voice barely a whisper. "And my sister?"

Jin-é nodded. "I take care of it. They get our message."

"And they'll be safe?" Julian asked.

George glared at him. "You made a promise!"

But Julian just turned his head away.

"He make right choice," Jin-é said. "He not trust your government."

George closed his eyes.

How did they know where we'd be?

He thought back to the flat: Julian curled up in the corner, the blanket wrapped around him, his eyes half closed, George and his dad talking in hushed voices.

He was listening – that whole time!

"You're a snake!" George spat. "I hope your sister disowns you. I hope your mother leaves you to–"

"All you care about is yourself!" Julian said, turning on George. "Don't pretend you actually cared about what happened to me. JP was right – it was all empty promises!"

George shook his head in disbelief. "I can't believe I tried to help you. I took pity on you. I should have let my father put you in a cell!"

Julian smiled. "That was the best part of your stupid plan."

"That enough," Jin-é interrupted. "We have deadline to meet. You ready?" she asked one of the triplets.

"We know where we can ambush JP," he replied. "We'll take them by surprise. They won't see us coming."

"And MI5?" Jin-é asked.

"They're expecting us to take Victor out in a car park in Dover," the other one replied. "They'll be waiting there, but we'll attack beforehand and deliver Victor to you."

The third triplet had reappeared from the back of the office with an armful of weapons. "Julian told us where Victor's trackers are. We'll deal with them."

George's heart sank. Victor, out on his own, out in the open, undefended and soon to be untracked.

"MI5 will be on you before you can destroy the trackers," George said, trying to keep the panic out of his voice. "You'll all be arrested. They have a whole team waiting to take you out. You won't get away with it!"

"We won't destroy tracker," Jin-é smirked. "We take them on little journey. MI5 go running around like mice chasing cheese."

George could feel the fuzz in his head again, but he shook it off.

I need to do something.

"You go now," Jin-é said to the triplets. "You call me when you have him."

"What about me?" Julian asked.

"You go too," she said, handing him a plump deli bag. "This is your reward."

"And my family?"

"You go with the boys. They tell you what to do," Jin-é said, turning back towards her desk.

"But…"

"You go," she repeated. "If all goes well, you see family again. I make sure."

With that, the triplets took Julian and vanished from the office, leaving George alone with Jin-é. She rounded the desk, her needle in her hand, and flipped open her laptop. George eyed the door. The triplets had done a poor job of binding his ankles. If he could just get a moment alone, he might be able to make for an exit, but looking back at Jin-é he realised one thing: he had to stay. There was only one way to get his mum back and that was to stick to Jin-é like glue.

George watched the clock above her head as the hands inched their way closer to dawn. Closing his eyes, he leant his head back against the shelves behind him. He ached all over, and although he didn't want to let his guard down, he knew that he needed to conserve his energy.

Tick-tock.

The clock taunted him. What would be happening out there? All the plans they'd made would be unravelling and falling apart. Dupont and Elías would be driving Victor towards a trap; JP would be wasting his time bashing up Victor's ankle; Sam and Cate would be waiting in Dover, looking out over an empty car park; none of them would be expecting the triplets to attack; no one would see them coming as they rammed into Dupont's van, and Cate and Sam would sit open mouthed as Jin-è blindsided them all.

Buzz!

The sound of the phone woke George from his daze. Jerking upright, he locked his eyes on Jin-é. She was up from her desk, wrapped in a fur-lined coat and making for the door.

"Wait!" George said, leaping from his chair. But forgetting all about his bound ankles, he stumbled forwards and collided with the nearest crate.

"Pah!" Jin-é laughed. "You stupid boy."

George slid to the ground. "I'm coming with you … take me with you. I want to see my mum … please!"

Jin-é turned.

"Here," she hissed, lifting her needle. "You'll get what you seek!"

But as George scrabbled to get out of the way, Jin-è kicked out at the crate beside him, and to George's horror, the side fell open and a body rolled out: slender, bound, her copper hair plastered across her face.

"Mum!"

Chapter 30: Keeping On Track

Like strokes of paint, the strands of her hair lay vivid against the white-washed canvas of her skin. George swept the hair from her face with his bound hands, and the warmth from her cheeks sent relief soaring through him.

She's alive!

Her eyes flickered and her chest rose and fell, deep and slow.

"What have you done to her?"

"She sleeps like baby," Jin-é chuckled. "She have no pain."

George levered his hands under her chin and tried to lift her head. There were no obvious signs of damage – no blood, no bruises; just limp, drowsy unconsciousness.

Buzz!

Jin-é's phone went again.

"We move now."

George looked up at her. "How are we supposed to move her?"

Jin-é leant down and slit the ties at George's ankles with the point of her needle.

"You drag her," she smiled. "Chop, chop."

With that, she scuttled out of the office, and George sat and listened to her footsteps as they disappeared into the cavern of the warehouse.

Frantically, he scanned the room, desperate to find something to cut through his and his mother's bindings, but he stopped himself.

I need to get her out, but…

He was stuck. Even if he could escape, he wouldn't get very far dragging his mother's unconscious body.

"Mum," he whispered, gently shaking her shoulder. "Mum, it's me, George."

She groaned and her eyes rolled in their sockets.

George leant out of the doorway. There was no sign of Jin-é.

"Mum, come on." He tried again. "Please, Mum, wake up."

Nothing.

Vroom!

An engine roared to life, and the warehouse lit up, as Jin-é maneuvered a small van around the lines of shelving.

Come on, George, think!

George checked all four walls of the warehouse. There were several exits, if only he could…

"George?" Her voice swept over him. "Is that you?"

Straddling the office threshold, George sat motionless – a lump in his throat. "Yes, Mum … it's …"

Squeal!

Tyres strained against the slippery floor.

"Mum, can you move?" He shuffled back towards her. "You need to get up."

Her eyes fought to stay open. "George, why are you here?"

"There's no time, you need to get up."

Pushing himself to his feet, he bent down in front of her, slung his hands over her head and wriggled his forearms under her armpits. Heaving her upwards as she pushed against the side of the crate, he managed to pull her to standing. Swaying to one side, she almost pulled him over, but he pushed the other way and rested her against the crates. "Can you walk?"

Like a rag doll, her head rolled on her shoulders and her knees buckled, but George braced himself and managed to keep her on her feet.

Squeal!

The tyres were coming their way.

"We need to leave," George whispered in her ear.

"No," she whispered back, "you go … leave me."

"What?" he said. "Mum, she's going to sell you to Ivan; she's going to get you killed!"

"No," she croaked, her head collapsing against his shoulder. "I have to..."

With that, she slid back down to the floor, pulling George down with her.

Slam!

"We go, now!" Jin-é shouted from outside the office.

Jin-é just stood and watched as George stumbled across the warehouse, dragging his mum backwards, her feet trailing behind her like limp ribbons. It took all his strength to heave her into the back of the van, and by the time he had climbed in himself, his side throbbed and his head pounded.

Jin-é had removed her bow and replaced it with a beanie that concealed her platinum hair. She wore dark blue overalls and large padded boots, making her barely recognisable. Slamming the van door closed, she sealed George and his mum in complete darkness. George ran his fingers over his cap – wet and sticky – his head was still bleeding.

Clunk!

They bounced out of the warehouse, and George could hear his mother groan. Feeling in the darkness, he lifted her head and slid it onto his lap. "I'm here."

The van trundled out into the autumn dawn, and George rested his head against its side. He needed to think of a way to get them both to safety, and that meant staying alert.

I need to know where we're going.

The van clattered over another bump, and George was taken back to Paris: trapped in the back of Austin's van, on their way to the art studio. He thought of his dad and how he'd managed to guess where the studio was from George's description. Steadying his mum's head with his hands, he closed his eyes and tried to take everything in.

A curve in the road, a steep hill, the sound of the gears, the shriek of gulls, the crash of waves. His eyes sprang open.

We're at the coast!

He listened closer. The bark of a dog, the faint tinkling of music, the clink of something against metal. It all sounded very familiar.

Margate?

The triplets, Julian – they had to be back in Margate.

George was just trying to imagine where exactly on the seafront they might be, when Jay groaned again and a small hatch between the driver and the back of the van slid open.

"You keep quiet now!" Jin-é barked. "No nonsense!"

George didn't listen, he just peered past her, trying to see out of the front windscreen. It was Margate alright. The ferris wheel loomed over the horizon ahead, and he could see the lines of beach huts at the edge of the promenade. The dawn light and thin mist made everything appear serene, but something was drifting in on the breeze, a noise that tore through the peace and quiet like the screeching drag of a chair in a church. Tyres squealing, engines revving … and the wail of a siren.

Jin-é pulled to a stop, and George lowered his mum's head carefully to the floor. Up on his knees, George stared in disbelief as two small vans careered around the corner, almost taking the bend on two wheels.

They've made the hit!

George watched in horror as one of the vans tore past them, one of the triplets at the wheel, but the other van skidded to a halt, and before George could reposition himself at the hatch to get a clearer view, one of the triplets was leaping out from the passenger seat and vaulting over the railings, down onto the beach.

Where's he going?

George pushed his face up to the hatch; his eyes, nose and cheeks squeezed through the tiny space, straining to watch the boy as he sprinted for a small boat at the water's edge; a small piece of Victor's overalls in his hand.

They've got the trackers!

George looked back towards the van and could just make out the other identical face in the driver's seat as it pulled off again and sped out of view. The triplets must have shredded the overalls, each taking a piece with a tracker and each going in different directions.

"No!" George gasped, making Jin-é slide the hatch door closed, nearly taking off the tip of George's nose.

George was thrown back into darkness as Jin-é restarted the engine, but no sooner had they pulled off, than George could hear the sound of the sirens steaming past.

Dad!

He held his breath, desperately hoping to hear the sirens coming back his way, but Jin-é drove slowly and steadily away from the scene, and soon they were trundling down the beach road and away from town.

George tried his hardest to imagine where they were heading, but soon the tarmacked road melted away and they were rattling down what felt like a stony path. The metal cabin sounded like it was under attack. It creaked and groaned as the stones pinged off its underside like bullets.

Trying to hold his mum as tightly as he could, George waited in the dark, only hoping that he would have another chance to make his escape once they stopped, but the longer they drove, the more he could feel the fingers of despair as they gripped at his chest.

How will Dad find us now?

Crunch!

The van had hit gravel.

Slam!

Jin-é was out of the driver's seat, and George could hear her crunching footsteps above the crash of the waves and the call of the gulls.

"Where are we?" Jay croaked.

George looked down but could only just make out the outline of her features in the dark.

"I think we're on the beach," he whispered, trying to help her sit up.

She shook out her head and pushed herself up against the support of the van's side. "You shouldn't be here, George."

George could hear disappointment in her voice and his heart sank. "I … I've come to get you out."

He felt foolish saying it in front of her. Even though it was true, something about it sounded stupid and childish.

"Does Sam know?"

George thought about his dad, and the hours they'd spent planning the sting, and felt even more embarrassed.

What on earth was I thinking?

"He's coming for us," he said, trying to sound assured. "It's the … plan … to get you out."

Jay sat in silence, but George could hear her breathing, short and irregular.

"Mum?"

"When Jin-é comes back, I don't want you to say a thing. You leave everything to me. I'll find a way to get you out of here."

"No," George said. "You don't get it. We have to get *you* out. Jin-é is going to sell you to Ivan, along with Victor and the weapon and–"

"Victor?" Jay almost toppled into George. "The weapon?"

"It's all part of the plan. Ivan wouldn't meet, so we staged an escape, and now Victor will lead Jin-é to the weapon and then she'll–"

"Wait a minute!" Jay was now wide awake. "Slow down! Did you say you staged an escape – for Victor?"

"Y… yes," George said, hesitantly.

"Victor is out … wait, and the plan is what?"

"To give the weapon and Victor to Jin-é so that Ivan will turn up at the trade."

"Is your father mad?" It sounded like Jay was on her knees.

"No … it was … my idea."

The silence returned.

"It would have worked, Mum," George insisted. "It was the only way to get Jin-é out into the open."

George felt the van shift as his mother sat back down and collapsed against the van's side. "And what, your father swoops in at the end and saves us all?"

George could hear the bitterness in her voice.

"Does it matter?" he asked. "That was the operational objective and … we're a team."

"And your father, in his wisdom, made you, his only son, part of that team, in what sounds like a risk-riddled sting?"

"Er, no," George admitted. "I was supposed to be in bed at home."

George could hear his mum's hair brush against the wall of the van as she shook her head. "So, how exactly did you end up here – in Jin-é's van?"

"Right," George said, "well, Jin-é may have got wind of the sting."

"Oh God, this is not—"

"Quiet," George interrupted, pressing his ear up to the van's side. "She's coming back!"

And before Jay could respond, the van doors flew open and Victor's half-naked body came tumbling in to join them.

"Say hi to best friends," Jin-é chuckled, before slamming the doors closed again.

"What the hell!" Jay said, recoiling.

Victor wriggled to upright on the opposite side of the van, chuckling in between his heavy breaths. "Well, this is a lovely surprise. Bet you weren't banking on spending your final hours with me, my dear Jay-Jay."

"I couldn't think of anything better," Jay snarled. "At least I'll get the chance to finish you off myself."

"I think you'll find that Ivan has other plans," Victor sneered.

"You'll be first on his list."

"Guys," George tried to interject, as the van jumped back to life.

"Not once I remind him that it was you that scuppered our deal," Victor went on.

"You won't get that far, I'll kill you first," she bit back.

"Come on," George said.

"Oh, I don't think so little Jaybird, you see I still have something he wants, but you have nothing – just your pathetic life that he can't wait to snuff out."

Jay flung out both her feet, catching Victor on the ankle that JP had bashed up.

"Argh!"

"Stop!" George screamed. "Both of you! No one is going to kill anyone. We need to work together; we need to have a plan."

Victor pulled in his legs and snorted at George. "Well, I don't believe that this was part of your plan, was it Master Jenkins?"

"It's not my fault!" George mumbled.

"Let me guess, Julian betrayed you." George said nothing. "I told you not to trust him," Victor sneered.

"Who the hell is Julian?" Jay asked.

Jin-é was now moving at pace, and a sudden corner sent them all tumbling to one side.

"Goddamn it!" Victor groaned, trying to right himself. "Your idiot of a son put all his faith in a Triad loyalist – one of Jin-é's foot soldiers."

They swerved the other way.

"Where are we going?" George asked, bracing himself as best he could with his hands still bound. "Have you told her where the weapon is?"

"I've sent her in the rough direction," Victor grunted as they slid around another corner, "but I won't be revealing that weapon to her unless she guarantees my freedom."

"That wasn't the plan!" George said.

"Well, since your plan fell apart, we have a new one and it's my plan."

"Jin-é doesn't care about your freedom," Jay said. "She only cares about getting in a room with Ivan."

"I'll help her get into that room," Victor said, "but I'm not letting Ivan get away with that weapon."

"Ha!" Jay snorted. "Do you seriously think Ivan will let you out of that room alive? Trust me, he has no scruples – he'll mow you down the minute he has what he wants."

"Not unless Jin-é kills him first," Victor chuckled. "Which I assume is her intention."

"She wants revenge. That's all she cares about. She doesn't care about us, but she's a fool, driven by anger, and Ivan will bring his snipers, he won't honour any deal, just like…" Jay paused.

"Like Calais?" Victor asked.

George thought of the dead boy, his mother at the grave and the bullet. He looked towards her in the dark and could feel a change in her – the speed of her breathing, the curve of her silhouette.

She was there!

He shivered.

"He won't let any of us live," Jay said.

"So, we need to stall her," George said.

"What does that achieve?" Victor asked.

"The longer it takes us to find the weapon, the more chance we've got of–"

"Of what?" Victor asked. "You still think Daddy is going to charge in and save the day?"

George could feel the dampness of the blood against his neck and he shivered again. "Yes – that's the plan."

"And how exactly will your father find us?" Victor asked. "If you didn't notice, I am without my tracking bracelet or my overalls."

George tried to pull his hoodie around himself. He fiddled with the zip at his waist, trying to pull it up, but with his hands tied, it just slipped from his fingers and clinked against the metal of his jeans' button.

My tracker!

His head snapped up.

It can still work – the plan can still work!

George thought of each step of the plan. They were still on track! Victor must lead Jin-é to the weapon; Jin-é must meet with Ivan; all the targets must end up in one place. They could still succeed.

He thought of Madame Wu's words. *'It will have to be you.'* She was right after all. He was going to have to be there at the end. He needed to stay in control, and he needed to take every opportunity to keep the plan on track – but he also needed his dad to do the same.

"He'll find us," he grinned to himself in the dark.

But as the van swerved around another corner, all George could hope was that someone had told Sam that he was missing, and that Jin-é wouldn't strip him of his clothes.

From: The Moth
To: The Flame
Re: The Jaybird {Encrypted}

Three birds in the cage and soon my basket will be full.
Nearly ready for checkout.

Don't be late.

End.

Chapter 31: The Moth to the Flame

George could still picture the map of Dover in his head. The wide, open car park; the clear vantage points where Cate and Sam would be watching Victor from; the two main roads that led away along the coast – a perfect place to start tailing their target. But as Jin-é opened up the van doors, there was nothing clear and open about the view that lay ahead.

Rocky outcrops, a bouldered beach, dark craggy caves. How the van had even made it down there was a mystery to George, but there they were; Jin-é, Victor, Jay and George, shivering against the early morning frost.

Victor shook out his legs as Jin-é sliced through the ties at his and Jay's ankles. Without his overalls, he'd been left with bare arms and legs.

"I'll die of hyperthermia," he complained. "The least you can do is give me something to wear."

Jin-é looked him up and down. "You right," she said, "I not want to look at this."

She grabbed a spare set of overalls from her van and threw them at him. Smiling, he raised his hands and motioned towards the belt at her waist. "You'll have to cut my hands free."

Jin-é looked reluctant.

"You can trust me," he promised. "We're partners, remember? We both want to see Ivan pay. Just like in Paris."

"Pah!" Jay laughed. "I wouldn't trust him as far as you can throw him!"

"I not trust any of you," Jin-è said, waving her needle at them.

"Don't listen to her," Victor said, sidling up to Jin-è. "She'd happily let Ivan take us all down with her."

"I need that weapon," Jin-è said, reaching for the knives at her belt.

"I'll get you that weapon and we'll do it together – you and me."

George rolled his eyes at Victor's attempt at charm, but Jin-è quickly sliced through his ties, letting him pull on his overalls.

No! I can't let Victor run. I need to keep all the targets in sight.

"We get moving," Jin-é said, readjusting her belt and looking at her watch. "How far is weapon?"

George looked at his mother, but her eyes were firmly fixed on Victor. She was obviously thinking exactly the same thoughts as George.

He can't be trusted.

"Follow me," Victor said, zipping up his overalls and striding off around the van. "See, George, I told you I still have friends," he whispered at George as he passed.

"Stop!" Jin-é's needle flew from her hand and lodged itself in the side of the van, making Victor stop short. "You not go anywhere." Retrieving her needle, she turned and poked it at Victor's ribs. "You make plans with the boy? Plans to cross me?"

"No!" Victor insisted, holding up his hands.

"We'll see," Jin-é said, grabbing more plastic ties from her belt.

"What are you doing?" Victor asked, as she grabbed Victor's wrist and bound it to George's.

"No!" Jay said, stumbling across the pebbles. "Tie him to me, not George. I won't run, you know I won't."

"Ha!" Jin-è laughed. "George not leave you; Victor not leave George, and," she said, binding her own wrist to Jay's in the same way, "you not leave me!"

"This is ridiculous!" Victor barked.

"We stick together – until we get weapon," Jin-é said, yanking at Jay's arms and pulling her across the beach.

"Please," Jay said, "leave George here!"

"No!" George said. "You need me!"

Jay scowled at him. "No, she doesn't!"

"Yes, she does!" George said, desperately trying to communicate with his mother. "You need me – all of you – I am your only hope of surviving this!"

Jin-é burst out laughing. "Come on!" she yelled, shoving Victor in the back. "We wasting time. You stay ahead. We follow you."

With nothing more to say, the bizarrely-bound band traipsed across the bay, following Victor towards the caves.

"Where we going?" Jin-é asked, poking Victor with her needle again.

"In here," he replied, stopping at the mouth of one of the smaller caves.

"You left the weapon here?" Jay asked.

"Yes, my dear Jay-Jay," Victor sneered back. "When I got wind of Ivan's plans to drag me off to the Russians, I buried the weapon in here and made the crossing with a trunk full of fakes."

George peered into the cave. It seemed to go on forever. He thought of his tracker and his wire and remembered how Cate had lost him under Chinatown.

How will she track me in there?

"Are we going into the cave?" he asked out loud, hoping that someone was listening to his wire.

"Yes," Victor said, turning towards Jin-é. "Did you bring the lights?"

"I got it," Jin-é replied, lifting two small torches from her belt and handing one to Victor. "We speed up now."

George felt a strong sense of unease as they started climbing into the darkness. The smell of damp stone, the crunch of rubble under his feet, the distant echo of their footsteps. It was all too familiar.

"This is where the tunnels led you to?" he said to Victor. "The tunnels you escaped from Chiddingham through."

Victor smiled, the torchlight deepening the creases in his face. "It's amazing how far you can go unseen, George."

They crunched on, deeper and deeper into the cave until the path narrowed and George could see a fork in the path up ahead – just like the tunnels back home.

Dad will never find us here.

Aware that he was unlikely to be able to get a signal out for much longer, George lowered his chin to his chest and stated as clearly as he could, "The tunnel splits up ahead."

The terrain was rockier and the tunnels had collapsed in places, meaning they had to climb over boulders and slip through gaps in the rocks.

George tried his hardest to relay their journey, step by step.

"Are you sure it's this first fork left?"

"Are we going right or left?"

"Why didn't we take that right turning?"

"Will you shut up!" Victor snapped. "It's like having an annoying toddler along for the ride."

"How much further?" George asked.

"I said, shut up!" Victor replied, tripping on some lose debris and pulling George to one side.

"Where are we meeting Ivan?" George asked, looking over his shoulder at Jin-é.

"It not far from here," Jin-è said, her voice bouncing off the walls.

"Not in these caves, I hope," he said, trying to laugh.

"No," Jin-é replied. "Somewhere where I am in charge."

George tried to focus on keeping upright, he tried to focus on the fact that the plan was still on track and he tried to focus on the hope that his dad would be able to track him to the meet point with Ivan. If he could just get all four of them there in one piece, and if he could ensure that Victor played ball and revealed the weapon, then the job would be half done, but as they trudged on, something prickled at his neck, a sensation that he couldn't shake, a feeling that something was coming, a distant whisper that floated in on the hush of the crashing waves.

George stopped dead, making Victor stumble and Jay and Jin-é nearly crash into them.

"What are you doing?" Victor growled.

"Can you hear that?" George asked, turning his head back towards the way they'd come from.

The others fell silent.

Sure enough, something was edging closer.

Dad?

But there was something about it, something about the pace of its approach, the aggression and confidence of its stride, that convinced George that it wasn't his dad.

He would come quietly.

George yanked at Victor's bound wrist and pulled him in close. "Did anyone else know where you left the weapon?" George whispered.

"No, not really, I mean…" Victor's eyes widened, "maybe … Angelika."

With that, the tunnel filled with the sound of gunfire, and George ran for his life, dragging Victor with him, hoping that he could outrun the enemy and hoping that Jin-é and his mother weren't far behind.

Chapter 32: Constant Sniping

Running seemed like the best option, but running only took them deeper into the network of tunnels, and the further they ran, the more they lost their bearings.

By the time they had outrun the gunfire, they had found their way to a cross junction. Four tunnels, four different directions. It reminded George of the tunnels at school: littered with rubble and crumbling at the seams.

"How on earth did Angelika know that we were here?" Jay hissed at Victor, as she searched down each tunnel, dragging Jin-é with her.

"You set me up!" Jin-é growled, lunging towards Victor, but Jay held her back.

"No, he can't have," Jay said. "He's been locked up at MI5."

"Exactly," Victor whispered back from the other side of the junction, "and anyway, she dumped me in Paris and ran off with the Rothkos, remember? I owe her nothing."

"The Rothkos were returned," George said as they congregated together at the centre of the cross.

Victor's already tense jaw, jutted out in anger.

"Angelika gave them back! She must have cut a deal with Ivan!"

"And I assume that you told Ivan that you were bringing him Victor *and* the weapon," Jay said, glaring at Jin-é.

"Yes, I offer him the whole package – only way to get him to show his stupid face!"

"Shh!" Jay said, peering back down one of the tunnels.

"But why wouldn't Angelika have just led him directly to the weapon herself?" George asked, looking over his shoulder.

"Because," Victor said, "she didn't know exactly where I'd hidden it. We split up here, at this very point, and I took the weapon."

"So, what do we do now?" George said. "They're in here somewhere, and it won't be long until they find us. We can't just hide."

"We need to find a way out," Jay said.

"I'm not leaving my weapon," Victor said.

"I stay too," Jin-é said, "if Ivan here, I face him. I get my revenge, once and for all."

George shook his head. "He'll kill you."

"Not if I kill him first."

"The warrior who seeks revenge…" George started.

"I already dug my grave," Jin-è spat, "long time ago. I not leave here 'til I have my revenge."

George could hear something coming up the tunnel behind him. "We need to move," he whispered.

"This way," Victor said, dragging George with him.

Slowly, they edged away from the crossroads. George tried to tread as lightly as he could, but Victor was storming ahead.

"Slow down."

"I can't let Ivan get his hands on that weapon," Victor said.

Crunch!

Jay stopped. "They're behind us!"

"That way!" Victor said, shoving Jin-é in the back.

"I don't suppose you have anything more useful than a few knives and a needle in that belt?" Jay asked as they ran down another fork.

"Not I give you," Jin-é replied.

Crack!

The gunfire returned and the bullet blew a cloud of dust into George's eyes, making him trip and crash into Victor.

"Stand up straight, you idiot!" Victor screamed, lunging to the left down another side tunnel.

Crack!

The bullets kept coming.

"Turn left!" Victor barked to Jay and Jin-é, who were ten paces ahead.

"What?" Jay screeched. "It's a dead end!"

George and Victor caught up and they tumbled out into a cave. Sure enough, they had found the only tunnel that had no other way out. The beams from the two small torches were sucked up by the vast space – a domed prison, littered with fallen rocks, stranded boulders, caved in from above.

George turned back towards the tunnel, but the footsteps were coming fast. "What do we do?"

"Get behind there," Jay barked, shoving George and Victor further into the cave and pushing them behind one of the large boulders. "I hope you've got a gun," Jay whispered at Jin-é as they ducked behind another boulder.

George squatted down with his face to the boulder and his back to the wall.

We're doomed.

"Turn off your torch," Jay whispered at Victor, and the cave dived into a pit of darkness. Not a pinprick of light, no shadows, not even a grainy outline – total blindness.

Trying to quiet his breathing, George listened to the approaching footsteps. They slowed, hesitant, unsure of what lay beyond the end of the tunnel, and then a faint light crept into the cave, awakening the shadows, rebirthing the outlines of the rocks that surrounded them.

"I know you're in there," a voice boomed out, filling the cave and rebounding off the walls. George held his breath and heard the click of a gun.

"It's rude to hide from your guests," the voice continued.

Smooth, deep, with Victor's accent, it could only be Ivan Pozhar.

George looked over at his mother: she was tustling with Jin-é, trying to drag her back down to the ground, but Jin-é had cut the ties that bound her to Jay and was fighting against her grip. She thumped the butt of her small handgun into Jay's cheek, making her collapse back to the ground.

No!

"I'm here," Jin-é said, slowly rising to her feet, the top of her beanie only just visible above the curve of the boulder and her gun pointed towards the tunnel.

George couldn't resist peeking around the side of his boulder, but all he could see was an arm protruding from the shadows. The watch, the rings and the gun glinting in his hand, Ivan was flattened against the tunnel wall with someone else holding a light at his back. George swallowed hard and slipped back into his hiding place.

"So, you have me here," Ivan said, "I suggest you show me what goods you have to sell."

"I have Jaybird," Jin-é said, dragging Jay to her feet and shoving her out into the open, her needle pressed into Jay's ribs.

"No!" George breathed, making Victor clamp his free hand over George's mouth.

"And I have Victor and … weapon," Jin-é continued, still crouched behind her rocky shield. "And as extra bonus … I have the Jaybird's son."

"I see," Ivan said, "and what is it that you want in return?"

George looked at Jin-é. Is this when she'd pull the trigger? She had Ivan right where she wanted him – or was it not a clean enough shot?

"The sniper that kill my son," Jin-é said.

What?

She'd gone to all this trouble, dragging Ivan out, just to get him to hand over his sniper.

Ivan's laugh rumbled around the cave. "You really are a fool."

"You don't play me!" Jin-é squeaked. "I deserve truth. I know you had my boy killed. I just want the one who pulled the trigger. You walk away with all the rest. I deserve that – my son deserve that. Now, you give it to me."

Ivan was still laughing. "My dear, you already have your sniper ... she's standing right beside you."

George looked at his mother.

The dead boy, the bullet, the grave!

'There are things I've done ... I must make amends.'

"No!" Jay screeched, turning towards Jin-é. "It's not true!"

Jin-é was standing upright, her gun now pointed at Jay. "You lie to me!"

"No," Jay said, backing up, her ankles turning on the rocks at her feet. "He's lying, he's trying to throw you off guard."

"You say you help me find the man who kill my son! You promised!" she screeched, ripping off her beanie and exposing her bleached hair like a beacon in the dark.

"I have the evidence!" Jay said, backing closer to George and Victor. "I can identify the man who shot your son. It was Ivan's nephew!"

"How you so sure?" Jin-é asked.

George struggled in Victor's grip, trying to free his mouth, trying to reach for his mother.

"Stop," Victor hissed in his ear.

"Because I was there!" Jay said. "I know who pulled the trigger, and I'm pretty sure you'll find him stuck to Ivan's side, even now."

George pulled forwards and glanced towards the tunnel again. Ivan's face had slid into the light. His golden hair; his broad, square face; his amused smirk and the shadow of another man, hanging at his shoulder.

"Why would you trust her?" Ivan said. "She's MI5 scum. She has no loyalty to you."

George could see the confusion in Jin-é's eyes, the gun trembling in her hand.

I have to do something.

He thought of the envelope in his wardrobe, the bullet, the pictures of Ivan, the dead boy and the man with the missing ear. He bit down hard on Victor's hand and tore his face away. "She's telling the truth," he cried. "The man who shot your son, he only has one ear. I have the evidence, back home. She can prove it."

Jin-é looked down at him and then turned back towards Ivan, her gun sliding over the top of the boulder. "You show him to me."

Ivan shook his head, and the shadow at his shoulder slid out of view. "Why would you believe a child?"

"Show him!" Jin-é screeched. "Or I kill them all and you never find the weapon!"

Ivan stood in the tunnel, his gun pointing at Jin-é and she crouched behind her shield, her gun on him.

George had seen a stand-off before, and he knew that someone always had to take the first shot, but as he flattened his back to the rock and looked up to the craters in the ceiling above, he realised that Jin-é had already lost.

"Angelika!"

Crack!

George froze.

Crack!

His mother dived towards him.

Crack!

And Jin-é fell to her knees, her eyes open and staring.

"No!" George gasped, as she tumbled forwards, and all he could think of was the red of her bow as the blood blossomed from her pale skin.

Chapter 33: There at the End

"Relieve them of any weapons," Ivan ordered, as he and his nephew strode out from the tunnel.

George couldn't help but stare at Ivan's nephew: his slim frame, his stern face, his missing ear.

They were surrounded and unarmed, but Angelika forced them out into the middle of the cave and patted them all down. George stared at Jin-é's body and could think of nothing but her warning.

The warrior who seeks revenge…

"You sold yourself out," Victor growled at Angelika, as she checked the pockets of his overalls.

"All I ever wanted was to get back home, you knew that," she replied.

"Everyone you come across eventually turns their back on you," Ivan said from a safe distance.

"Oh, and you think she has any loyalty to you?" Victor sneered. "She only looks after herself."

Angelika shoved Victor to his knees, and George was forced to kneel too. "I could never rely on you," she snorted. "All you ever cared about was getting your revenge on *her*." She glanced at Jay. "That's what got you caught in Paris – your ego. You promised me a ticket home and you failed – because of your obsession with her."

Victor clenched his jaws, and George could hear the grind of his teeth.

"What makes you think Ivan will keep his promises?" Victor asked.

"She knows a real businessman when she sees one," Ivan said. "Not the kind who backs out of a deal."

"You were going to sell me out!" Victor spat.

"Well, that's another thing about good businessmen," Ivan said, "they know a good deal when they see one, and I was offered a deal I couldn't refuse. A deal that would have secured my protection by the Russian Government for the next ten years, but thanks to you two, I was made to look like a fool."

"You are a fool," Jay mumbled.

Angelika turned and smacked the butt of her gun into Jay's ribs, making her collapse to the ground.

"Stop!" George shouted.

"Quiet," Angelika growled, "or you'll be next."

Happy that they were no longer a threat, Ivan wound his way between the rocks, with his nephew at his side, and came to stand in front of his three hostages.

"From where I'm standing," he said, "I think you are the fools. Did you really think I'd let Jin-é get anywhere near me? Did you really think I'd hand over my only nephew, my most skilled sniper, my most loyal soldier? Jin-é was doomed from the moment she took over the 14D and decided to play games with me."

"You didn't need to kill her son," Jay said.

"I don't *need* to kill anyone," Ivan said. "I do it because I don't like being made a fool of, so I suggest you listen carefully. You will take me to the weapon, and I *may* consider letting you live."

"Ha!" Victor roared. "You expect me to believe that!"

Jay shuffled up next to George and edged her bound hands towards his. Reaching out her fingers, she squeezed his as best she could. He looked up at her, hoping to see the usual reassurance and determination in her eyes, but all he saw was sadness.

No, Mum, don't give up!

"You're all out of choices," Ivan sneered.

George tilted his head away from Ivan's gaze and thought of his mum and dad in the hangar in Paris; how they'd manage to communicate without words; managed to formulate a plan to get out. He wriggled his fingers out of her grip and slowly lifted them towards his zip, trying not to pull too hard on Victor's arm and trying not to draw anyone's attention other than his mother's. Her eyes drifted down to his chest and then straight back up to meet his gaze. He nodded and she smiled, the faintest curve of a smile.

She understands.

As they were herded back out of the cave and towards the maze of tunnels, George figured that the best he could do was stretch things out for as long as he could; keep Ivan talking; delay him from finding the weapon and give his dad as much time as possible to track them down, just like his mum and dad had done in Paris as they waited for Dupont and Elías to return with Mr Steckler. He wasn't sure whether it would work, but it was their only hope.

"Ouch, I've got something in my shoe," George said, hopping to a stop. "It stings like mad."

Still tied to Victor, he dragged him to halt. Angelika was behind them, her gun inches from their backs, and Ivan's nephew had Jay by the arm.

"I don't care about your pain," Ivan called from the tail. "We keep moving. The longer this takes, the more likely you are to feel real pain."

Victor yanked at George's arm, and George hobbled on.

He needs to slow down.

"Argh!" George tripped on a rock and tumbled to the ground, stopping Victor again.

"What are you playing at?" Victor hissed.

"I'll make you carry him if you can't keep him moving," Ivan said. "How much further?"

"Not far," Victor replied, heaving George to his feet again. "A few more turns."

Building up a pace, they marched on, the crunch of their footsteps ruining any chance of hearing anyone else approaching. George strained his ears, desperate for a sound, any sound, but nothing came. He thought of tripping again but daren't test Ivan's patience any more. He needed to do something, anything, to stall, but before he could come up with an idea, they emerged from the tunnel, into the crossroads and Victor stopped dead.

"Here?" Ivan asked, pushing forwards.

"I just…" Victor turned full circle, dragging George with him.

George took his chance. "I thought you said it was this way."

"What?" Victor said, looking at him sideways.

"You know, when we were here before, you said it was this way," George said, raising his arms towards one of the tunnels.

Victor frowned. "I said nothing…"

"No, he didn't," Jay said, locking eyes with George. "I'm sure he said it was that way."

Ivan stood between them, looking from one branch of the crossroads to the other. "Well, which way is it?"

"Um," Victor hesitated, and Ivan lunged at him with his gun, making him and George both stumble backwards.

"You better not be messing with me. I swear I'll make your death more painful than you can imagine," Ivan said.

"If you're going to kill me anyway," Victor snarled, "why should I let you have the weapon? I'd rather die knowing that you've failed."

Ivan slammed his rifle into Victor's chest and pushed him and George up against the wall.

Clunk!

George felt something hard at his heel.

As Ivan and Victor eyeballed each other over the barrel of the rifle, George slid his eyes to the ground. There, just poking out from beneath a large pile of rubble, was the sharp corner of a rigid metal box.

George lifted his head.

Do something!

"It was definitely that way!" George said, pointing to the tunnel through which they'd first arrived.

We need to get out of here!

"And why should I believe you?" Ivan asked, releasing the pressure on the rifle and standing back.

"Because … I have nothing to lose," George replied. "I don't owe Victor anything. In fact, I hate him! It's his fault I had no mother for seven years, it's his fault my father barely speaks to me and it's his fault that I'll probably spend the rest of my pathetic life in therapy!"

Ivan smirked. "See," he said to Victor, "everyone eventually turns their back on you." Ivan grabbed George by the arm. "You better not be playing me, boy."

George shook his head and tried to clench the shaking from his hands. He could feel his mother's eyes on him.

"He's got no reason to lie," she said.

Ivan let go of George's arm, but pressed his rifle up under George's chin. "I won't hesitate to kill you … slowly."

George tried to swallow and could feel the cold of the rifle against his throat.

How much longer can I keep this up?

Ivan ran the rifle's nose down George's arm towards his hands. "A finger for every false turn; a finger for every wasted minute, until you have no fingers left and then we'll start with your toes. Do you understand?"

George tried to nod.

"Good," Ivan said, shoving George out in front of him, with Victor dragging behind. "No more stops."

"I hope you know what you're doing," Victor breathed in George's ear.

"I'm trying to keep us alive," George whispered back.

I need to get us back to the beach.

With every step, George knew that he was marching closer to a point of no return. He was running out of time; playing a dangerous game with a dangerous man. A game that only one of them could win, and right now, George could feel the whisper of victory slipping through his fingers like sand.

Where's Dad?

What on earth had made him think that he could outsmart Ivan? He had put all his hope in his dad finding them, but as the seconds cascaded away, the reality of their situation began to close in on him.

The sound of Ivan's heavy stride stalked George from behind, and he struggled to control his breathing. His heartbeat drummed loud in his ears, his head thundered and the familiar crush of panic was clamping down on his chest, but then he saw it – seeping down the wall of the fork ahead – light.

The beach!

George surged forwards, dragging Victor with him.

"No," Victor said, yanking George back.

What is he doing?

George pulled at the ties that joined them.

"It's … this way," George said, nodding towards the light.

Victor glanced down the other fork.

"No," Victor said, leaning away. "This is not the place."

"Yes – it – is."

They yanked each other back and forth like contestants in a tug of war.

Crack!

Ivan blew a hole in the ceiling, and a cascade of rubble showered down on them from above, making them collapse into the dirt. "Your time is up!"

"Wait!" George choked, pushing himself to his hands and knees, but Ivan stood towering over him, his rifle pointed at George's outstretched fingers. "Which finger do you like the least?"

"No!" Jay screamed, fighting against Ivan's nephew's grasp. "Take mine! Leave him!"

Ivan turned towards her, a broad grin on his face. "So, be it. I've waited long enough to make you pay for what you did."

George tried to scream but his voice clung to his throat.

No!

Ivan glided his rifle towards Jay. "In fact," he said, striding towards her, "I don't see any point in wasting time with your fingers."

George's feet grappled with the loose stone. "No!"

"You are no use to me, anymore," Ivan continued, as he raised his rifle.

George pushed himself to his feet. Time was up. He'd messed up; failed. He should have made her run, dragged her from the warehouse. He shouldn't have trusted Julian, he shouldn't have trusted Victor, he shouldn't have believed Madame Wu. He was no warrior, and in the end, it would be him that lost it all.

Ivan aimed, George lunged and Jay dived.

Boom!

George felt everything around him shift – the air, the rocks, the bodies that fell to the floor – and the cave filled with a thick, choking smoke.

"Run!" he heard his mother scream, and he scrambled back to his feet, yanking Victor with him, head down, pounding through the haze, towards the light.

"Don't stop!" she shouted from behind. "Whatever happens, just keep running!"

His ankles jarred, his wrists burnt as the ties tore at his skin, and his eyes streamed as dust and smoke blurred his vision, but he managed to stay on his feet.

Crack!

Ivan was on their tail.

Crack!

Angelika too.

The tunnel widened out into the cave and George lunged from one boulder to the next, Victor stumbling to keep up.

Crack!

George could feel his heart straining at his ribs; his breath tearing at his lungs.

Crack!

He dived for the cover of a boulder.

Crack!

There was a clear path to the beach; a path that wound between the rocks – protected, shielded.

"Keep moving!" he called to Victor, but as he lunged for the next boulder, his arms jarred and twisted, and he fell to the ground, the weight of Victor's body holding him back. "Get up!" he yelled at him, but Victor was down: his eyes shut; blood seeping from his knee; his head beaten by the fall.

"Come on!" George screamed, but Victor didn't move.

Crack!

The bullets kept coming, and the rocks around George splintered under Ivan's attack.

We need to move!

George dug his feet into the stones and tried to drag Victor's body towards the beach, but with every shot, more chunks of rock rained down on them.

"Hey!" someone cried, and George turned to see his mother dashing across the cave, diving from one outcrop of rocks to the next, drawing Ivan's fire.

George looked down at his ties. Twisted and gnarled, the plastic had thinned in places. Scrabbling around at his feet, he found the sharpest stone he could find, and using every ounce of his energy, he secured it between his feet and hacked at the plastic at his wrists. Back and forth, rough and jerky, the plastic started to notch.

Victor groaned. Someone screamed. The waves crashed.

Crack!

George's hands were raw: the cuts from the glass, the sharpness of the stone, the chill of the wind, but he pushed harder.

"Argh!" he screamed, ramming the edge of the stone against his ties one final time.

Boom!

Something exploded deep within the tunnels, echoing around the walls and sending more smoke billowing out into the cave.

Snap!

His hands were free. Victor's arm flopped to the ground, and George was up. With his back flat to the rock, he inched around its side and peered out across the cave. Angelika and Ivan's nephew were buried in the smoke, their bullets spraying like a fountain into the darkness of the tunnels behind them. George searched the shadows of the cave for his mum, and as the smoke cleared, he could see her huddled form: unarmed, barely protected by her rocky shield, and out on her own.

"No one plays me for a fool!" Ivan roared, unleashing a storm of bullets in her direction.

She won't survive!

George turned.

I have to do something!

He could see the mouth of the cave.

I can make it.

Without stopping to think, he leapt to his feet, grabbed the nearest rock and flung it in Ivan's direction.

"Hey!" he hollered, lunging for the next boulder.

"You!" Ivan bellowed. "I'll kill you first so your mother can watch!"

Crack!

George turned and readied himself to run again.

"Wait!" Victor yelped, his eyes now open wide; his hands outstretched. "Don't leave me!"

Crack!

The rocks between him and Victor erupted, and George stood frozen still, staring down at the man he hated; the man that had brought him so much misery.

He doesn't deserve to live.

But George thought of Jin-é.

Be careful of what you seek.

And he thought of Madame Wu.

The warrior who seeks revenge.

And he thought of all the lives that had already been lost, and before he could change his own mind, he fell to his knees, crawled across the stones and grabbed Victor by the arms.

"You better run fast," he said, pulling Victor to his feet.

Crack!

Eyeing up the last ten feet between them and the beach, George wedged his shoulder under Victor's armpit and wrapped his arms around his chest. "Now!" he screamed.

Victor lurched, George lunged, Ivan fired, and as they dived towards the next refuge, George looked back. His mother was out in the open.

"No!" she cried.

Ivan swivelled.

Crack!

Jay stumbled.

Crack!

George shoved Victor towards the next boulder and screamed, "Noooo!"

Crack!

The bullet flew. It raced across the cave, and George felt the pain sear through his shoulder, splintering like ice and fire through his veins. His body collapsed hard against the stones, flat and cold, out in the open, laid bare to Ivan's attack.

He could hear his mother's screams, he could smell the blood that seeped from his shoulder, and he could feel the weight of Victor's body as Victor lunged towards him and threw himself over George, absorbing the hailstorm of bullets, covering him like a blanket – heavy, limp and crushing.

'I failed', was all George could think as his mind began to slip away, but as his eyes closed, he could hear the roar of the gunfire coming from the tunnels behind him; he could hear the shouts of the officers that were racing across the beach; he could hear the whirr of the helicopter blades that were descending from above, and he could feel his father's touch as he rolled Victor's body aside and cradled George in his arms.

Chapter 34: Into the Darkness

There was no light, just darkness – solid, deep, unending – and George floated: bobbing, drifting away. Somewhere in the distance, a voice called to him and drew him back, like the flow of the tide.

Still blind to the world around him, all George could feel was the throbbing in his head, the stiffness in his neck, the sting at his shoulder, the aching in his arm, the tingling in his fingers and the soft, warm cocoon of her hand, enveloping his like a fine silk glove.

"Oh, my Georgie," she whispered.

Gran?

She circled her thumb around his palm, slow and gentle, and he tumbled back into the darkness.

Where am I?

The next thing he knew was the closeness of bodies; the shuffle of feet; the sound of hushed voices.

"Will he be ok?"

Lauren?

"When will he wake up?"

Felix?

"He looks so pale."

Francesca?

"He'll be fine, he just needs time to heal."

Dad!

"He's tougher than anybody."

Will?

"He'll be back causing trouble in no time."

Jess?

"He better not have a more impressive scar than me."

Josh?

George could feel a smile try to wake his lips but his mind was slipping away again, far away. He tried to fight it, desperately snatching at the voices that surrounded him, trying to stay in the present, but he lost grip and floated away. He floated out of his bed and out of the room, and soon he was sitting on the end of the seesaw, looking into his mother's dark eyes, but this time she wasn't beside him, steadying him with both her hands; she was at the other end, a look of panic in her eyes.

Mum!

The seat beneath him jolted and he looked down. He was hovering in the air, his legs dangling over an abyss, and with every breath, he slid a little further down, a little closer to the edge.

"Hold on!" his mother cried, reaching out her fingers, grasping for his hand, but the seesaw just kept tipping, and everything was sliding; sliding down towards the darkness below. Towards the dark swirling water, rippling like oil and towards the bodies. George could see them now; their blank, lifeless faces peering back up at him: the guards from the vault, Mrs Hodge, Alex Allaman, Jin-é ... and Victor.

"No!" he screamed, as he lost his grip and plummeted towards them.

"No!" he screamed as his eyes shot open and everything blurred into a mess of colour. Balloons and flowers, cards and letters, his dad's battered cap; a jumble of shapes and silhouettes: light and dark, soft and hard, curved and straight, and there sitting next to him, a face – the face of his dad.

"George!"

Sam's eyes were pink with veins; puffy and swollen. George opened his mouth to speak, but before he could form any words, his dad's arms were around him, his body swamping George's.

"Thank God," Sam choked in his ear. He pulled away and clasped George's face in his hands. "You're back."

George's eyes adjusted to the light in the room and all he could think of was one thing.

"Mum!" he croaked. "Where's Mum?"

"It's OK, George," Sam said, glancing at George's monitors, which were softly bleeping. "Just stay calm."

George tried to push himself up. "Dad, where is she?"

"She's fine, George, I promise," Sam replied.

George thought of all the voices he had heard. "Has she been here?"

Sam shook his head. "Not yet – she's had … some questions to answer."

"What?" George said, the pain flaring from his shoulder. "Argh!"

"Take it easy," Sam said, reaching for a gas mask. "Here, this will ease the pain."

George grabbed the mask but didn't put it to his face. "Dad, she's innocent! You know she is!"

"I know," Sam said, "but there are accusations she needs to … address."

"Jin-é's son," George said.

"Among other things," Sam said, trying to get George to sit back. "Come on, George. I'll call the nurses in if you don't relax."

George sank back into his pillow and took in a lungful of gas. His head swam. "Did you know, Dad?"

Sam looked down at his hands. "I knew that she had been accused of murder, yes."

"She didn't do it, Dad. That's what the evidence in my wardrobe is. Ivan's nephew did it, the guy with one ear, the guy—"

"Yes, we know," Sam said, placing a hand on George's arm, "and we got him – Ivan and Angelika too."

"And the weapon?" George asked.

Sam nodded. "Yes, and the weapon."

George looked down at the bandage at his shoulder and took another suck on the gas.

"Bullet wound," Sam said. "Quite an impressive one but no permanent damage."

George's mind flashed back to the cave.

"Victor?" he asked, screwing up his face.

Sam shook his head.

"JP, Dupont, Elias?"

"They'll survive," Sam replied.

"But the triplets, they…"

"Yeah, we caught them too – all three of the little blighters."

"And … Julian?" George asked, trying to suppress the anger in his voice.

"He didn't make it out of Margate."

"How?"

"You," Sam said. "All you, George. You told us everything we needed to know."

"You were listening – that whole time?"

"No, not until Gran's 999 call filtered through to us. Luckily, Cate had your wire on auto-record, so we had everything we needed."

"And the tracker?"

"It was difficult to pinpoint your exact location because of the cliffs," Sam said, "but … it didn't matter."

"What? Why?"

"We had Ivan under survcillance, remember?"

"Right," George said. "So, you knew he was in there – in the caves with us?"

"We may have lost track of Victor, but as soon as Ivan started to move, we guessed that the meet was on and we followed him."

"But … if you knew…"

Sam shifted in his seat. "We had to hang back, George. We couldn't make a move on Ivan until we were sure that Jin-é and your mother were with him. We needed to strike all three targets at once."

"But … Jin-é died, Dad … Mum could have died … I could have–"

"I know," Sam said with a quiver on his lips. "I wanted to move sooner, you know I would have, but…"

"The operational objective," George said.

Sam's eyes drifted to George's shoulder. "I'm sorry, George. I should have just got you out, I waited too long, I will never–"

"It's OK," George said, resting his hand on Sam's shoulder. "You promised me you'd finish it, and you did."

Sam cleared his throat and sat up. "You finished it, George. You made it happen."

"I don't know about that," George said, blushing.

Sam reached over and grabbed the bloodstained cap from George's bedside table and plonked it on George's head. "Your mother said you were a true hero."

George looked out of the window. "I wouldn't go that far."

"Hmm, you only have to look at these cards to see what people think of you."

George scanned his eyes over a few of the messages: his friends, his teachers, Eddie, Elías and Dupont, even JP.

"Who's this one from?" George asked, picking up an official looking letter signed by a TOD.

"Ah, that you'll find is a letter of commendation from the chief of MI5, Tim O'Donnell," Sam said, breaking into a genuine smile.

"O'Donnell?" George said, looking down at the signature.

"Yes, I believe you may know his daughter," Sam grinned.

Miss O'Donnell!

"Is that why … you wanted me to…"

"It's best to keep these things within the organisation," Sam winked. "I thought she'd understand you better than any old high street counsellor."

George's head spun and he sucked on the gas and air again.

"When can I go home? When can I see Gran and … Mum?"

"Soon, George," Sam said, patting George's knee. "You just need to focus on recovering, OK."

It was three days before George was allowed to go home. More cards and gifts waited for him at the cottage, as well as the hugest chocolate fudge cake that he'd ever seen.

"Oh, my boy! When am I ever going to be able to let you out of my sight again?" Gran said, engulfing him in a hug.

"Be careful with him," Sam said, as he helped George through the front door.

"That goes for you too," Gran said, flicking her tea towel at Sam.

Gran settled George into his bed, plumped his cushions, surrounded him with extra blankets and plied him with endless hot chocolate and cake until he dozed off to sleep.

When he woke, he could feel the weight of someone sitting at the corner of his mattress. Sure that it was Marshall, he thought about swatting him away, but when he opened his eyes, his Mum was sitting quietly at his feet, smiling down at him. George stared at her. With her hair back to its natural hazelnut, just like his, and her eyes warm and soft, she looked just like the photos that lined his bedroom wall.

George's voice caught in his throat.

"You're here," he croaked, unable to keep the dampness from his eyes

"Yes, George, I'm here."

"Right here, at home," he said, sitting up.

"Thanks to you," she smiled.

Having her there, in his room, felt so surreal; like a dream – a dream he'd had a thousand times. Not daring to blink, in case she vanished, he tried to soak up her warmth; inhale her presence. Then panic hit him.

Is she here to stay?

"Are you off the hook ... with MI6?" he asked.

"Pretty much," she said, looking around his room.

"You didn't kill Jin-é's son," George said. "That was the evidence you sent me, wasn't it?"

She nodded. "I'm sorry I had to put that on you, but I didn't know who else to trust. I knew that Cate already had her suspicions, and I didn't know who your father would believe."

"But you were there … in Calais?"

Her eyes dropped to the duvet. "Yes, I was there."

"But I don't understand. If you knew who killed Jin-é's son and you had the evidence, why did you need to make amends?"

Jay swallowed and looked up at him. "I was there because I was *supposed* to kill him, George. Victor had given me to Ivan as part of their deal. Ivan had given Victor everything he needed for his attack on London – weapons, money, contacts – but all Ivan had was the promise of the weapon, so he took me as collateral, and he wanted me to prove my loyalty." She sighed and stared at the ceiling. "Jin-é's son was trying to repay a debt, a debt of money that Jin-é had stolen from Ivan out of revenge for their ongoing feud. Her son turned up in good faith, George. He wanted to repay the debt and get back a hostage that Ivan had taken." She shook her head. "But Ivan had no intention of letting him live."

"But it still wasn't you that killed him," George said, confused.

"No, George, I couldn't. When I saw how young he was, I just fell apart. All I could think of was you, and I couldn't do it."

"So, you owed Jin-é nothing."

"I didn't pull the trigger, George, but I still sat there and watched Ivan's nephew kill that boy. I sat back and did nothing. I just watched his body fall to the floor, and then, even worse, I turned my gun on Ivan's nephew, stole the money and ran." Her head was in her hands. "I didn't stop to see if the boy was dead, I didn't stop to find out who he was or if he had a family, I just thought of myself. I thought of my own freedom, my own life."

"That's how you finally escaped?" George asked.

"Yes, that's when I went on the run; got away from Victor and Ivan. But it hasn't stopped haunting me since, so when Jin-é grabbed me in Paris and told me why she wanted to trade me with Ivan, I knew that that was my chance to make things right. I didn't know it was her son, but once I knew, I swore I'd help her get the man who killed him."

George sat back and thought of the boy's young face.

"She never got her revenge," George said.

"No, but you got it for her, George. Because of you, Ivan and his nephew will never see the outside world again. They'll spend the rest of their lives in prison. You got her the revenge she deserved."

Jay repositioned herself on the bed and clutched her side.

"What's wrong?" George asked. "Were you hit?"

"Just a scratch. Could have been a lot worse," she said, grimacing, "especially if you hadn't had been there as my back-up."

George thought of the weight of Victor's body on top of his. "I couldn't save everyone though, could I?"

His mum frowned. "I hope you're not feeling sorry for Victor, George. He brought all this upon himself."

"But he died saving me," George said, shaking his head, struggling to understand why a man who had done nothing but show him hatred and contempt had sacrificed himself for him.

"Well, maybe it was you that saved him, George. Maybe he saw in you the kind of man he never was. He only clamoured for wealth and fame, power and revenge. You lost, you suffered, but in the end, you didn't seek revenge."

"Like the proverb," George said.

Jay nodded. "And maybe by saving you, he was finally able to do something good – something that brought him balance."

George rolled his head on his shoulders, stretching out the ache in his neck. "Maybe."

Jay picked up the box that Sam had given George for his birthday and pulled a drawing from the top of the pile. It was a picture of a dog: all scribbly, black, crayon fur and smiley, radiant, felt-tip sun.

"You always wanted a dog," Jay chuckled.

George sat silent and watched her as she placed the picture back into the box. "George, I know it doesn't mean much, but I'm sorry. I'm sorry for everything I've put you through. I don't expect you to ever forgive me…"

"It's OK, Mum," George said, "it was…"

"No," Jay said, looking up. "I heard what you said in the cave, and I know that you hated Victor and Jin-é and all the others that caused you pain, but it should be me that you hate. If I'd turned around and run that day in Scotland, if I'd put you first, before my own desperation to stop Victor, none of this – these past seven years – none of it would have happened."

George placed his hand on his mum's. "But, Mum, it was your job. If you didn't take these people down, who would?"

Jay smiled. "There are plenty of young officers coming up the ranks, ready to take my place – more capable than me, braver, brighter – like you," she said, smoothing down his wayward hair.

Creak!

Someone was outside George's bedroom door.

"Cerys?" Jay asked, winking at George.

With that, the door peeled open and Gran's beaming face peeked through the gap. "Didn't want to interrupt," she said, "but tea's ready."

George smiled inside – even now, Gran was watching over him.

"We're coming, Gran," he said, sliding his legs out from under his duvet.

"Can you stand?" Jay asked, helping George to his feet.

"I'm pretty sure," he replied.

Jay held his arm and propped him up as he hobbled down the stairs. As they entered the kitchen, Sam was at the breakfast bar stirring the steam out of his bowl.

"Cheesy pasta," Gran beamed. "Your favourite!"

George gingerly lowered himself onto the free stool at the bar, and Sam jumped up to offer his to Jay.

"No, I'm good," she said. "Let Cerys have it."

Gran and George sat elbow to elbow as Sam and Jay cradled their bowls of pasta and leant up against the counter on the opposite side of the bar. No one spoke as they all shovelled down the warm goodness.

George lifted his head and looked at his family, their heads buried in their bowls. Even Marshall had slunk into the room and was licking at the remnants of his supper. George could feel a lump of pasta stick in his throat, and a tear ran down his cheek. It clung to his jaw, but before it could tumble into his bowl, Gran's soft finger was catching it. She smiled at him and ran her thumb over his damp cheeks.

"It's good, huh?" she said, nodding at the bowl in front of him.

"It's great," George smiled, "really great."

Jay stayed at the house for several hours, and as night approached, George offered her his bed.

"I'll sleep on the couch," he insisted, but she refused.

"Thank you, George," she said, glancing at Sam, "but … I … have some things I need to sort out."

Before she left, she disappeared into the garden with Sam. It was dark, but the flood lights filled the garden with enough light for Gran and George to spy on them from the kitchen window.

Sam stood with his hands in his pockets and his head hanging low. Jay seemed to be doing most of the talking. She stood upright and strong again, and George watched every tilt of her head; every move of her hand. When she reached out and placed her hand on Sam's arm, George held his breath, but Sam didn't flinch or pull away.

"Do you think they still love each other?" George asked Gran.

"Love comes in many forms, George," Gran sighed, "and seven years is a long time for two hearts to be apart." She looked at him. "Do you still love her?"

George stared out at his mother. She felt less of a stranger to him now, but really, he barely knew her. He searched his heart and knew that there was warmth inside him, a warmth that he only felt when she was close. Honestly, he didn't know what he felt, except that the ache inside him had gone and he knew that he didn't want it to return. He didn't want her to ever go away again. He wanted her to stay, and he wanted his family to be whole – forever.

"Will we be a family again?" he asked Gran.

She turned and wrapped her hands around his. "You never stop being family, George, however many miles and however much time stands between you, family is an unbreakable bond."

George looked out at his parents and realised that his family would never be normal – they would never fit the mould – but he couldn't be prouder of who they all were and what they had all achieved, and he now knew that, although he wasn't like any other teenage boy, he did have something to offer; something to say, and even though he was different, he didn't need to change. He no longer wished to be someone else, anyone else, because he stood for something; he stood for what was right and just, and even if he didn't stand out for any other reason, he wouldn't change who he was for the world.

From: Chief
To: J21
Re: J14 {Encrypted}

You were right. He is more than capable.
He coped with everything that was thrown at him. He
showed courage, determination, integrity and ingenuity.

I will put forward the recommendation that he enlists for
training on his 16th birthday.

We look forward to having him on board.

End.

Thank you for reading **The Undergrounders & the Malice of the Moth**.

That is the end of George's story, for now…

In the meantime, I am writing a new adventure, so please do follow me on:

Website: ctfrankcom.com
Twitter: @ctfrankcom
Facebook: CT Frankcom
Instagram: CT Frankcom

And please do leave a review on Amazon or Goodreads. I would love to hear from you xxx

Printed in Great Britain
by Amazon

54632464R00194